CARVING FOR MISS COVENTRY

BOOKS BY DEBORAH M. HATHAWAY

A Cornish Romance Series
On the Shores of Tregalwen, a Prequel Novella
Behind the Light of Golowduyn, Book One
For the Lady of Lowena, Book Two
Near the Ruins of Penharrow, Book Three
In the Waves of Tristwick, Book Four (Pre-Order)
Book Five, Coming Soon

Belles of Christmas Multi-Author Series
Nine Ladies Dancing, Book Four
On the Second Day of Christmas, Book Four

Seasons of Change Multi-Author Series
The Cottage by Coniston, Book Five

Sons of Somerset Multi-Author Series
Carving for Miss Coventry, Book One

CARVING
FOR
MISS
COVENTRY

———— ∽ ————

DEBORAH M. HATHAWAY

For Derek and Nikki—

Here's the thing.
You guys made the pandemic bearable,
even if you do like sharp cheese.

Here's to our next fifty-two game nights
in fifty-two weeks.

CHAPTER ONE

Inglesbatch, Somerset – May 1816

Briarwood Estate was the ideal location for a cricket match. Extensive grounds, lush green fields, no trees to cast distracting shadows. The house itself stood pristine and polished, the east and west wings of the edifice extending past the center, as if the tan walls were outstretched arms, welcoming the guests and cricket players to its abode.

Edward Steele peered up at the front of the house with a wary eye. He was neither guest nor cricket player. To him, the home's wide-open arms were nothing short of barriers flexing their dominance.

Doing business with the man who owned such a property should be flattering for anyone, but for Edward, working with Lord Ryecombe had been an unsettling experience from the start. Edward had far too much to lose, and more often than not, those with greater power and wealth were the ones who could damage a person the most.

Pulling his attention away from such discouraging thoughts, he focused on the cloudless, blue sky instead. The sun shone brightly that morning after weeks of rain, drying up the last of the dew and warming his shoulders and those of the attendees who'd already arrived to watch the match.

Gentlemen in fine suits and ladies in pastel gowns and flowery bonnets gathered at one side of the field, separated from the much more humbly—and sensibly—dressed families of the opposite team, the team made up solely of working class men.

Edward had been invited to play alongside them this year, but he hadn't the time to engage in such merriment. At least until his situation changed.

With an impatient sigh, he swapped the large package he carried in his right hand over to his left then tugged at his cravat. He shouldn't have worn his best jacket. Well, his only fine jacket. But Mother had encouraged him to avoid appearing even poorer than he was.

"Unfortunately, appearances matter to these sorts of people," she'd said.

Edward had obviously agreed. But that still didn't mean he enjoyed overheating in the jacket he barely found occasion to wear more than once a month.

The last of the carriages drove away on the long, circular path, having deposited the final guests at Briarwood. Lord Ryecombe had promised to retrieve the package from Edward the moment the guests had all arrived. Where was—

"Mr. Steele."

Edward should've expected punctuality. Most gentlemen exhibited the admirable trait. How unfortunate it was that other desirable qualities did not make more of an appearance in their lives. Like humility. Or honesty.

He bowed, clearing his throat. "Lord Ryecombe, my lord. Good day."

The man was nearly balding, but what hair he didn't have atop his head was made up for by the thick set of side whiskers that carried from his hair, past his ears, to midway down his jaw.

"I take it that is my order?" Lord Ryecombe motioned with a tip of his head toward the leather-wrapped package in Edward's hands. Apparently, he was as uninterested in exchanging pleasantries as Edward was.

He extended the package forward. "I trust they will meet your expectations."

Lord Ryecombe huffed in disbelief as he took the bundle. The man had no faith in Edward. That much had been evident when he'd made the commission in the Steele's woodshop a week before.

"Typically," the man had said, "I would hire a *proven* woodworker. But seeing as how I need these by next week, you are my only option."

The words still chewed at Edward's patience. He'd been working at Father's shop—now *his* shop—for nigh on twenty-three years, since the tender age of five. He'd proven himself and then proven himself again.

Of course, what with his sullied name, it was very unlikely Edward would ever *not* have to prove himself again.

Lord Ryecombe untied the twine around the bundle. "I trust you had no trouble accomplishing the task in the allotted time?"

Edward nodded in silence. He didn't miss the pointed words. When the man had hired him, Edward had at first declined, saying he could not finish in seven days.

Lord Ryecombe had raised his chin. "I find that difficult to believe. From my understanding, your workload is not what it once was."

He wasn't wrong. But no man appreciated having his failing business pointed out by another. Even still, Edward had no choice but to accept the job.

Lord Ryecombe removed the twine and unfolded the top half of the package. He pulled the leather back, and it fell down around his other hand holding the bottom half, revealing the top of two cricket bats.

Edward had not enjoyed creating what were essentially glorified oars. Like most of his rare, latest commissions, they had required all function and very little finesse. How he longed for the days when he used to carve intricate designs into frames, shelves, and signs. Blast this world for turning stone statues into more of a fashionable commodity than wood.

If only stone was the sole reason he continuously found himself without work.

Lord Ryecombe continued to examine the bats, running his wrinkled fingers across the smooth edges of the flat, burnt-colored wood.

Edward had longed to carve even the smallest design on the bats, but he knew he'd be criticized. Instead, he'd branded his business name near the handle.

Steele and Son
Woodwork

He really ought to change that name. But what would the business be called without Father?

Steele and No Son?

One Steele and One Steele Alone?

"Will they suffice, my lord?" Edward asked, ready to be done with this whole affair.

Lord Ryecombe waited another moment to respond. "What type of wood is this?"

"Real English willow, my lord." As if he'd use anything else.

Lord Ryecombe was clearly well-versed in cricket and knew exactly what wood was needed to prevent cracking under the pressure of hitting fast-moving balls. He was no doubt simply testing Edward with the question. Yet another condescending action often used by the upper class.

Finally, the man looked up with a nod, the ends of his eyebrows sticking out like a tomcat's whiskers. "Yes. These will do. I admit, Mr. Steele, you've impressed me. I did not expect such high-quality work."

Typical patronizing flattery. Edward was not one to unnecessarily boast of his capabilities, but he was also not unaware of his own talents. He could beautify a piece of wood with a dinner knife if he was required to do so.

Very well, that was a bit of a stretch. But still, it was not in his nature to perform half a job. He'd spent longer than he cared to admit studying depictions of cricket bats and staring at them through shop windows. He'd even expressed a feigned interest in purchasing one in order to hold it to recreate the latest style, size, and weight.

"I'm pleased they will do, my lord," Edward responded as humbly as he was able to. It would not do to offend the man who had not yet paid him. Speaking of being paid. "If you are satisfied, Lord Ryecombe, shall we settle accounts so I can leave you to your guests?"

He'd always felt just a twinge of discomfort bringing up payment to his employers, but lately, he had to forgo his embarrassment. He couldn't *afford* to be embarrassed.

"Certainly," Lord Ryecombe said, wrapping up the bats in the leather once again, "just as soon as the match finishes and we are assured that the bats withstand the rigors of the game."

Edward blinked. "My lord, I was under the impression that we had agreed for the payment to be settled the moment the package was delivered."

Lord Ryecombe's brow wrinkled, forming more layers on his forehead than Mother's trifle. "Why in heaven's name would I pay you before your work has proven itself?"

Edward's chest tightened. He was already months behind in paying his rent for his woodshop. If he didn't receive that payment, he would lose the shop and then bid farewell to his one source of income. He and Mother would have nothing. No food, no home, no prospects.

Edward drew in a steadying breath. "As you can see, I have already expended the wood and completed the bats. Should one of them fail, it would not be due to my craftsmanship."

"Do you think the bats will falter?"

Edward straightened his spine. "No, my lord."

Lore Ryecombe smiled wryly. "Then you really oughtn't be concerned."

"Lord Ryecombe, I—"

"Do not forget, Mr. Steele, that I am doing you a favor. After what has been said about your father, it is a miracle, indeed, that I even requested the job of you at all."

Edward's jaw twitched. All who knew him—inconsequential woodworker that he was—were not blind as to where he stood in regard to the rumors surrounding Father. Unfortunately, Lord Ryecombe was just like everyone else, listening to the tittle-tattle of gossips around Bath instead of knowing Father's character and what he stood for.

Lord Ryecombe raised his chin in a challenge. What little remaining sprigs of hair he had atop his head floated about in the breeze like wheat in a field.

Would that Edward could tell him such a thing.

"Do you understand, Mr. Steele?"

If Edward did not need Lord Ryecombe's commission—and if Mother did not wish to eat that evening—Edward would have very much liked to introduce the man's pristinely tailored breeches to the lush grass they stood upon.

"Perfectly, *my lord*," he said with fisted hands.

Lord Ryecombe gave a satisfied smile. "Very well. You may seek me out after the game. You may remain here or return later, I care not."

With a firm nod, he ended their conversation, leaving with both bats gripped in his hands.

Those bats were a mere pittance to a lord. Not even a dent would be made against the man's boundless wealth if he paid Edward now, so why would he not?

With an irritated shake of his head, Edward swept his gaze around him. The large area in front of Briarwood had filled with even more individuals.

The scent of cucumbers, strawberry turnovers, and cheese drifted past his nose, and Edward's stomach rumbled. The table nearby nearly overflowed with silver trays filled with pastries, biscuits, and rose-painted cups near a large serving bowl of lemonade.

The corners of Edward's lips raised.

If the bats did break, which they wouldn't—*they wouldn't*—and Lord Ryecombe refused Edward payment for his troubles... then Edward knew just how to make his money back—through his stomach.

Perhaps he'd stay at the match after all.

With an appetite the size of Somerset, Edward helped himself to his first plate of food, consisting of a plain pastry biscuit, stewed fruit, and a few pieces of cheese.

As he ate, his heart threatened to sink at the guilt knocking at his chest, but he refused to give answer to it. He did not need to feel badly for eating his weight in Lord Ryecombe's food. He was now, for all intents and purposes, the man's guest, and he would behave as one.

He munched on what he hated to admit was the most delicious food he'd eaten in months, all while the men gathered on the green in their respective teams.

The gentlemen's team laughed gleefully, clapping one another on their backs as they stretched their arms in circles.

On the other side of the field, the working-class men huddled together, listening intently to the man who was clearly their captain, Mr. Reginald Sinclair, whom Edward recognized as the nephew of the postmaster.

From what Edward had heard of Mr. Sinclair, they had both had similar experiences with their fathers being treated poorly by the upper class. But where Edward held onto a grudge, Mr. Sinclair did not. At least, as far as Edward was aware.

Either way, Mr. Sinclair's team admired him, hanging on to his every word with nods of devotion and understanding.

By the time the game began, Edward had nearly finished with his second plate—jam puffs, blancmanges, and a plum cake —and was more than ready to fill his third with two pieces of pound cake.

He wasn't a gluttonous man. He merely enjoyed a small taste of revenge now and again. No, no. Not revenge. Equality and fairness. Even though he hardly knew what fairness in life was.

As the points increased for both teams and the bats held up under the pressure of the game, Edward's confidence grew. Yes, he would be receiving payment that morning, and all would be well.

For the time being, of course. Lord Ryecombe's promised payment would hardly cover half of February's rent. Past and future rent would still need to be paid, broken tools would still need to be replaced, and food would still need to be purchased. He couldn't afford any of it.

He ate his newly plated pound cakes, the sugar turning to sand in his mouth. This was all due to men like Lord Ryecombe. Selfish, heartless. Did he not know he injured Edward's mother by withholding the payment, too? Either way, the man obviously didn't care.

But Edward cared.

He meandered back to the table, slipping pieces of plum cake and sponge cake and a strawberry turnover into his handkerchief. Securing the pastries in the now-stained white folds, he then placed the food into his leather satchel. Mother would appreciate these, even if they were a bit dismantled by the time she could eat them.

After stashing away his pilfered-for-a-good-cause pastries, he looked around to ensure he'd remained unspotted. All eyes were focused on the game.

That is, all eyes except for a stunning pair directed straight at him.

His heart dropped. Had the young woman who boasted such eyes seen his thievery? He glanced away but could still feel her gaze on him.

As casually as possible, he took a few steps back and slid into the crowds, the food twisting round in his stomach like a spiral auger. Suppose she told Lord Ryecombe? The man would never pay Edward then.

The usual crack of a ball against the bat echoed around the field, but instead of the usual cheers, screams bore out, and Edward's pastries were forgotten.

"Lord Ryecombe!" came a voice above the rest.

"Is he injured?" cried a man from behind.

"Who hurt him?"

"Blast and wretch!"

Edward leaned forward with the rest of the crowd, both teams racing toward the seats where Edward managed to catch a quick glimpse of Lord Ryecombe rocking back and forth, holding his hands to his mouth.

"Is there a physician?" shouted someone standing beside the injured man.

"Make way, please!" A man with sandy-brown hair pushed forward. "I'm a doctor."

Lord Ryecombe swatted him away. "I'm more than well, Cooper," he grumbled. "Continue with the match!"

"Forgive me, my lord, but I must insist that you allow me to see to the wound, if only to ensure nothing worse comes of it."

"You are thimply trying to end the game now your team ith winning," Lord Ryecombe growled, his swelling lip impeding his speech. "Upon my honor, he'll pay for thith!"

Lord Ryecombe was clearly referring to the man who had struck him. Edward glanced around, but he could not see a single soul who bore the regret and guilt he ought to for hitting a member of the gentry in the face with a cricket ball.

"Did you see the accident?"

Edward paused. A female voice was close to him, but clearly, she wouldn't be speaking with Edward.

He kept his focus on the crowd gathering closer around Lord Ryecombe, his view of the man now gone.

"Excuse me, sir?"

Her voice sounded closer. *Was* she speaking to him? He glanced over his shoulder, startled when those stunning eyes—green, now that he could see them closer—watched him again.

Heat poured into his cheeks. Did she recognize him as the pastry pilferer? "Pardon?"

"I merely asked if you happened to see the accident."

Perhaps she *didn't* recognize him. Her expression was innocent enough. "Yes. I mean…That is to say, no. I *heard* the incident."

A touch of disappointment flickered in her eye. "So you did not see the culprit?"

"I am afraid not."

She pulled her lips to the side and peered around him at the working-class team. Edward hesitated, facing forward again.

"Do hold still, my lord," the doctor was saying, though Edward could no longer see them.

"Are you a supporter of the game?"

Was she speaking to Edward again? He turned around, and sure enough, her focus was still trained on him.

He glanced from side to side. She had to be at least twenty, still in need of a chaperone. Where was her family? Would they think it was he who had prompted the start of their conversation?

"I enjoy watching a match every now and then," he replied simply.

She nodded in silence.

Wishing to avoid any misconceptions or condemnations, he gave a nod to end their conversation then faced forward again.

Most of the crowd had dissipated from around Lord Ryecombe, the teams already returning to the field. So the earl had gotten his way, and the game would continue. Not that that came as a surprise to Edward. Wealthy gentlemen always received everything they—

"Have you played cricket yourself?"

Edward started at the woman's voice piping up directly beside him. When had she moved up there?

"I have," he responded.

As strange as she was, he could not deny her pretty features accentuated by a blue spencer and white dress—clearly the dress of a gentleman's daughter. Her bonnet matched with small sprigs of minute, blue flowers tucked into a darker blue ribbon.

But never mind her charming appearance. His discomfort grew and spread as rapidly as an infectious wood disease. Never had a person, let alone a lady, taken such an interest in him before.

"Did you enjoy playing the sport, Mr....Sir?"

So that was where she drew the line of propriety, avoiding asking him his name because they had yet to be formally introduced? Perhaps if he answered apathetically, she'd take the hint and leave. "I suppose."

A pleased twinkle shone in her eye. "Do you live here in Inglesbatch?"

"No, I do not."

"Then where do you live?"

She was mad. She had to be. Should he really be alerting a mad woman to where he lived?

She looked at him expectantly until he relented. "I take up residence in Bath."

Her eyes shone even brighter. Apparently, he was giving her all the correct answers this morning. "Were you born and raised there?"

He glanced at the crowd nearby. Fortunately, no one seemed concerned with their conversation in the slightest, all eyes focused on the cricket match. "Yes, I was. But if you'll excuse—"

"Do you have friends playing today?"

For heaven's sake. What was next? Would she ask after his parents? How he had been brought up? What his family's darkest secrets were? "Yes, I do."

"Is that why—"

"Marianne?" called a feminine voice from within the crowds.

The woman's eyes rounded, looking past Edward's shoulder.

Was that her name? Marianne? He looked over his shoulder but could not find who had called out.

"Is someone looking for you?" he asked, turning back to the woman with the green eyes.

She gave an uncomfortable laugh. "Oh, I hardly know. At any rate, I must be off. It was a pleasure to meet you, sir. Good day."

With a swift curtsy and a smile that revealed small dimples at the ends of her lips, the woman disappeared into the crowd the opposite direction of where the other woman had called for her.

Edward remained still for a moment, trying to process what had just occurred. What was this woman planning to do with all of this newfound knowledge?

With a quick exhale of breath, he faced the cricket match once more, carving out the memory of the woman and replacing it with his attention on the bat—the bat that held his fate within each grain of the wood he'd smoothed.

His work would hold up for the rest of the game. It had to.

After all, he couldn't afford for it to do otherwise.

CHAPTER TWO

Marianne Coventry circled back around, slunk past the refreshment table, then slipped into her chair behind her parents without a hitch.

A point was made for the gentlemen's team, and Father stood, cheering with delight just as Beatrice emerged from the crowds.

"There you are, sister," Marianne said, feigning surprise. "I'd wondered where you'd gone."

Beatrice eyed her suspiciously. There was no fooling her. "I was sent to find you, Marianne. Mama was worried."

Mama turned around at the sound of her daughters speaking. "Ah, you have finally returned. I trust the lemonade was worth the lengthy time it took you." She raised her eyebrows knowingly.

Marianne knew she shouldn't have taken so long. Speaking with two gentlemen had been pressing her luck. Three was just asking for trouble.

"I was merely taken with Lord Ryecombe being injured, that's all," she said.

"Oh, yes. Poor man." Mother faced forward again. "I do hope he will be all right."

"I'm sure he will be, my dear," Father said, patting her hand that she laced through his arm.

Another crack echoed around the field, and Mother and Father both faced the game once more. Unfortunately, Beatrice wasn't so easily distracted, her blue eyes boring into Marianne.

In every way, the sisters were opposites. While Marianne had green eyes and dark brown hair, her older sister was blue-eyed and blonde. Marianne's nose was littered with a sprinkling of freckles, and Beatrice had not a blemish to be seen.

Truthfully, Marianne was more than happy with Beatrice being the prettier of the two. Having such beauty meant that Beatrice would marry sooner. Or at least, it was supposed to have meant that.

"Where were you, really?" Beatrice asked, leaning toward Marianne so their parents couldn't hear.

Marianne smiled innocently. "By the refreshment table." That wasn't a lie. Each man she'd spoken to *had* been by the refreshments.

"And what were you *doing* over there?"

"Why, getting refreshment, of course."

Beatrice frowned, though no wrinkle formed in the middle of her brow. "Very well. I'll allow you to keep your secrets, only because I'm too tired to pull the truth from you." She stifled a yawn, covering her mouth with her laced glove. "Do you have any idea how much longer the game will last?"

"I imagine another hour or so. Lord Ryecombe's injury delayed us a good deal."

Beatrice grimaced.

"Are you not enjoying yourself?" Marianne asked.

Beatrice glanced sidelong. "What is there to enjoy about a cricket match?"

Marianne nodded with understanding. Though cricket was

an exciting game to her, and she would die for a chance to play herself, Beatrice had never liked the sport. But after her parents had become acquainted with Lord Ryecombe at the assemblies last evening in Bath, their family had been invited to watch the match at Briarwood. Beatrice had protested the idea, but Father never passed on an invitation to improve his standing with gentlemen.

Marianne couldn't complain about the match herself. For once, the sun was bright and warm, she was away from the confines of her home, the happy chatter around her buoyed her spirits, and the food was delectable.

The last man she'd spoken to had apparently thought the same thing.

She smiled, looking past Beatrice to try to spot him again, but he was hidden amongst the others. Shame.

"Who are you staring at?"

Marianne hesitated. "Oh, no one. I was just admiring gowns and such."

Beatrice eyed her with suspicion again, but Marianne leaned forward, clasping her knees in her hands before Beatrice could press her for more information. "Perhaps you and I could take a walk to the refreshment table. I'm certain we could meet some interesting people on our way."

Heavens, but she was laying it on thickly.

Beatrice shook her head. "I'm not one for socializing at the moment."

Marianne couldn't understand it. If she were Beatrice, she wouldn't hesitate to speak to every man within ear shot. Heavens, Marianne wasn't even out in Society yet, and she'd already brashly approached three different men.

If Father discovered her improper behavior, there certainly would be consequences. He was taken with appearances, especially as of late. But truly, Marianne's behavior was as much for her sister's sake as it was for her own. Ten years had passed since Beatrice's search for a husband began—and five years since Marianne had believed *hers* would begin. She wanted Beatrice to be happily settled. Was it so very wrong for Marianne to wish for the same herself?

"If you are so very bored with cricket, perhaps we could play a game of our own," she suggested next.

"What do you have in mind?" The usual, perpetual somberness dimmed Beatrice's eyes.

She had not always been that way. When they were children, she was as energetic and enthusiastic about life as Marianne. But Beatrice had become far more serious once she had entered Society at fifteen, when Marianne had just turned ten. No doubt she felt the pressure to marry and marry well.

"I shall bring to your attention a few men in attendance here, then you will tell me if you believe the two of you would make a fine match," Marianne offered.

Beatrice frowned, staring at the field in silence. Had she seen through to Marianne's true motives?

"I do not know if I am up for such a game, Marianne," Beatrice said.

Marianne scooted to the edge of her white chair. "Come now. It will be fun. Here, I shall find the first for you."

She pointed out a gentleman nearby with a red waistcoat—the first man Marianne had accosted with her questioning that morning. "He is charming, is he not?"

He was also clearly wealthy and had answered all her questions without fault. Born and raised in a renowned city, did not care for cricket, enjoyed reading. All of these added up to what could potentially be a very fine match for Beatrice. If the match was realized, Marianne would finally be free.

Yet, with Beatrice's disinterested gaze, Marianne's hope floundered.

"You don't find him the least bit attractive?" she asked.

"Certainly. But he's too tall." This was exactly why Marianne had taken it upon herself to narrow down the potential candidates. Beatrice had become unbearably fussy with prospective husbands. She had to be aware what her hesitant behavior was doing to Marianne, did she not?

Marianne wasn't sure she wished to know the answer. Either Beatrice knew and willingly continued to injure Marianne—or she didn't, thereby revealing her lack of consideration for her sister.

Marianne shook the demoralizing thoughts from her mind. "Very well, what about him?" She pointed out the second gentleman she'd questioned, a man with fair hair and a chest reminiscent of a barrel.

Beatrice nodded. "He is handsome. But he does not appear as if he would enjoy reading."

"He enjoys reading," Marianne blurted out before thinking better of it. "I mean, I'm certain he would." She was certain because he'd told her as much.

"Even still, you know I am more partial to darker hair on a gentleman."

Marianne bit the inside of her cheek. Each man had answered her questions hesitantly but none so much as the third. He was dark-haired and by far the handsomest of all the men she'd spoken to.

She strained her neck forward, and to her delight, she caught sight of him making his way to the refreshment table again. Would he hide another bundle in his satchel?

"What of him?" she asked next.

"Who?"

"The man at the refreshment table."

Beatrice's eyes lingered on him before pulling away. "He is of a lower class, Marianne."

"And?"

Beatrice gave her a dubious look. Obviously, Marianne knew exactly what the issue was, but he was perfect. From what she'd gathered in the few moments she'd spoken to him, anyway.

"You know Father would never approve." Beatrice raised her chin. "Nor would I. Papa worked too hard to leave behind that life, only for his daughter to return to it."

Marianne sighed. She was right, of course. As a young family, the Coventrys had never been truly destitute, but there were moments she recalled her parents voicing their fear of not having enough money for food. Before Marianne was ten, Father had realized his dream of making money through trade and various investments enough to purchase an estate of his own. But if the working class was where Father had started—was how he had become who he was today—how terrible could it be?

"He still appears to be relatively wealthy, does he not?" Marianne pressed, eying the man's fine jacket.

She hardly cared about wealth. She could go without new gowns and the latest fashions if she was simply around the people she loved.

Beatrice didn't look at him again. "You and I both know wealth only plays a small factor in all this. Father is adamant about keeping up appearances."

Marianne knew this to a fault. It was the very reason she was still not out in Society. When Father had first made his fortune, he'd been snubbed by a certain number of upper-class individuals. Not wishing to be looked down upon, he swore to obey Society's standards to a fault, whether that was in his daughters' best interest or not. Marianne obviously believed the latter, though she did her best to do what Father requested of her.

"As I said before," Beatrice continued, "I shall not marry anyone I do not love, especially if he is not a gentleman, and neither shall you." She stood abruptly, clasping her hands before her. "Excuse me. I'm tired of *both* games now."

Marianne's shoulders fell as she walked away. Her sister had said neither of them would marry anyone less than a gentleman. But then, would Marianne even have the *chance* to marry if her sister never chose a spouse?

As it was, it was probably for the best that Beatrice had not fallen for the working-class man. Marianne wouldn't like having a man so handsome for a brother-in-law.

CHAPTER THREE

L ord Ryecombe was upset. When the working-class team won and the bats held up without so much as producing a splinter, he handed—rather *flung*—Edward's payment at him with a begrudging look.

"Ath promithed," he grumbled. His lip had swollen large in an angry, purple bruise.

"Thank you, my lord," Edward said, clutching the payment as he battled with his lips to thwart a smile. Was his chipper tone far too pointed? Was it terrible that he did not care if it was? Having the earl humbled—in appearance and in paying Edward —was simply too satisfying. As Mother always said, "Injustice has a way of working itself out."

"Excellent cricket match," Edward said. He motioned to Lord Ryecombe's mouth. "I am sorry to see you injured, though."

Lord Ryecombe muttered a few unintelligible words, clearly seeing through Edward's fabricated sorrow.

At the earl's dejected tone, Edward's mood lifted even higher, like leaves raising toward the sun. His day had turned out immeasurably better than he'd thought it would, especially when the odd woman had finally left him to his pastries in peace. He was more than fine not having seen her again once she'd darted away from whoever had called out for her.

Lord Ryecombe shifted away from Edward without another word, turning to speak to a gentleman with fair hair who had come up beside the earl.

As they engaged in their own conversation, Edward slipped the payment into his satchel with a satisfied smile. Mother would be pleased to see the amount. They would live to see another day at the shop now.

"Well done with the bats, Steele."

Edward looked up as his friend, Michael Cavinder, walked past, sweat still beading his brow from the match.

"Thank you," Edward returned. "And well done on your victory." He glanced to Lord Ryecombe, who was still occupied with the gentleman. Lowering his voice, he said, "Did you see who hit the ball at Lord Ryecombe?"

Michael paused, laughing in his throat. "Does it matter who did, so long as we all got to witness it?"

Edward shook his head in amusement. He and Michael had been friends for years now, having first bonded over their shared love of the arts—Edward with carving, and Michael with painting.

Michael rubbed his jaw, his eyes still shining with mirth as he spoke in a hushed voice. "You know, my father painted the earl's portrait. I do wonder if he should make an adjustment to Lord Ryecombe's likeness now that he'll have a proper scar on his lip."

Edward chuckled, and the men tipped their heads to each other in departure.

Securing his satchel closed, Edward made to leave Briarwood Estate, but Lord Ryecombe stopped him, calling out from behind.

"Mr. Thteele?"

Edward turned to face him again, the other gentleman still at his side, focusing his attention on Edward.

"Is this the maker of the bats then?" the man asked.

Lord Ryecombe nodded, his voice taut as he spoke. "Mr. Coventry, thith ith Mr. Edward Thteele. Mr. Thteele, Mr. Jacob Coventry."

Edward greeted the gentleman with a short bow. Mr. Coventry responded with an observing eye, looking Edward up and down as one would examine a new milk cow.

"I'm quite impressed with your work, Mr. Steele," he said. "I happened past your shop last week and viewed your fine carvings from the window."

Edward quite liked this man, despite his being a gentleman. "Thank you, sir."

Lord Ryecombe looked green in the face. Whether that was due to the praise Edward had received or because of the obvious pain the man was in due to his purple lip, Edward couldn't decipher.

"Excuthe me," the earl said with a bow.

He wandered toward two working men waiting nearby. A mention of a pair of bay horses drifted to Edward's ears, and he focused on their interaction, distracted by their looks of dismay. Eventually, the earl walked away, and the two men were left with scowls.

"...ever come through with the blunt..." one of them said as the other shrugged.

Was Lord Ryecombe trying to swindle them, too? If only that came as a surprise.

"They do not look very pleased with their conversation."

Edward darted his gaze to the man Lord Ryecombe had introduced him to, having nearly forgotten that Mr. Coventry still stood beside him.

Edward cleared his throat, embarrassed at having been caught prying in another's affairs.

Mr. Coventry shifted his body to face him. "Have you a moment to speak, Mr. Steele?"

"Of course, sir." So long as more praise would be given.

"I will not take much of your time. I merely wished to inquire of your schedule. You see, over the last few years, I've hired numerous cabinetmakers to refinish one of the libraries in my house that was damaged from extensive underuse and lack of care. The entire room has been refurbished with new wood—the ceilings, the bookshelves, the flooring."

Edward nodded, leashing his hope to his side.

"It has taken longer than I'd hoped it would," Mr. Coventry continued, "but I should like to see its completion this year. The final touch will be, of course, the carving. I'm sure you've surmised as much, but I should like to hire you for the job."

Edward blinked to ward off his surprise.

Lord Ryecombe had hired Edward out of sheer desperation, and any other orders from the upper class were next to nonexistent. The only way Edward had been able to keep a small amount of food on his table was working for those in the city who were unaware of the rumors and had happened upon his shop. Apparently, this was the category into which Mr. Coventry fell.

"It will be a long task, mind," Mr. Coventry said. "Perhaps three or four months."

Three or four months. Three or four months of a solid, steady income. Three or four months of carving, designing—doing the thing he loved most. This had to be a dream.

"I believe I could manage such a task," he answered as apathetically as possible.

"I would need you no later than next week," Mr. Coventry said, then he hesitated. "In Ashwick."

"Ashwick?" But that was nearly twenty miles away.

"Yes, I hope that will not be a problem. You would need to stay in the village, of course. But I am more than happy to pay for your room. And I will compensate you for the work generously."

Edward's hope lapped at his heart. With such work, he might then be able to satisfy the four months of rent he owed. He would certainly be daft to decline such an offer.

But how could he leave Mother for so long?

"When would you require an answer, sir?" he asked. "I have a few items to work out beforehand."

"Within the next few days would be ideal, but I understand if you need more time to put your affairs in order." He pulled out his golden watch, eying the time. "When you decide, send me a note at Queen's Square. We will be there until the end of this week."

"I'll have a decision to you before then," Edward agreed.

The men nodded in departure, and Edward struggled to hide his smile. Now all that was left to do was tell Mother—and hope she would agree to his decision.

But of course, she did.

The moment he spoke with her about the opportunity, she began eating his smuggled pastries and jumped straight into planning.

A week later, Edward was adjusting his leather satchel around his shoulder and carrying a portmanteau out of their small home on the outskirts of Bath.

"You'll send word the moment you arrive safely?" Mother asked, readjusting his cravat for the second time—something she'd always done with Father.

He nodded. "You will be all right here without me?"

She patted his cheek. "The three months will be long, but we shall do what we must."

Edward was still hesitant about leaving Mother for so long, especially with the landlord, Mr. Chapple, breathing down their necks. Edward had managed to ward off the penny-pinching man for months with compliments and promises. But he feared Mr. Chapple would take advantage of Edward's absence and threaten evicting Mother.

Worry stirred in the center of his chest, producing unsettling images of begging for money on the streets and carving from a cheap house in the middle of the countryside. He'd promised Mr. Chapple he'd deliver a month's worth of rent by the second week of June—after a month of working for Mr. Coventry.

This was all contingent on Mr. Coventry keeping *his* end of the bargain, of course. Would he do the same as Lord Ryecombe had done? Or would the man simply refuse to pay Edward altogether?

Edward shook the thoughts from his head. Mr. Coventry had seemed more than trustworthy. Edward needed to believe him. He had no choice *but* to believe him.

"Do take care of yourself, son," Mother said, "and be sure to eat often to maintain your high spirits."

"I will, Mother."

"And be sure not to work yourself too hard. But take care not to dawdle. And express your gratitude to the Coventrys every moment you have the opportunity." She hesitated. "And... and be sure to take special care with your behavior. We wouldn't wish for the rumors to only grow."

Edward listened to her advice. One would think he was a boy leaving for school for the first time and not a twenty-eight-year-old man.

If he was being honest, though, he was as anxious as if it *was* his first day of school. He knew his actions were constantly under scrutiny after all that had occurred with their family. Mr. Coventry didn't appear to be aware of any such rumors, but Edward feared that someone—Lord Ryecombe, perhaps—might alert Mr. Coventry that the Steeles were nearly out of business. Or worse, *why* the Steeles were nearly out of business.

But three months working for a reputable gentleman could change the rest of their lives forever. Though, whether that change be positive or negative was still yet to be seen.

CHAPTER FOUR

After spending a restless night at the Blue Boar Inn, whittling away at a spare stick to release his nerves, Edward rose early and traveled the distance on foot from the village to the Coventry's home.

With its columns and spires and light brown stones, Daffley Park easily rivaled Lord Ryecombe's estate. To the west of the house, a small pond nestled in a grove of trees. Beyond that, fields of sheep bordered with grey stone walls lined the countryside. In truth, he far preferred the grounds to the house. But then, what did Edward know about stone?

He strode toward the structure with his leather satchel over his shoulder, his tools tucked inside. Knocking against the front door, he removed his hat and waited to be greeted.

A few moments later, the door swung open without a sound, and the butler stood before him with an impassive expression. "Yes?"

"Good morning. My name is Mr. Edward Steele. Mr. Coventry has hired me to—"

"You are the woodcarver?"

"Yes, I am."

The butler opened the door wider. "We've been expecting you, sir. I am the Coventrys' butler, Mr. Morley. Do come in."

Edward entered with a grateful nod of his head. He forced his eyes away from the grand marble entryway, the chandelier at the top of the room shimmering with crystals, and the two circular staircases winding to the upper floors.

He'd been slightly uneasy with the sheer amount of money Mr. Coventry had agreed to pay him via their next correspondence. Now, Edward was certain the man could afford to compensate him even more.

Mr. Morley closed the door and faced Edward. "Mr. Coventry has been called away on a business matter, so he has tasked me with showing you to the library."

Edward shifted his feet tensely. Mr. Coventry had been more than kind to Edward. Would the rest of the household welcome him so openly?

They were sure to, if they did not know about the rumors.

"If you will follow me, sir."

Edward trailed after Mr. Morley through the various corridors, losing count of the number of rooms they passed until they reached the east wing of the house.

From there, Edward could have found the room himself. Mahogany tended to lose most of its aroma as time passed, but the woody scent still pervaded the area, growing as they drew closer to the library.

Edward preferred that smell to any other cologne or fragrance. It spoke to his soul with warmth and whispered clarity to his mind.

He stepped into the library after Mr. Morley, his eyes captured at once by the sheer amount of deep, reddish-brown wood covering the room. The ceiling was split into simple, squared sections, and the bookshelves circled about the entire space from floor to ceiling, excepting the large windows at the end of the room, which poured bright sunshine into every inch of the library.

Edward certainly had his work cut out for him.

"As far as I'm aware," Mr. Morley said, "the cabinetmaker hired before did an excellent job creating the shelves and ceiling, but he failed to meet Mr. Coventry's expectations in regard to the detailing." He pointed to a small section of the bookshelf where a foot of the wood had been carved into a rather unwieldy design.

It certainly needed a more graceful touch. Luckily, Edward could provide just that.

"You are welcome to come and go as needed through the servants' entrance," the butler continued, "but Mr. Coventry expects a full day's work from you every day apart from Sunday. Of course, he is not averse to you needing an extra day or two to await supplies or to recoup from your work."

That was fair enough.

Edward placed his hands on his hips as he distractedly examined the ceiling. He could create a very elegant design along the edges of the squares, yet still showcase the masculinity of the wood. Perhaps a grand floral design with wave-like shapes would serve him well.

"I was told Mr. Coventry discussed the matter of payment with you?" Mr. Morley asked.

"Yes, he did." Mr. Coventry had promised to pay Edward after a month's worth of work, which was more than generous. Shocking, really, in comparison to Lord Ryecombe's behavior.

Still distracted, Edward continued to glance about the room. In the corner was a dark-red, oversized chair pushed up against the window that featured a spectacular view of the estate. Beside the chair, a small table was situated with a stack of books and...were those crumbs spread about the top of them?

Mr. Morley's words cut through his musings. "There will be meals available from our own cook, providing you agree to have a small fee taken from your income."

Edward nodded. "That would be most appreciated." Especially after the stale meal he'd consumed at the Blue Boar last evening.

Mr. Morley extended a piece of paper folded three times. "Here is a list of Mr. Coventry's requirements. I hope you have been warned of the work ahead of you, Mr. Steele."

Edward scanned the items requiring detailing. Just as Mr. Coventry had said, this was easily three months' worth of work, if not more.

He smiled. "I am more than ready, Mr. Morley. I assure you."

A flicker of approval flashed in the butler's eyes. "This end of the house is usually silent, so you will be left relatively undisturbed. Should you be in need of anything, simply alert us with the bellpull and someone shall be sent to help you." He walked to the door. "Now, if you'll excuse me, I must make ready for Mrs. Coventry's callers."

"Thank you, Mr. Morley."

The butler departed with a nod.

When Edward was left alone, he drew in a deep breath and took in the work ahead of him. His hands tapped anxiously against his leg, itching to feel that smooth wood with his fingertips.

He hoped Mr. Chapple would be patient with the rent due. He hoped Mother would be all right without him. And he hoped Mr. Coventry would approve of his work.

But Edward? He was going to be just fine.

He removed the satchel from his shoulder, laying it down on a nearby table. As he pulled the tools out, lining the chisels and mallet neatly in a row, footsteps padded outside the door.

He paused. Had Mr. Morley forgotten a part of his instruction?

But the butler never appeared.

"Hello?" Edward called out.

Silence replied.

He walked to the door with narrowed eyes, poking his head around the corner, but no one was there. Perhaps he'd simply imagined the footsteps. Or maybe the house was haunted.

He smiled, amused with himself. He certainly was in a good mood.

With an indifferent sigh, he returned to the bookshelves crying out to be beautified. This was going to be a dream realized, carving these shelves, and he couldn't wait to get started.

───────── ∽ ─────────

Marianne pressed up against the wall, blood rushing in her ears. Who was that man, and why was he in her house?

She'd been distracted walking to the library that morning, so eager to continue reading about Hamlet and Ophelia—for the third time—that she hadn't seen the imposter until she'd rounded the corner. Thankfully, she'd pulled back before he'd seen her.

She chewed on her lower lip, contemplating what to do next. Should she scream? Alert Mother? Ring for a footman to expel the ruffian from the premises?

No. There was no time. He was obviously there to steal something. She needed to act swiftly.

Moving to stand right outside the door, she raised Shakespeare's greatest work—in her opinion—over her shoulder. If words were dangerous, then thirty thousand of them should do the trick.

This was it. This was her time to defend her home. She drew in a deep breath and bounced up and down on the balls of her feet, finding the energy and courage she needed to confront the rascal. The rascal who was...*humming*? What sort of thief hummed while he thieved?

She stilled, the tightness in her chest loosening. Slowly, she peered around the edge of the door.

His back was turned to her as he rolled up his shirtsleeves and stared at something on a table covered with a white sheet. He propped his hands on his hips, his dark brown waistcoat spreading nicely across his shoulders. Then he peered up at the shelves and retrieved something from the table.

A tool? From where had that come?

As he moved toward the shelves, pressing what looked to be a chisel against the wood, her questions were answered.

Of course. This must be the woodcarver Father had mentioned wanting to hire. He was dressed far too nicely to be a common criminal, and he certainly wouldn't have been humming or calling out earlier if he'd been trying to sneak about in silence.

Beatrice was right, Marianne let her imagination run amok too often. Slowly, she lowered her weapon. Rather, *Hamlet*. This woodcarver certainly had a fine set of shoulders. His strong jaw was reminiscent of—

She gasped. The man turned just enough for her to see his face, and recognition struck like a flash of fire in the darkness. This time, instead of hiding behind the wall, she raised her skirts, clutched her book in her hand, and darted down the corridor far away from the library.

It was him, the man from the cricket match. She was sure of it.

She pressed a hand to her brow to settle her spinning mind. After the cricket match, she'd realized how fortunate she'd been that Beatrice had not wished to pursue any of the men Marianne had spoken to. The men surely would have told her family of her odd behavior. Father would have been furious.

Father *was going* to be furious, for now that the woodcarver was in her home, the truth would most certainly come out.

Unless, of course, she could stop him from ever saying a word.

CHAPTER FIVE

E dward was settling into his new routine nicely. After four days, he'd finally found a way to receive a better night's rest at the Blue Boar by avoiding the uneven lumps in the inn's mattress. He'd also learned to leave the window open just a crack to ease the stale smell of the countless number of individuals who'd slept in the room before him.

Each day, after he completed his work, he would return to the village, have a drink at the inn, converse with a few local farmers, then spend the rest of the evening whittling, writing to Mother, or walking around the town. In the mornings, he frequented Mrs. Hill's bakery, and rather than using his waning funds for a heartier morning meal, he spent the pennies buying discounted tarts, cakes, or biscuits and bringing them to Daffley Park to enjoy throughout his day of work.

He was also making steady progress in the library, having almost forgotten how greatly he preferred carving flowers, leaves, and curves rather than creating unembellished, old-fashioned furniture made of oak.

Among other things, he'd even learned to deal with the ghost of Daffley Park. Although, she was rather less like a ghost and more of an actual female with flesh and bones. A female who had taken to staring at him every day without fail at nine o'clock in the morning.

He had yet to catch a solid glimpse of her, but he'd seen the swish of her skirts as she darted away from the room every morning he tried to confront her for staring. She was no doubt a maid. Whether she was simply intrigued by what he was doing or was watching him for another reason, his patience was growing as thin as the metal of his smoothing chisel.

After receiving a tray of food one midday, Edward had asked the footman if he knew the maids for the east wing of the house.

"There's one maid who cleans up here, sir," he'd replied. "She does so on Mondays. Early morning, I believe."

Edward had nodded, though his confusion had only grown, as well as his determination to confront the girl and end her stares once and for all. He was finished looking over his shoulder, having her gawk at him like he was a caged bear at the Royal Menagerie.

The next morning, he worked steadily, forcing his eyes to remain on the leaf-like design he was carving next. He took a bite of his pale Shrewsbury cake then continued with his work.

It was nearing nine o'clock. She would arrive any minute now.

Sure enough, only moments later, the girl's footsteps stopped just outside the door. If he hadn't come to expect her appearance, there was no way he would've heard her, her movements as quiet as a petal falling from its flower.

He drew in a steady breath. Every time he had called out to her or attempted a glance at where she stood half-hidden behind the doorframe, she had startled like a newborn fawn and swiftly fled.

This time, he'd attempt a different route.

Little by little, as he tapped his mallet against the chisel along the mahogany, she leaned farther around the door frame.

He had to time this perfectly, wait for just the right moment or his plan would fail.

Finally, when half her shoulder was visible from the corner of his eye, he spoke. "Were you in need of something, miss?"

She gave an almost indiscernible gasp and pulled back.

He continued carving inch by inch, all the while listening for any retreating footsteps. Had he missed them, or was she being exceptionally bold that morning?

"I know you are there, miss," he lied.

Still, she remained out of sight. He didn't blame her for doing so—if she was, in fact, doing so.

"I will tell no one that you are shirking your duty," he continued. Was he embarrassing himself now, speaking to an empty room and corridor? Or was she, in fact, listening to him? "Though, I highly doubt a maid ought to be neglecting her work every morning as you do."

He watched the door expectantly, but she didn't appear.

With a sigh of disappointment, he returned to his work. Then a movement flashed in the corner of his eye, and the girl stepped into the doorway.

Only, she wasn't a girl.

"I am not a servant."

Edward stared. Those stunning green eyes were unmistakable.

"You," he said, his jaw slack. "You are the woman from the cricket match."

She raised her chin, her hands held behind her. "Yes. But I am not a servant," she repeated.

No, of course she wasn't. She was a gentleman's daughter, through and through. Except, what gentleman's daughter would approach a perfect stranger and ask personal questions of him? No doubt the same gentleman's daughter who would hide behind a wall and sneak stares at a woodcarver.

"I apologize for the mistake, Miss..." He stopped with a prompting for her name.

"Marianne Coventry," she stated.

He swallowed. "You are Mr. Coventry's daughter?"

"One of them, yes."

Anxiousness grasped his chest and squeezed tightly. His employer's daughter. He'd been hoping for a friend of the family or a distant relation. Never his daughter.

He couldn't afford to be alone with this woman. It was too risky, too foolish, given the rumors already surrounding the Steele name. Suppose someone thought he was capable of...

He cleared his throat, the air between them as thick as the mahogany he should be carving right now. "It is a pleasure to meet you, ma'am."

He nodded and turned away, hoping his signal was obvious enough for her to leave but polite enough that she wouldn't be offended.

Unfortunately, she didn't move an inch. "I did not know who you were at the cricket match."

"Pardon?"

"I did not know who you were when I spoke with you at the cricket match."

He felt only slightly better. At least she hadn't been spying on him then, too.

"In truth," she continued, "I do not even know who you are *now*."

That was the one question she *hadn't* asked him before. "Edward Steele. Your father hired me to finish this room."

"I gathered from the shavings." She motioned to the shredded wood scattered about the floor and atop his boots.

Her tone was clipped, especially when compared to how cheerful she'd been at the match. She had good reason to be in a poorer mood, he supposed. She *had* just been mistaken for a servant.

He shook his boots back and forth to be rid of the shavings. "I apologize for mistaking you as a servant, ma'am. It will not happen again."

Her eyes brightened as slowly as a sunrise. "I suppose I can hardly blame you. I haven't been behaving very ladylike, have I? Asking imposing questions and staring unabashedly." She ended in a soft, twittering laugh.

He watched her carefully, unsure of how to respond. There was not a single penitent wince or embarrassed blush on her face. Not even a flicker. How could she be perfectly fine with her behavior? She had to be one of the strangest women he'd ever met. Her twinkling eyes made her one of the prettiest women he'd ever met, too.

"I did have reasoning for my staring, though. You see, this is where I come to read every morning." She pulled her hands out from behind her back, revealing a book.

He waited for her to explain further, but she looked at him expectantly, as if he was supposed to know the magnitude of her words already.

"I'm...sorry?" he said, ending in a question. She looked perplexed. Was he not the one who ought to be confused? "Is there, perhaps, another location where you might read?"

"But I always read here. From nine o'clock to ten o'clock."

He stared. What did she expect him to do, stop working, leave the house, and come back when she was finished?

Her silence spoke measures. He should've known. All people who came from wealth were the same. "I suppose I could speak with your father to ask him if..."

She shook her head with wide eyes, ending his words. "Oh, heavens, no," she blurted out.

Perhaps word of their conversation alone together would not reach her father then. That was a relief.

Checking her volume, she continued softer. "He wouldn't

understand my desire to read here. At any rate, he is still away on business."

She looked longingly at the corner of the room, and he followed her gaze to the oversized chair he'd noticed on his first day, the crumbs no longer visible. Had she been the one to put them there?

Her continual stare in that direction answered his question.

He wiggled the tools in his hands. Every moment that ticked by increased the likelihood of them being discovered. Mr. Coventry may be absent, but that would not stop Mr. Morley or any other member of the household from telling him that the woodcarver was possibly fraternizing with his daughter.

She needed to leave. Now. "Ma'am?"

Miss Coventry blinked, withdrawing from her daze. "Do you, perhaps, know for how long you will be carving?"

Edward hesitated. If she was that attached to the library, how would she react to the truth? "I'm afraid my work here may take some time. A few months at least."

Her shoulders fell. "I see."

He certainly was not to be blamed for his presence there, but the disappointment on her face tugged at his conscience. He needed to help her. Especially given that one negative word to her father might persuade Mr. Coventry to send Edward home without a shilling.

"I leave before six o'clock every day. Perhaps you could read here then."

"No, that is when I visit with my family, providing they're not out."

She certainly wasn't making this easy on him. "I could take an hour's long break in the afternoon if that will suffice? One o'clock, perhaps?"

She shook her head. "I am occupied all afternoon. And one o'clock is when I paint, not read." She clicked her tongue in disappointment.

Edward wasn't sure if the absurdity of the situation was getting to him or if he was simply attempting to cope with the strangeness of it all. Either way, a stitch of humor sidled through his defenses, and he fought hard to keep his smile at bay.

"I'm terribly sorry," he responded.

She looked up at him, catching his eye and pausing for a moment without speaking. "Oh, that's all right."

He watched her expectantly, thinking she would finally excuse herself, but she remained.

"You must be an accomplished woodcarver for my father to have hired you. He is quite particular when it comes to whom he employs."

Suddenly, Edward didn't mind her lingering. "I'm humbled that he would use me, then."

She nodded, her eyes searching his, then she abruptly curtsied and turned on her heel. "Good day, sir," she murmured over her shoulder, then she was gone.

Edward stared at the empty doorway, blinking. That woman was just as odd as he'd remembered, and she would certainly prove to be a terrible distraction.

So how was he to keep her out of the library?

CHAPTER SIX

Marianne was not one for dramatics, but staying away from the library the following morning was one of the most difficult tasks she'd ever had to accomplish.

Very well, she *was* one for dramatics. But not going *had* been extremely challenging. She'd tried reading in the orangery, the drawing room, and then in the rose garden, but she missed the scents of the wood and the books mingling together like old friends, and she longed for the soft way in which the light from the library windows illuminated her pages.

She was well aware of how ridiculously she was behaving, but nothing had disrupted her schedule this way in months, apart from when they were in Bath.

She sighed deeply as she lay in bed that night. How she longed to return to the city. She'd been kept indoors for the most part while there, too, but at least her family had been together more often.

It had almost felt the way things had once been. The four of them together at home. Father reading to them at night as Mother brushed the girls' hair before a warm fire, Beatrice and Marianne giggling over the silly voices Father used.

But those days were gone and had been for some time. Now, Father spent most nights in his study, poring over ledgers, Mother was busy running her large household, and Beatrice pottered off to her friend Miss Clark's home multiple times a week.

If only Marianne was allowed the same freedom. If only Beatrice would choose a spouse so Marianne could...

She pressed her hands to her face. This was precisely why she stuck to her schedule. Not doing so allowed her mind to wander too greatly.

The next day, she threw herself devotedly into her daily routine, walking for two hours instead of reading to avoid the dilemma altogether.

But then another issue arose. As she wandered on her walk, so did her eyes wander toward the library windows. She couldn't make out much with the overcast skies glaring off the glass, but she could just imagine the woodcarver, Mr. Steele, creating grooves in the wood with his tools, his sleeves rolled up and his dark hair falling over his brow.

She was daft to have continued spying on him, and speaking to him had been an even worse decision. It was only a matter of time before Father discovered her poor behavior.

Although, if she carried out her plan, she just might convince Mr. Steele to do otherwise.

After her walk, a light meal, a ride around the estate, and adding to her landscape painting of the view from the parlor window, she set about her plan.

She was supposed to be practicing her needlework that hour, but for her own well-being, she abandoned adding a few white roses onto her handkerchief and headed down to the kitchen.

A few moments later, she returned upstairs with her newly acquired stash in a small basket. She swung it lightly in her hands, traipsing across the entryway with a grin. There was no possible way this Mr. Steele would not accept her bribery. She had an inkling that he had a sweet tooth as unquenchable as hers.

She'd nearly made it to the stairs when the front door clicked open. Swiftly, she jerked the basket behind her back and faced whoever was entering Daffley Park.

"Beatrice?"

Her sister looked up, her smile disappearing and surprise rounding her eyes. "Marianne." She looked away, unbuttoning her spencer. "Where are you off to?"

Marianne tightened her hold on the basket behind her. "Oh, nowhere in particular. I was simply stretching my legs."

"But it is only half past. I thought you would still be stitching."

"I decided to finish early today."

Beatrice removed her spencer and bonnet, handing them to a passing footman who accepted the outerwear then left the sisters alone in the entryway. "That hardly sounds like you, sister, changing your schedule in such a way."

Perhaps Marianne had made it known to too many people how dutifully she repeated her routines. "I suppose it's never too late to change." She laughed guiltily. "Where were you?"

Beatrice looked away, her cheeks rosy. It must be quite cold out of doors today. "Only visiting Miss Clark. Mr. Henry Clark wished to give you his regards."

Marianne nodded. Henry Clark, Miss Clark's younger brother, was a kind man. He was only a few years older than Marianne and had always made an effort to include her and Beatrice both in conversation and greetings.

"I trust he is well," Marianne said.

"I believe so."

They stood in silence for a moment. Beatrice had never been one to speak much, but today she seemed remarkably quiet.

"Did you enjoy yourself with Miss Clark?"

"I did, thank you. Where is Mama?"

She was quick to change topics, too.

Marianne adjusted the basket she still hid. "She is planning the menu with Mrs. Roberts."

"I will join her." She walked the opposite direction from where Marianne had been headed then paused. "But first, I have a proposition."

Marianne tipped her head to the side. "And what proposition would that be?"

"If you do not tell Mama that I was with Miss Clark this afternoon, I will not tell her that you've been sneaking Cook's pastries again."

Marianne's mouth dropped open, and she pulled her basket from behind her back. She needed to stop sneaking. She really was terrible at it.

"I suppose I have no choice but to agree," she said. Should Mama discover her indulging again, Marianne would certainly receive another stern scolding. But then... "Why do you not wish for Mother to know you were visiting with the Clarks?"

Beatrice hesitated, then she stretched her lips in a smile. "I was supposed to be practicing the pianoforte."

"Oh, I see." But Marianne was not fully convinced. Beatrice was hiding something more. Then again, so was Marianne. "Very well. I accept your proposal."

"Perfect." Beatrice outstretched her hand, palm up as she wiggled her fingers. "Now you may compensate me for my excellent idea."

Marianne huffed out an exaggerated sigh then slipped her hand beneath the cloth covering her basket. A moment later, she withdrew a cherry tart and extended it to Beatrice. "Here you are, madam. I do hope you will be satisfied."

Beatrice took the tart and promptly bit into the pastry, backing away from Marianne. "I will never be satisfied with a single tart. Just like you." Her eyes wrinkled slightly at the edges with her smile. "Now remember, not a word to Mother."

Marianne nodded, watching her sister practically skip down the side corridor. That visit with Miss Clark had done wonders for Beatrice's mood.

Now here was hoping Marianne's tarts would do the very same for Mr. Steele.

CHAPTER SEVEN

Marianne paused just outside of the room. Was she utterly ridiculous for doing this? Should she leave matters as they were and simply hope Mr. Steele wouldn't speak with Father?

"Have you come to spy again?"

She started at Mr. Steele's voice. Blast it all. It was about time she'd learned her lesson about thinking she was being covert.

Slowly, she stood in the doorway. "No, not at all."

Muted light from the heavily clouded skies streamed in through the large windows at the far end of the room, illuminating the carver, who stood on the fourth rung of a ladder that leaned against the bookshelf. His shirtsleeves were again rolled halfway up, and he held a tool in each hand. He'd been making steady progress on one side of the bookshelf, the design swirling more than halfway up the height of the shelves.

His eyes dropped to the basket in her hands. "Is there anything I can do for you today?"

His stern brow had lessened somewhat from what it had been at the cricket match, and a shadow of facial hair brushed against his jawline—a jawline so angled, it appeared to have been carved by the very tools in his *very* masculine hands.

"Ma'am?"

She blinked, forcing her eyes away from his features. "Yes, I hope you forgive my intrusion."

He pulled his tools away from the wood and leaned his left arm against the ladder. His waistcoat was halfway unbuttoned, his cravat loosened enough to reveal the lower half of his throat.

She cleared her own throat and looked away. "I've been considering my actions lately and realized they may have been lacking in propriety. So, I thought I'd make amends by bringing you these." She raised the basket, unveiling the pastries with her free hand. "I hope you enjoy them."

Mr. Steele peered down at the basket, his lips twitching before he looked back up to her. "That is very kind of you. But you needn't have gone to such trouble."

She shrugged, stepping forward and placing the basket on the table beside his perfectly aligned tools. "Perhaps for one mistake. But I've made three."

Still standing atop the ladder, he narrowed his eyes. "Three?"

She nodded. "I bombarded you with questions, spied on you for days, and then hinted very conspicuously for you to leave Daffley Park for an hour so I could read here. So you see, cherry tarts are the very least I could do." She motioned to the tarts. "Why do you not take a moment and enjoy one while they're warm?"

He watched her for a moment in silence. "I don't believe your father would approve of my stopping work to eat a pastry."

She narrowed her gaze. "Did my eyes deceive me when last I was here? I'm certain I saw a pastry of your own situated just there." She pointed to where his handkerchief had rested the last time she'd been in the room—the same place his handkerchief was now located, fresh crumbs atop it.

If she didn't know any better, she'd say the man was more obsessed than she was.

He seemed to contemplate her words before nodding. "Very well. I will gratefully accept your offer. If only because I've no chance of denying the fact that I have been eating on the job."

Cherry tarts. They always did the trick.

He descended the ladder and approached where she stood at the table, rubbing his hands together as small shavings of wood drifted to the ground.

She took a step back as he retrieved the largest tart. She'd forgotten how tall he was.

"I do apologize for how few there are," she said as he took a bite. "I'm afraid my sister pilfered one. And I may or may not be guilty of fishing out one or two for myself before I arrived here. You see, I have very little self-control when it comes to pastries." She clenched her teeth together and sent him an awkward grin.

He gave a half-smile in return and swallowed, his throat bobbing. She'd never taken any special note to a man's neck before. There was something intriguing, even captivating, about the angles.

"I don't believe I would have been able to stop myself either," he said.

So she'd been right about him. "I thought so, especially after you swarmed Lord Ryecombe's refreshment table like a bee to a wildflower."

He coughed, holding one of his hands to his mouth as he leaned forward, trying to catch his breath.

"Heavens, are you all right?" she asked.

He continued to cough.

"I'm terribly sorry. Was I supposed to have kept that knowledge to myself? And that I also saw you slip a handful of cakes into your satchel?"

His coughing increased.

Oh dear. She'd taken her teasing one step too far.

Eventually, Mr. Steele let out one more thorough cough then straightened, clearing his throat and averting his gaze.

"I do apologize," she mumbled.

He shook his head. "I feared you had seen me doing such things," he said, his voice husky from the coughing attack she'd induced. "I have no reasonable excuse for eating as much as I did. But to be clear, I did not take the cakes for myself. They were for my mother."

A warmth flowered in her heart. "Oh, how very kind of you. I'm sure she appreciated them."

He cleared his throat again. "Well, the cakes were more or less a handkerchief full of crumbs by the time she partook of them. She was very gracious, though she had to scoop them into her mouth."

Marianne gave a little laugh. He glanced at her then back at his tart. "Am I allowed to continue eating, or are you to reveal something else unsavory about me first?"

She waved a hand. "Oh, no. By all means, eat."

She tried not to stare as he took another bite. When had swallowing a cherry tart become such a mesmerizing action? Did he really need to have his cravat loosened so much? She supposed the room was a little warm.

"Do you like them?" she asked, if only to keep her eyes from where the contours of his neck disappeared into the slackened cravat.

"Very much. I've enjoyed much of your cook's food and am always impressed. I also enjoy Mrs. Hill's pastries from the village."

Marianne clicked her tongue as he took a final bite. "Oh, you would be wise to not let Cook overhear you say that. She might scorch your food on purpose."

He watched her, intrigue lighting his eyes. "Why is that?"

"I'm afraid Cook and Mrs. Hill have a rivalry. When we first arrived in Ashwick and hired Cook, her proficiency became well known, but Mrs. Hill is not one to accept defeat easily. Everyone in town looks forward to the rural festivals because Cook and Mrs. Hill create so many delicious pastries to compete with one another, we all eat ourselves sick."

A smile cracked on his lips. "That must be quite enjoyable." He finished off his tart and brushed the crumbs off onto his handkerchief.

"Oh, very much so. Perhaps you will be here during one of the festivals."

"Perhaps." He looked back to the bookshelf, as if contemplating beginning work again, but to her delight, he continued speaking instead. "You mentioned earlier about first arriving in Ashwick. Did you live elsewhere before?"

She tapped her toe anxiously on the ground. Now would be a good time to share with him the real reason she'd come upstairs.

"Yes. Father purchased Daffley ten years ago. We lived in a small town in Berkshire before this."

"I see." He was no doubt wondering why they had moved, and Marianne would have gladly told him, had he asked. Unlike Father, she didn't feel shame for their past.

But Mr. Steele remained silent.

Now. She needed to speak now. Before her opportunity was lost. "Mr. Steele, there is another reason why I've brought the tarts to you."

He didn't respond, his eyes narrowing a fraction.

"You see, I'm afraid I am using them to bribe you."

His eyebrows raised. "To do what exactly?"

She drew in a deep breath. The worst he could do was deny her request and tell Father. Nothing more terrible than that. Then Father would keep her indoors for longer, and she'd be doomed to remain shut away at Daffley Park forever.

That was all.

She groaned inwardly. "I wish for you to not tell my family

that I spoke with you at the cricket match and to keep to yourself the fact that we are acquainted at all."

He remained still. "You do not wish for your father to know you've been here?"

She shook her head.

"And you will not speak to him about me?"

"No, Mr. Steele."

His shoulders visibly relaxed. "You have my word then, ma'am."

Well, that was easier than she'd expected. "Do you not wish to know my reasoning as to why?"

He shrugged. "I imagine you have a very valid reason. But it is not my place to question it." He reached for the basket on the table. "May I have another tart, or do you wish to eat the rest?"

She pulled her eyebrows together. Why had he agreed so quickly? Rather than pressing the issue, she ought to be happy. But she couldn't understand it.

"I brought them all for you."

He nodded, snagging another tart and taking a bite as he moved toward the ladder. "Off to read, then, are you?"

She struggled to set aside her confusion. "No, I only read in the mornings. Right now, I ought to be practicing my needlework." But she'd chosen to forgo the activity in order to speak with this near stranger.

That made sense.

He popped the rest of the tart into his mouth, his jaw working as he chewed. So now she had an obsession with the way this man swallowed *and* chewed?

"Do you practice your needlework in here?" he asked.

"In the library? Heavens, no. I work on it in the drawing room where the light is not so brightly reflected against the whiteness of the cloth."

"A valid reason." Why did his brown eyes twinkle so amusedly? "What explanation do you have to read in the library? Apart from the obvious answer of being near books, of course."

She tore her eyes from the gentleman and swept her gaze around the room. "I've always loved it in here, but ever since Father had the room refinished, the smell of the wood is intoxicating." She shrugged. "I do not know how to explain it, exactly. It is soothing in a way. Almost like an embrace. To have that mixed with the comforting smell of old books, it will be utter perfection in this room. If only they could bottle that smell more frequently instead of roses or jasmine."

His eyes fixed on her. Had she done it again? Said something to make him uncomfortable? Overstepped her bounds?

"What is it?" she asked.

The amusement in his eyes had faded, replaced with a wary brow. "I must simply return to my work, or your father will be displeased. That is all."

Embarrassment pinched her chest. Why did she linger when her task was already accomplished? "I will leave you to it then, Mr. Steele. Good day."

She left the library and the woodcarver behind.

There. She'd done it. She'd apologized, delivered a peace offering, and made an agreement to keep their communications secret. Now she could forget about the man and move on with her life and her routine.

Oh, but she would need to retrieve the basket from him at some point. Now, when could she fit that into her schedule?

CHAPTER EIGHT

Marianne looked forward to Sunday every week. She didn't mind sitting on the hard pews in the freezing temperatures of winter nor the boiling heatwaves of summer. She didn't mind listening to an hour-long sermon of scriptures she already knew by heart. She didn't even mind when her legs begged to be stretched or her eyes began to droop.

Because on Sunday, Marianne was free. Well, as free as she could be. Without Father there, she was even more so.

When normally, she would patiently await the end of the sermon, today, she used every last ounce of her willpower to not leap from the pew and dart outside to speak with as many people as she could while Father was not present. Inwardly at times, she felt like a puppy free from her restraints for the first time, ready to lap at strangers simply because she was happy to see them. Outwardly, however, she was as calm and collected as Beatrice.

No, she could never be that calm. Beatrice hardly ever showed any emotion now, apart from boredom.

When the sermon finally did end, Marianne followed behind

Beatrice and Mother as they moved to pay their respects to the vicar, Mr. Ellison, who stood just outside the church doors.

Once they'd moved on, Marianne lingered behind, taking any chance to speak with someone other than the members of her household.

She'd always liked the vicar and his wife. Mr. and Mrs. Ellison were some of the few individuals who did not treat her like a social recluse. Not that she blamed the rest of town for doing so. She was the only one of her age who was not yet out in Society, married, and having children of her own.

"Mr. Ellison," she greeted. "Thank you for your sermon. Your words always carry me through each new week."

The middle-aged man gave her a kind smile. "Miss Marianne, you truly are a light. There are many times I receive gratitude and compliments, but with you, I know they are always sincere."

He patted her hand warmly, and she curtsied before returning to Mother and Beatrice, the two of them having continued down the path toward the carriages.

Marianne was not yet ready to leave her one social event of the week, however, so she slowed her pace and breathed in the fresh scent of the morning air. The rain had halted for a moment, and though the sun did not break through the clouds, nothing could mute the brilliant green of the grass nor the glorious pink of the rose bushes surrounding the churchyard. Birds chirped in the ash trees behind them, and the soft chatter of friends and family members greeting each other warmed her heart.

How she loved Sundays.

"Marianne?" Mother called from up ahead.

Marianne finished the final distance between them. "Yes?"

"We must pay our respects to the Abbotts."

Marianne nearly groaned. Father insisted that they seek the approval of the Abbotts, the foremost family in Ashwick. But each time, the elderly couple ignored Marianne entirely and stared down their noses at everyone else. Indeed, they were the ones who'd encouraged Father to keep Marianne from Society until Beatrice married. Father had instantly agreed, not willing to risk anyone looking down on his family.

Marianne tried very hard to like everyone. But the Abbotts held a special place in the "strongly dislike" portion of Marianne's acquaintances.

"Mama," she began in a soft voice, "might I stay behind this time? I could greet the Clarks instead."

Mother hesitated. She understood Marianne's plight and was more willing to bend the rules of Society than Father was. She'd been the one to convince him that Marianne no longer needed a governess at eighteen.

But still, in this regard, she had her hands tied. Father had requested each of his family members to prove that they, the prior working class Coventrys, were worthy to mingle with gentlemen and ladies. Marianne hardly cared *whom* she mingled with, just so long as she got to speak with someone.

Except for the Abbotts, of course.

Mama pulled her lips to the side. "Very well. But not a word to your father about this, understood?"

Excitement's broad doors opened wide inside Marianne's chest, allowing even more light to enter. "Oh, thank you, Mother!"

She gave her a quick embrace then retreated toward Miss Clark nearby with a lilt in her step.

As she approached, Miss Clark greeted her with outstretched fingers. "Miss Marianne, it is so lovely to see you."

Marianne smiled, taking her hands. Miss Clark had always been kind to her, though she was better friends with Beatrice, being closer in age and in similar circumstances. Well, they *had* been in similar circumstances. Now, Miss Clark removed her hands from Marianne's and laced her arm tightly through her betrothed's.

After the usual greetings, Marianne faced them both. "This was the second time the banns have been read, yes? You must both be eager for the coming week to be accomplished."

"Indeed," Miss Clark said, beaming up at her soon-to-be-husband. "Are we not, Mr. Morris?"

He grinned right back. "Absolutely."

Marianne felt as if she was imposing, so long did their gaze last. She couldn't blame the couple, of course. She would be just as excited, should she ever be in the same circumstances.

Mr. Henry Clark then came up to stand beside his sister, his usual happy smile taking up half his face. "Good morning, Miss Marianne."

"Mr. Clark, how do you do?"

The man—having just returned from Oxford that year—was charming in a boyish sort of way.

"Are you enjoying being home again?" she asked.

His grin had yet to falter. "Very much so."

"I'm terribly sorry we have not been to call in so very long, Miss Marianne," Miss Clark said. So she *was* able to pry her eyes from Mr. Morris's. "We've been so busy with our wedding preparations, you see."

"Entirely viable excuse, of course. I fear I must apologize, as well, though. My sister calls upon you so often without my knowledge. I've not been able to send my regards."

Miss Clark tipped her head. "Oh, but she has not called these last few weeks."

Marianne narrowed her eyes. That couldn't be right. "She told me she visited with you twice only this past week."

Miss Clark looked to her brother. "Have I missed Miss Coventry's calling?"

"I do not believe so. Though, she is more than welcome to call, of course." He directed his grin once more at Marianne. "Or you are welcome to come on your own, if you wish, Miss Marianne."

She shifted her feet uncomfortably. Miss Clark shook her head at her brother then gave Marianne a sympathetic look. Was Mr. Clark unaware that she was still not out in Society? It was true that most of Ashwick—excepting the Abbotts, most likely—had thought perhaps Father would allow Marianne out when she was twenty. Even Marianne herself had hoped that. All of her friends, and most of her friends' younger siblings, had already married.

Obviously, Father had other plans.

She nodded an awkward thanks to Mr. Clark then turned back to Miss Clark. "You are certain Beatrice did not visit you this last week?"

"Yes, my dear. Quite certain. I've been occupied all week with Mr. Morris's family who have just arrived for the wedding."

Marianne stared off, revisiting the conversation she'd had with her sister. She was certain Beatrice had said she'd called on the Clarks. But then, Marianne *had* been distracted by her upcoming visit with Mr. Steele—and with hiding the pastries. Perhaps she'd heard wrong.

Unless, of course, Beatrice had made the agreement with Marianne to keep her location a secret from Mother because Beatrice had not, in fact, been at the Clarks.

Marianne inwardly shook her head. She was once again letting her imagination run wild. Beatrice had no reason to be untruthful.

A movement at the corner of her eye pulled her attention away from the Clarks. Mother and Beatrice waved her over to the gate leading toward the carriages.

Already? Her high spirits slipped from her grasp before she even had time to gather them.

With a half-hearted smile, she bade farewell to the Clarks—

Mr. Clark's grin also fading fast—and returned to her family's side.

"Must we leave so soon?" she questioned.

"I'm afraid so, dear," Mama said with a look of compassion. "Beatrice has the beginnings of a headache."

Marianne looked to her sister, who winced. "If one more person interrogates me about whom I wish to marry, I fear I shall go mad. Why is it so difficult to believe I will marry for love, but that love is difficult to come by?" She walked toward the carriages. "I am sorry to cut your socializing short, Marianne. You may join me in visiting the Clarks this week."

Any other day, that would have satisfied Marianne's desires. But now, she could not help but think, would that visit really happen? She had a mind to confront Beatrice about her potential falsehood, but Marianne had promised not to tell Mama.

Together, the three of them made for the carriages, Marianne's footsteps slow and heavy.

"Chin up, my dear," Mother whispered, taking her arm in hers. "I'm certain things will change soon. Your obedience will bless you in the future."

She wanted to believe Mother, but Marianne's unending optimism faltered. Sundays kept her afloat, but what was she to do with her socialization cup veritably empty?

"Who is that man?" Mother asked under her breath.

Marianne looked up at the same time her heart dropped.

Mr. Steele was standing nearby with his eyes trained on them.

CHAPTER NINE

Dressed in the same jacket he'd worn to the cricket match, Mr. Steele stood near the gate leading from the church-yard—the gate Marianne and her family walked straight toward.

"Who is he?" Mother repeated in a whisper.

Beatrice remained silent. Marianne couldn't say a word even if she tried. Her head spun in circles.

This did not bode well. She may have bribed the man to keep their knowledge of each other silent, but how was he to do so when he would inevitably speak with them that morning? If Mama knew, she would be inclined to tell Father. Marianne was done for.

But then, she had no reason to believe Mr. Steele would *not* keep her secret. Was that not so?

They reached the gate, her family pausing as they took in the sight of the large puddle that had grown to cover more than half of the pathway. Marianne glanced back to Mr. Steele, who stood beside it, his eyes still fixed on her. Is that why he stood there, to help them cross it? Perhaps he wouldn't say a word to them.

"Might you allow me to help you cross, ladies?" he offered, removing his hat with a bow.

So much for not saying a word.

Mother stepped forward first. "That would be very kind of you, Mr...."

"Mr. Edward Steele, ma'am. Your husband hired me to carve within the library at Daffley Park."

Mama's look of intrigue changed to understanding. "Oh, yes, of course. My husband has been searching quite some time for someone of your caliber."

Mr. Steele's eyes flicked to Marianne.

Marianne glanced at Beatrice.

Beatrice watched Mr. Steele.

Did she recognize him from the cricket match? Heavens, this was turning into a disaster.

"I certainly hope I can live up to his expectations," Mr. Steele said.

"I'm certain you will." Mother turned with a motion of her hand. "Won't you allow me to introduce my daughters? Miss Beatrice Coventry and Miss Marianne Coventry."

Marianne curtsied alongside her sister, keeping her eyes averted. Would Mr. Steele now tell Mother that he knew Marianne? Or worse, *how* he knew her?

"It's a pleasure," he said with another bow of his own.

Her heart thumped. His eyes caught hers. Then he stood off to the side. "Well, I shouldn't like to take up more of your time. If you will allow me."

He offered his hand first to Mother, who accepted it graciously.

Relief rushed through Marianne's limbs, causing them to feel as weak as the sculpted jelly they'd eaten last night for dessert. How could she have ever doubted Mr. Steele would keep his word?

As he helped Mother around the large puddle, Beatrice nudged Marianne. "What was that about?" she whispered.

Marianne gave her an innocent expression. "What do you mean?"

"I mean, all those stares between you and the woodcarver. Do you know him?"

Beatrice didn't remember him?

The tension in Marianne's shoulders disappeared entirely. "Of course not." She didn't *really* know him either, apart from the fact that he had to be the most honorable gentleman who was not, in fact, a gentleman.

She focused straight ahead, ignoring Beatrice's questioning gaze and trying very hard not to run her eyes across the framing of Mr. Steele's broad shoulders or smell the musky cologne that softly pervaded the area around him.

He returned soon for Beatrice, and after she was safely delivered to Mother's side—she and Mother walking toward the carriages—Mr. Steele reached out his hand for Marianne.

Gently, she placed her fingers in his, and their eyes met as his thumb pressed lightly on her knuckles. She directed her eyes forward and stepped around the puddle.

"Thank you," she murmured, releasing her hand and walking beside him toward her awaiting mother and sister.

She ought to say something more, but her tongue felt too thick in her mouth. What was this foreign feeling of shyness weighing down on her like a heavy, woolen blanket?

"Did I manage to keep to our agreement?" he whispered.

She glanced up at him, her words finally coming. "I believe so."

"Excellent. I'd hate for you to think those cherry tarts went to waste."

He gave her a knowing look, then after delivering her to her family, he bowed and walked away.

Mother stared after him. "What a charming man. How

unfortunate he's of a lower class. He might've made a fine match for you, Beatrice."

Marianne paused. She'd once thought the very same, but now, her stomach clenched at the image of her sister and the woodcarver together.

She shook her head. What was she thinking? If Beatrice considered Mr. Steele a match, Marianne would be free.

"Yes, well, we all know Father would never allow it," her sister said. "Neither would I."

She entered the carriage, and Mother nodded, following after her.

Marianne stared after them then returned her gaze to Mr. Steele, who had stopped to speak to Mrs. Hill. The baker had her hands on his, a delighted grin on her wrinkled face as Mr. Steele smiled down at her. That smile of his was so elusive. And attractive—*very* attractive.

She knew Mother didn't really mind what class a person was, but Father and Beatrice both had inflated opinions simply because of Father's income. Marianne couldn't understand it. What did it matter if a man was a gentleman or a member of the working class? Before Father had elevated his status, he had still been just as wonderful a man. Just like Mr. Steele.

She shook her head and entered the carriage. No, Beatrice would never fall for a working-class man. With amiable, eligible gentlemen becoming scarcer in Ashwick, it was very unlikely that Beatrice would marry at all.

So where did that leave Marianne?

CHAPTER TEN

E dward had spent the better part of ten minutes searching the Coventrys' library for his forming chisel before realizing he'd left the tool at the inn.

Frustrated with this setback, he jogged halfway back to the Blue Boar, retrieved the tool, then made for Daffley Park once more. This would certainly teach him not to make the mistake again. He'd lost more than an hour of his time. After finishing only a side of one bookshelf in a fortnight, he couldn't afford to waste a single moment. He would certainly be consuming every last week allotted him to complete the design.

He turned along the lane that led to Daffley Park, his musings propelling his feet faster. He needed to accomplish much more to prove his worth to Mr. Coventry, and dawdling on the path would do nothing of the sort.

The dirt road shifted to gravel, his feet crunching against the road to the estate. He had all of his tools, his stomach was filled with Mrs. Hill's pastries, and the temperature breathed even cooler that day. Nothing would distract him from finishing his work now.

Except for the clopping hooves coming up behind him.

Halfway to the house, he shifted to the side of the road to allow the rider past.

"Good morning, Mr. Steele."

Miss Coventry pulled up beside him, sitting tall and regal in her riding habit atop her bay gelding. Her groom rode a healthy distance from her on his own horse.

"Good morning," he returned.

Her emerald eyes smiled as she looked down at him, though his attention was stolen by a swipe of green paint along her jawline. His lip twitched.

"You are late this morning," she stated, no hint of judgment in her tone.

His eyes dropped to the paint once more. The green not only enhanced her eyes, but it also drew far too much attention to the smoothness of her skin.

He raised the chisel in his hand. "Yes, I forgot this at the Blue Boar, so I had to go back and fetch it for my work today."

"You ought to have asked for a horse. You would have made it in half the time." The paint on her jawline darkened as the clouds in the sky shifted.

"That is all right. I did not mind the walk."

The usual anxiousness that accompanied being with Miss Coventry did not appear that afternoon. Not only did he trust the woman to not speak disparagingly of him to her father—she seemed to have not an unkind bone in her body—but he also had taken matters into his own hands by presenting himself to Mrs. Coventry under the guise of helping them across the puddle. Having the woman introduce her daughters would lead to far fewer questions should someone discover his strange acquaintance with Miss Coventry.

He'd felt badly sending the young woman into a panic at the churchyard, but he was grateful for the chance to prove to her that he could be trusted, despite the unsavory rumors he hoped to keep the family ignorant of for the duration of his stay.

Her gelding stomped on the ground, bringing his attention back to the present.

Miss Coventry leaned forward and stroked the horse's neck, and the animal instantly calmed. "How goes the work in the library?"

He glanced at the groom, who stared toward the stables, no doubt bored of their conversation. "It's moving along smoothly. I've never worked with such fine mahogany."

She sniffed a laugh, still stroking the bay's brown coat. "That is my father for you. He would never settle for anything less. Only the finest mahogany for his library. Only the finest material for Mother's curtains. Only the finest silk for sister's dinner party dress."

He waited. "And for yourself?"

She stared down at him, her brow pursed beneath her elegant, blue hat. "Oh, I am in need of very little."

Her silence spoke measures, though questions still arose in his mind. Was she neglected? Not given the same treatment and fine things as her mother and sister were? How could that be so with Mr. Coventry being as kind to Edward as he had been?

"How long have you been carving, Mr. Steele?"

He hesitated, knowing she was simply changing the subject to avoid his questions. But he wouldn't press her to speak more on something she didn't wish to.

The horse stomped again, despite her settling strokes.

"All of my life. My father started his business when he first married my mother, and I was born soon after. The first gift I remember receiving as a young man was a chisel."

The dimples near the edges of her mouth deepened as she smiled. "Truly? How delightful."

Of course, she would think that was delightful. *She* was delightful. He had certainly eaten his own disparaging words. She was a bit strange, but she wasn't at all like most wealthy individuals. She was a woman who preferred the smell of old books and carved mahogany to roses and jasmine.

The horse stamped on the ground again, snorting impatiently.

Miss Coventry seemed to notice, as well. She turned to the groom. "Would you mind very much taking Rosencrantz to the stables for me?"

"Of course, ma'am."

She then turned to Edward with an expectant look. Heavens, she was looking for him to help her dismount.

He stepped forward, hesitating just a moment before dropping his chisel to the ground—unwilling to risk carving Miss Coventry's skin—then reached his hands forward. He may be more comfortable speaking with the woman, but touching her? That was another matter entirely. Suppose someone saw them? Hopefully, the groom would vouch for Edward's innocence.

Miss Coventry modestly raised her right leg up and over the lower pommel, then leaned forward, pressing her hands gently against Edward's shoulders. As she slipped down from the horse's back, his fingers wrapped around her slight waist, and his heart skipped a beat. The feel of her so close to him felt natural. But it shouldn't.

The second her feet settled on the ground, he tore his eyes away from the paint accenting her delicate jawline then released her and moved back. Willing his heart to pump properly, he retrieved his tool from the ground.

"Thank you," she said.

She extended the horse's reins to the groom, who made his way across the grounds with both animals, leaving Edward alone with Miss Coventry.

Perfect, he could bid farewell to the man vouching for him now.

"Would you see me back to the house?" she asked. "You are going in that direction after all."

He cleared his throat. "Of course."

The worst that could happen was Mrs. Coventry spotting them from the window. He was doing nothing untoward. It was not as if they were alone in a room together. They were out in the open. Nothing improper about this at all. Nothing he could be blamed for. Nothing he would lose his payment over.

"So, tell me more about the carving you do. You enjoy it greatly, yes?" She stood a good distance away on his right side, the paint still clearly visible. Should he tell her about it or leave it be?

"I do," he replied, gripping the chisel more firmly in his hand. "The work I've been completing here is far more fulfilling to me than simply creating plain furniture."

"What is it that makes you prefer one over the other?"

Edward hesitated. Did he truly wish to delve into his likes and dislikes? To create a connection with this woman even more than he already had? Then again, there was no way to kindly refuse to respond.

"There is slightly more finesse involved in detailing a piece of furniture rather than joining them together, which is difficult in its own right, but far less satisfying for me to accomplish."

"You do come from *Steele and Son*, do you not? What does your father prefer doing?"

A sorrowful ache cut through his heart. He knew he should've changed that sign. "He preferred the opposite of me, which was why we worked so well together. But he...he passed a few years ago."

"Oh." A line formed between her brows, the shimmering in her eyes vanishing. "I'm so sorry."

"Thank you," he said, looking away. He didn't wish for pity. He was tired of pity. But then, was it pity she was extending or simply compassion?

"It must be so difficult to carry on the work without him,"

she said softly. "But I'm certain you are making him proud by continuing the business."

The ache struck deeper, as if a chisel had been driven straight through his heart. *Steele and Son* was failing. Edward had yet to prove to Bath that the rumors were false, that the Steeles could be trusted. He was not making his father proud. Father would be ashamed.

They reached the house, and to his relief, instead of walking him to the library, she stopped. "I must go to the stables to ensure Rosencrantz receives a good brushing."

He nodded. "And I must see to the carving."

She studied his eyes for a moment before nodding her goodbye and walking past him, the paint standing out once more.

He really ought to just go straight upstairs, but his conscience got the better of him. "Before you go…"

She turned back to face him. "Yes?"

He touched his lower jaw. "You've something there. Paint, I believe."

"Oh, thank you." She rubbed at her cheek. "I do wonder why the groom did not tell me so. Did I manage to clean it off?" She leaned her jaw toward him, the creamy texture of her skin calling out to be stroked.

He startled at his thought and looked away. "No, it's still there."

She again attempted to wipe it clean, this time with the palm of her gloved hand. "Now?"

"No, you've missed it again." This would be much easier if he could simply reach out and stroke—*wipe* it off for her.

She huffed out a sigh and scrubbed harder, finally removing the mess.

"There you are."

"Thank you," she said with that appreciative smile she was so quick to give.

He pulled his lips in and nodded. Most women would be horrified to be seen in such a manner, but Miss Coventry had seemed entirely unaffected. "So, I take it you paint before riding every day?"

"I do, always at eleven o'clock," she replied, as if there was nothing out of the ordinary about her behavior.

He supposed there wasn't, really. But it was rather strange that she so religiously followed her schedule. Was she avoiding something? Beholden to a routine because of her father? Perhaps Mr. Coventry was not as respectable as Edward previously thought.

"Well, I shan't keep you from your work any longer, Mr. Steele. Good day."

She curtsied then headed for the stables once again.

"Good day, Miss Coventry."

Before he could ascend the steps to the house, she spun around, her brow furrowed. "What did you call me?"

He hesitated. What *had* he called her? "Miss...Miss Coventry?" That was her name, was it not?

Her frown did not ease. "I am Miss Marianne. My older sister is Miss Coventry."

Was that the first time he'd said her name aloud? How could that be so? He looked around them. "But...is your sister here now?"

"No."

"Then are you not Miss Coventry?"

She stared at him, her expression unreadable.

"I apologize if I've caused offense," he said. Though he had no idea how he could have done so. "I will refer to you as Miss Marianne, if you prefer."

She shook her head, still staring at him. "No, that is all right. You are correct, of course. I simply don't believe I've ever been called that before."

He tried not to gawp. "Never?"

She shook her head, still appearing in a daze.

How could that be? Surely, she'd been out without her sister before. She could not always be in her presence during balls and dinner parties.

"Are you well?" he asked when she remained silent.

Her eyes continued to study him before her features softened. "Of course. But I believe it really is time for me to let you depart. Good day."

Then she curtsied and with a growing smile left for the stables.

Thank goodness he was free to continue with his work. When next he saw her—that is, *if* he saw her, he would be certain to leave before any more time could be usurped from his carving.

Just so long as there was no green paint to distract him.

CHAPTER ELEVEN

Years ago, Edward and his father had been commissioned to create a sign for an inn in Devonshire. They'd traveled to the Golden Mermaid and delivered the sign—a mermaid with her tail diving into the water—before spending the night there. It had been the warmest, friendliest, and cleanest inn Edward had ever stayed at.

Perhaps that was why the Blue Boar seemed so dreadful. Or maybe his opinion was due to the plate full of inedible food sitting before him. The beef was black, the carrots were yellow, and the boiled potatoes were as hard as the rocks pebbling the road outside.

If he was still hungry after seeing such unappetizing food, he wasn't any longer once the scent of burnt apple pie at the other end of the table reached his nose.

The cook at the Blue Boar could take a pointer or two from the Coventrys' cook or Mrs. Hill.

He gently pushed the plate aside and scooted his chair back from the table, heading to sit at the bar. Instead of drinking the ale he'd requested, he stared out of the window at the rain splashing against the glass.

He'd received correspondence from Mother that day that had both worried and soothed him.

I've been telling everyone that our fortunes have changed. First, Lord Ryecombe hiring you to create cricket bats, and now Mr. Coventry requesting your services for months. Word has spread, and now, I'm pleased to say, you have a growing list of projects to see to upon your return home. Apparently, the good word of a gentleman helps a person as greatly as a poor word destroys one.

Mr. Chapple has requested to call on you, but I've managed to ward him off at present. I suspect he is anxious to receive his rent—and rightfully so—but he will simply have to wait.

If anything, taking more commissions for you has helped my days to speed along more quickly, which, I fear, is most needed. I find I grow rather bored when you are not here, my son. But worry not. I am more than well.

She seemed hopeful in her words, if not a little discouraged, which only added to Edward's guilt. There he'd been, enjoying pastries left and right, complaining about the bed at the Blue Boar, and doing the job he loved entirely, all while Mother was suffering alone. Lonely, no doubt hungry, yet still taking commissions for them to stay afloat.

How had he turned out so selfish with such a mother?

He sighed, longing for a distraction from his discouraging thoughts, so he turned his attention to the various conversations around him between gentlemen, farmers, and servants alike.

"Well, my Jimmy just purchased a cow…"

"The Clark's stable hand Charlie Macrae has been eyin' up some fine lady. Heaven knows who…"

"I'll be headed to Town, come July…"

"Mr. Coventry has always been that way…"

Instantly, Edward pulled on the reins of his focus, settling on the mention of the Coventrys.

"It is a terrible shame," the first man said, a voice Edward didn't recognize. He glanced furtively over his shoulder but could not place the gentleman speaking. "But we've known what Mr. Coventry has been like since he moved here. All about appearance, prideful man. He believes he is better only because he rose above his lower class."

Edward's eyes rounded. Mr. Coventry had been working class? Previous conversations with Miss Coventry swirled into focus. Of course. That's why they'd lived in a smaller town before. That's why they'd moved into Daffley Park. That's why he only wanted the best in décor and clothing—to prove his worth.

The second gentleman piped up. "I only hope the pride ends with him, though we know it has already infected his eldest. Miss Marianne is the exception, of course."

Edward had lost all sense of propriety. He didn't care a lick that he was eavesdropping right now.

"Indeed. She's a lovely girl. Shame Mr. Coventry has kept her out of Society for so long."

Edward paused. Miss Coventry was not yet out in Society? She had to be at least twenty years now. She *had* to be out. Yet…

Once more, information, memories, and thoughts flew about his mind, bouncing against the edges as he tried to make sense of it all. The schedule to be kept, keeping their conversations a secret, behaving so oddly, having never been called "Miss Coventry" before. That was all because she hadn't been out in Society yet?

He knew of the upper class refusing to allow their daughters out until the older sisters were married, but refusing to allow a woman to socialize, to call, to dance, or to attend dinner parties at twenty, simply for the sake of appearances? How unthinkably cruel.

With a heavy heart, he left his drink untouched and wandered to his room, pulling out the stick he'd been whittling away at and plopping back onto his bed.

It truly was a wonder that Miss Coventry was still so happy, despite her hardships. Then again, perhaps she wasn't.

CHAPTER TWELVE

"It is wonderful to have you home again, Papa."

Marianne stood with her father in the entryway of Daffley Park as he was handed his hat by a footman. Father had arrived just that morning but was now going out with Mama and Beatrice to the Abbotts' dinner party.

That was one party she truly did not wish to attend.

"It is wonderful to be back," he responded, smiling down at her. "I assume you've been keeping to your routine in my absence."

"Of course," she said. As much as possible, anyway.

He placed his hat on his head. "Excellent. I do know how happy it makes you."

She looked away. Keeping to her routine usually did make her happy. She'd discovered long ago it was the best way to cope with her life. If only Father could understand that that was her reasoning behind creating the schedule in the first place.

"Now," he said, glancing up to the empty stairs, "before your mother and sister join us, I have some exciting news to share." She leaned in as he motioned her forward. "I do believe I have finally found a gentleman your sister will marry."

For a brief instant, Marianne's heart lifted. Could it be true? Or would this be yet another failed attempt at the Coventrys' efforts to help Beatrice find love?

"He is the second cousin of Lord Ryecombe," Father said. "I met him at the cricket match but was unsure of his merits. After meeting with him again in Bath—that was my business for my most recent trip, you see—I am convinced he will be perfect for her. Can you imagine? Your sister, related to a lord? *Our family* related to an earl?"

Marianne forced a smile. Father had been enthusiastic once at the prospect of his eldest daughter being married off to a very distant relation of a baron. But these things never worked out.

"You do not seem excited, my dear," Father said. "What is the matter?"

Marianne shook her head. "Nothing. I *am* excited."

He frowned, obviously catching the hesitance in her tone. "Surely you must remember that you will benefit more than anyone with your sister finally marrying."

Didn't she know it.

He reached for her hand, placing a soft kiss to the back of it. "You have been unendingly patient throughout all of this, my dear. But you shall one day have the attention you deserve."

Marianne looked away. She didn't wish for all the attention. Heavens, she didn't need *any* attention. She only wanted to be free of her schedule, of Daffley Park, of not speaking to whom she wanted to speak.

"We must simply remember," Father continued, "following Society's rules benefits us all. We wouldn't wish for the upper class to look down upon us because we started beneath them, would we?"

Marianne shook her head, but only because she did not agree with Father's shame over his past. Making a name for oneself was anything but shameful.

Still, she held her tongue. Father felt as strongly about

proving himself to the upper class as she felt about wanting to be in Society.

"I will continue to be patient, Father," she finally said.

He gave her hand a squeeze then released it. "That is my sweet, obedient Marianne. Always doing the best for her and her family."

The words skittered up her spine like a spider. She was obedient. She was always obedient. If that was what was best for her and her family, then why was she so miserable?

"Will Beatrice truly choose this man, then?" she asked, desperate for even an ounce of hope to cling to.

"We shall see soon enough." He leaned in closer, his eyebrows raised conspiratorially. "I've managed to secure him an invitation to the Abbotts' party this evening."

She struggled to push her grin wider. "Then I look forward to a full report when you return."

Footsteps sounded on the stairs above as Mother and Beatrice appeared.

"I will be sure to keep you informed," he whispered with a wink. Then he turned to his wife and eldest daughter. "There you are. Come, we mustn't be late."

"Yes, we mustn't upset the Abbots," Beatrice said.

Marianne thought perhaps Beatrice had said the words in a mocking tone, but her expression remained unchanged.

"You both look lovely this evening," Marianne said.

Mother reached Marianne's side and gave her a kiss on the cheek. "Thank you, darling. I've instructed Cook to make an extra helping of sugar biscuits just for you tonight."

"Thank you, Mama." Mother always did something special for Marianne on the evenings they attended parties, whether that was requesting pastries from Cook, purchasing new paints, or finding a different book for Marianne to read. The gestures always made the sting of being left at home a little less potent.

"Extra sugar biscuits?" Father chuckled. "You and your pastries, Marianne."

She wouldn't need to eat *her pastries* if she was allowed into Society.

She ignored Father's teasing and turned to her sister. "Enjoy yourself tonight, Beatrice." The words lodged inside her throat as if she'd swallowed a cherry pit. Perhaps she wished to join them after all.

"I hardly think that's possible," Beatrice said, readjusting her shawl around her shoulders. "You are fortunate enough to be allowed to stay home, Marianne. Dull conversation and forced merriment will surely be the order of the evening for us."

Marianne always tried very hard not to be envious of Beatrice and her freedom. But it was in moments like these where she despised her sister's apathy. Did Beatrice not know her own fortune?

"Come along," Father said, clearly finished with the conversation.

He moved to the doorway, but footsteps above stopped their progression. The family turned toward the stairs as Mr. Steele descended them.

His eyes fell on Marianne first, and her spirits instantly raised. What a thrill it was to have a man as handsome as *he* watching her.

"Mr. Steele," Father said at once, "it is good to see you again."

Mr. Steele reached the landing, coming up to stand near Marianne. That foreign shyness she had felt in his presence before slipped back onto her tongue, and she was rendered mute.

It was just as well. She shouldn't be speaking with him anyway.

"I hope your business in Bath was completed satisfactorily, sir," Mr. Steele said.

"Oh, very much."

Marianne understood Father's grin all too well. He clearly believed he'd found his daughter's future husband.

"How fares the carving?"

"Very well, I believe," Mr. Steele responded.

"Do you always work this late?"

"No, sir. I typically leave before six o'clock, but I lost track of the hour."

"A man truly dedicated to his work." Father nodded in approval. "I am sorry I've been unable to see your progress thus far. I would do so now, but we are just about to leave for a party."

Instead of responding or looking at any other member of her family, Mr. Steele's gaze found Marianne's. She stood, taken aback at his lingering gaze. It was filled with understanding. But how?

"In that case, I will bid you farewell," Mr. Steele said. After another glance at Marianne, he departed.

Her family bade farewell to her shortly after, and Marianne was then left alone in the entryway with only her thoughts for company—and only sugar biscuits to look forward to.

CHAPTER THIRTEEN

The soft crunch of wheels against gravel stirred Marianne from her restless slumber. She sat up, blinking to gain her bearings. She hadn't realized she'd fallen asleep.

She slipped off her bed, covers still up, and peered down at the drive. The lantern glowed from the carriage below as her sister and parents spilled forth from within then disappeared from her view as they entered the house.

Thank heavens Marianne was awakened by their arrival. She was desperate to hear how the evening went. Might Beatrice be even remotely interested in father's gentleman?

After a moment, she donned her dressing robe and made for Beatrice's chamber, knocking softly on the door before being bade to enter.

"Marianne?" Beatrice said, her brows arched. "I thought you were Patton. Why are you not yet asleep?"

Marianne shrugged. "I wished to see how you fared at the party." She held her breath. Dare she hope the evening was a success?

Beatrice watched her for a moment then sat down before

her mirror, removing her necklace herself. "I'm afraid you would have been better off sleeping. I have nothing to report."

Marianne should have left that moment. Beatrice was clearly not in any mood to speak. But Marianne was desperate for any sign—even miniscule—that perhaps her sister had connected with Mr. Wakefield.

"Nothing at all?" she asked, taking on a light tone. "Come now, Beatrice. You know how I long to hear all the happenings at a dinner party." Specifically the happenings with gentlemen.

"I cannot imagine why."

Could she not? How Marianne missed the old Beatrice. The one who had been filled with life. The one who'd knocked on *Marianne's* door years ago to tell her about the first gentleman who had flirted and danced with her after her coming out.

"Please?" Marianne pressed.

Beatrice sighed, her petite shoulders falling forward. "It was the same as every dinner party. People mingling in their finery. Discussions at the table about the same weather we've been having for months. Praise over one woman's pianoforte playing and another's high-pitched singing." She looked back at Marianne. "You say you would enjoy such things, but I know you, Marianne. Your taste for adventure, your spirited personality, they have no place at a dinner party."

She turned back around, removing her right earring.

Beatrice didn't know Marianne as well as she professed, or she would have never said something so damaging as Marianne not fitting into Society.

Tears pricked her eyes, but she blinked them back. "I think I'd rather enjoy being out in Society simply to see beyond the walls of Daffley."

Beatrice sniffed. "It is not as freeing as you mistakenly think."

Impatience bubbled within Marianne. How could her sister be so unfeeling? "In what way are you not free?"

Beatrice removed her final earring then swiveled in her chair to face Marianne directly. "You are aware that Father has chosen a new gentleman for me to pursue."

There was no question in her voice, nor did Marianne deny her words.

"Father has spoken highly of Lord Ryecombe's second cousin, Mr. Wakefield," Beatrice continued. "He is handsome, wealthy, of good breeding. But I cannot love him."

Marianne hadn't known the amount of hope she'd allowed to grow within her heart until that very moment, for it left in one fell swoop, leaving her chest to sink in its absence. How could Beatrice simply brush away the man so swiftly? "Surely you are making a hasty decision. You might fall in love with him the better you know him."

Beatrice looked away. "What is love, anyway? I'm sure I shall never know."

Marianne's breathing came in small, short puffs of air. Beatrice would never know love, yet she demanded love in order to marry. If Mr. Wakefield—a cousin to an earl—was not good enough for her, then who would be?

Her chest was tight, and her logic, flawed. The hour was not so very late that she was not aware of that fact. Yet, with her patience waning and her hope all but gone, every shred of common sense slipped through her fingers.

For reasons she could not begin to understand, Mr. Steele's image popped into her mind. What if Beatrice was looking in all the wrong places for love? What if a gentleman wasn't who would make her happy, but a working-class man *was*?

Mr. Steele was wealthy, kind, and charming. He also behaved more gentlemanly than any gentleman Marianne knew. If anyone was deserving enough to marry a lady, surely it was Mr. Steele.

"Perhaps...perhaps you are simply looking for love in the wrong places."

Beatrice didn't respond.

"Perhaps you ought to consider a working man instead of a gentleman."

Beatrice whipped her head around to meet Marianne's gaze. Was that fear in her eyes?

Marianne needed to stop, but her tongue had already been set loose. "Perhaps a moderately successful, respectable man like Mr. Steele might make you the perfect husband."

At her own words, a strange, angry stirring awoke in her heart, akin to jealousy. But it was forgotten in a moment as Beatrice's startled expression shifted to a relieved smile and easy laughter.

"Oh, Marianne. You have always been a dreamer."

Annoyed with her condescending tone, Marianne scowled. "I do not jest."

"Are you hearing yourself, sister? Me, marry a woodcarver? As I've said before, I would never stoop so low."

Marianne balked at the pretentious words. Did Beatrice truly think herself so much better than the man?

Of course she did. So did Father. Simply because of great wealth and an estate in the Coventry name.

With a shake of her head, she left for the door. "Of course not," she murmured. "Forgive me for such a ridiculous suggestion."

"Marianne?"

She paused with her hand on the door, turning back to face Beatrice.

"I am truly sorry for not marrying yet," she said, her tone soft and sober once more. "I know how greatly you desire to be out in Society. But know this—even should I not marry, Mother and Father cannot keep you in forever. Your time will come."

Marianne didn't respond, nodding her head in silence before leaving. She knew her sister was trying to understand, but honestly, Beatrice *couldn't* understand. She was too free to understand. Marianne was desperate. There had to be someway out of her current predicament. Someway she could speed the process along.

Now, perhaps it was time to take matters into her own hands with the only man she could access—even if the thought of Beatrice marrying Mr. Steele made her stomach swirl.

CHAPTER FOURTEEN

The day after Edward had happened upon the Coventrys going out, Mr. Coventry joined him in the library, expressing his pleasure over Edward's progress.

"You've done a beautiful job," he said. "Not that that comes as any surprise to me."

He admired the work up close, nodding his head in approval and voicing his gratitude for Edward before leaving.

That visit thankfully gave Edward the validation he needed to continue with his chosen design. He moved on to the lower half of the opposite side of the bookshelf now. This was the most difficult part, as he was required to lie on the floor in order to reach the base of the shelves.

With his finger, he traced over the pencil markings he'd done one of the first days at Daffley Park, ensuring the lines met up and followed the same pattern as the rest of the bookshelf. Then he lay sideways at an awkward angle, tapping his mallet against the chisel in slow, succinct taps.

"Mr. Steele?"

He stopped, looking beneath the table he lay beside. Long

skirts appeared in the doorway, and an airiness took hold of Edward's heart, as if it flapped about in a cool, summer breeze.

He popped up from his place on the floor and brushed off the shavings from his arms.

Miss Coventry started as he appeared, placing a hand to her chest. "Oh, heavens. I did not see you there."

"My apologies. I was working on the lower portion." He placed his tools on the table and brushed more shavings from his trousers. What would she think of him, appearing so dirty?

She watched him in silence, her customary twinkling eyes and smile missing. Did she disapprove so heartily of him? Not that it mattered, of course.

"Is everything all right?" he asked.

"Yes," she responded softly.

She said nothing more. It had to be nearing eleven o'clock. Should she not be painting according to her schedule? He didn't know what to make of the fact that he remembered such a detail.

"I was speaking with my sister last evening," she finally stated.

Understanding flooded his mind. Of course, that was why she seemed out of sorts. He'd seen the look in her eyes when her family had left her to attend the party. Mr. Coventry was a good man, Edward was sure of it. But what did it matter what Society thought of Mr. Coventry if he was making his own daughter miserable?

"Beatrice is so very charming," Miss Coventry continued. "She is one of the most amiable women in all of Ashwick."

How on earth was he supposed to respond to that? "I'm sure she is."

"You do not know her very well," she stated.

"No, I haven't had the opportunity."

"Well, you ought to." Her eyes focused on anything but him.

"She's lovely, kind, obedient. Intelligent and talented. Did I mention she is charming?"

Edward nodded warily. "Yes, you did."

This was beginning to feel like the cricket match all over again. Miss Coventry, behaving strangely, bombarding him with odd questions and facts.

Then she looked at him head on. "Do you think she is beautiful?"

If Edward had been eating another cherry tart, he would have certainly choked to his death that time. He couldn't very well tell her the truth. Her sister *was* beautiful.

But he preferred dark hair and green eyes.

He cleared his throat. "She is very lovely, just like all the Coventry women."

There, that was diplomatic enough. Wait, had he just said...

But it was too late. Miss Coventry's expression softened at his compliment before a frown tainted her brow. He'd overstepped his bounds, making her uncomfortable. What was the matter with him? He should not be allowing her into his private thoughts. He should not even be *entertaining* such thoughts.

He was a lowly carpenter with a tainted name. To associate even by conversation with the Coventrys was a risk. If they discovered the truth, Mr. Coventry would certainly fear their own reputations being sullied and would remove Edward from his position in an instant. Where would that leave him and Mother?

"Beatrice is accomplished in every degree of her life, far more than I am," she said, her eyes on the doorway where she still stood. "She will make someone an excellent wife one day."

Edward paused. What on earth was this woman getting at?

"You are unattached, are you not, Mr. Steele?"

For reasons he could not explain, he longed to lie, unease taking over residence in his insides. "Yes, that is correct."

"That is good. Because…" She swallowed. "Because my sister has taken a liking to you."

Had Edward not been so shocked, he would've laughed aloud at such an obvious falsehood. The elder Miss Coventry, like him? Preposterous.

So why would Miss Coventry claim such a thing? Why would she tout her sister's many talents and…

Oh. Oh, of course. Understanding poured upon him more swiftly than the rain slipping down the library windows. If her sister married, Miss Coventry would be free.

"Miss Coventry…" He paused. The hopelessness in her eyes, the look of sheer despondence, scorched his soul like a burning iron. How could he speak the truth and break her heart further?

He lowered his voice further. "I apologize, Miss Coventry, but I do not believe I would be a good match for your sister."

She did not miss a beat. "But why?"

"We are of two different worlds. She is a lady, and I am but a humble woodcarver."

She clasped her hands together, holding them to her stomach, as if she were quelling a storm of her own inside. "Surely you must be aware at this point that we also hail from a lower class. Such matters ought not be a concern, for you have clearly risen above poverty as well."

He stared at the tools laid out across the table. If only she was aware of how closely he trod the line between poverty and destitution—and how her father was a deciding factor in all of it. Two more weeks. Two more weeks and he'd have enough money to satisfy Mr. Chapple. At least for a month.

He set aside his worrisome thoughts and focused on Miss Coventry. "I am aware that your father came from humble beginnings. I am also pleased you do not believe class matters so greatly. But I'm afraid it does matter for many."

Guilt encompassed him as her shoulders sank forward. "Yes. Yes, you are right, Mr. Steele. I never should have suggested…"

For the first time since he'd known her, a blush graced her cheeks. "I apologize for wasting your time, sir."

As lovely as the red made her appear, he did not wish to see her embarrassed. "It is more than all right, Miss Coventry, I assure you."

But she did not seem to hear him, delivering a curtsy before leaving the room without a word.

Edward longed to call out for her, to *chase* after her, but did he really have a right to? Mr. Coventry had risen above his station. While Edward did not believe Mr. Coventry to be better than himself, Society did.

And the rumor around his name was not something he could rise above—nor could he bring Miss Coventry down because of it.

CHAPTER FIFTEEN

Marianne leaned back against the old beech tree at the edge of her family's property, pulling her knees closer to her chest so she could balance her sketchbook closer.

Her drawing today was rather depressing. But then, she felt rather depressed. The woman in the sketch also sat against a tree, her face void of any smile. But where Marianne's hands were occupied with a pencil and a sketchbook, the drawing's hands were shackled together with a tight chain.

She sighed, allowing the book to fall back onto her knees as she leaned her head against the smooth, grey bark of the tree. The air was still around her, and the nearby pond sat motionless, reflecting the calm, dark green leaves above her.

Greenfinches chirped their warbling songs to one another as they swooped from branch to branch, their soft, emerald feathers muted in the dimming light of the lowering sun. Bluebells and violets grew in vivid patches around the pond and beyond, carpeting the other side of the pond in a blanket of blues, purples, and greens.

This was her safe space. The place she'd seek out whenever she needed peace or a moment to clear her mind. It was also where she found herself whenever her family held a party at Daffley Park, which was the case that evening.

She did not often allow herself to dwell on her hardships. After all, so many others had it far worse than she did. But there were moments when it was easier to allow the negativity to swallow her hope whole. For what hope *could* she have, knowing Beatrice would never marry—knowing Marianne might end up unmarried, as well?

A light breeze pushed the pond water into rows of never-ending ripples, subdued light shining across the crests. Darkness would fall before too long, and Marianne would have to return indoors. Then again, perhaps she ought to remain outside all evening. No one would notice she was gone. No one would care. No one would—

"Miss Coventry?"

Her shoulders jumped against the tree, and she swung her eyes round to where Mr. Steele stood in the grass a few paces away.

She had not seen him since she'd lied to him about Beatrice four days ago. What sort of desperation had gripped her senses then was beyond her. Would she do something to make her regret this evening, too? "Mr. Steele. You are working late this evening."

He looked away. "Yes, I must have lost track of the hour again." Grey half-circles underlined his eyes, as if he wasn't receiving enough sleep. Had he truly lost track of time, or was he staying later for another reason?

He motioned to her lap, taking a few steps forward. "Do you typically draw at this hour?"

Blast, her sketchbook. She hadn't hidden it in time. She closed the book and set it to the side of her, anxious to ignore the fact that he'd more than likely seen the drawing interpreting her life.

"No, at this late hour, I am typically in bed reading."

"But not in the library, as that is reserved for morning reading."

She nodded, and a heavy silence followed, weighing upon her chest. She could almost hear his thoughts.

Why does she follow such a rigid routine?

What a strange woman.

Clearly, she's mad.

"I have my reasons, you know, sticking to such a schedule."

He studied her, still standing a few paces away. "Why *do* you, then?"

His question was soft, no judgment in his tone.

She contemplated not responding, hiding the truth as she did even from herself. But she could not keep such things in any longer. Her heart wasn't strong enough to do so.

She reached for a pebble and tossed it into the pond, ripples radiating toward her. "Because keeping to such a rigid routine helps me to forget how empty my life truly is."

Surely, he would leave now. What man in his right mind would wish to speak to such a ridiculous female?

Instead of leaving, however, Mr. Steele approached, laying his jacket on the ground and sitting beside her. The strong scent of mahogany lingered around them.

"The ground is still wet," she warned. The moisture from the rain had already seeped through her doubled-up blanket.

"That's all right." He shifted against the ground, pulling his legs up and resting his arms on his knees before linking his fingers together.

They sat in silence for a moment, both staring at a greenfinch swooping low across the water.

"That drawing…was it of you?"

Again, she hesitated. How much of her weaknesses did she really wish to expose to this man? "I suppose."

"This is because you are not yet out in Society?"

Her gaze darted toward him, but he remained focused on the water. So, he knew, then?

As if he heard her silent question, he responded, "I overheard a conversation at the Blue Boar."

She should have known. It was not as if she was trying to hide it from him. Besides, all of Ashwick seemed to discuss her life with everyone but her.

"Yes, that is precisely why I feel trapped," she said. "Which is why you must think I'm mad whenever I speak to you. Asking all sorts of imposing questions, urging you to work faster so I can occupy the library again, lying about my sister taking a liking to you." Heat flushed through her cheeks. "I am ashamed of my behavior."

Why was he not leaving? After everything she'd said to him, after the way she'd treated him, why did he remain at her side?

"I do not think you are mad. But I am glad to hear the reasoning behind your actions." He looked over at her, his dark eyes searching her face. "I assume everything you have done was for the sake of your sister? If she marries, then you may enter Society yourself?"

She cringed at how selfish the words made her sound. She wanted Beatrice to be happily settled, but then Marianne also wanted her own chance at a happy match. The older she became, the more difficult that would be.

"Yes," she responded. "I asked you those questions at Briarwood because I thought I could sort through men faster than she would. Then I lied to you in the hope that you might have convinced her to fall in love with you. But I was a fool. She'd never marry a—"

She stopped herself, but it was too late. Curse her wretched tongue. She glanced at Mr. Steele, but he merely gave a saddened half-smile.

"She'd never marry a lowly woodcarver," he finished for her.

She grimaced. "Not lowly. But a member of a lower class, yes."

He nodded his understanding, remaining silent.

How she longed to dive straight into that pond and swim away from her troubles forever.

As if synchronized with her mood, a cool wind blew past them, sliding across her shoulders like a chill, unwelcome embrace. She brought her knees to her chest and rested her chin against them, securing her shawl more tightly around her.

"I'm sorry," she said. "I did not mean to…We were once of a lower class, too. I suppose we still are."

He nodded. "There is no need to apologize. I'm flattered you would even consider me worthy to marry your sister. But in truth…I'm not worthy."

"You are being too modest, Mr. Steele."

"I wish I was." His eyes sought hers. "But there are things…" He broke off with a sigh, rubbing the back of his neck.

His struggle to speak played out on his face as he grimaced.

"You needn't worry about sharing if you do not wish to," she offered.

But he shook his head. "No, you deserve the truth." He drew a deep breath. "*Steele and Son* was once a thriving, prosperous company. Father and I ran our business with ease and had many loyal, returning clients. After he died, however, things deteriorated. We lost almost all of our work, and I fell behind on our rental agreement with the shop. To make up the difference, Mother and I moved into a smaller home, but that only helped for so long. We are still months behind in our payments, with our landlord at the very end of his patience." He glanced at her sidelong. "I am not wealthy. Your sister would never wish to attach herself to me."

Marianne sat in stunned silence. She'd had no idea how destitute he was, nor how greatly he'd been suffering. She should've noted the way he only ever wore his one jacket, or how his boots were never polished, or how his cravat had been worn thin. How could she have been so selfish as to think she had a difficult life when he and his mother were worrying about not having a *home* in the next few months?

"I'm so sorry," she said, her brow pulling together. "I can ask my father to advance his payment to you or..."

He instantly shook his head. "No, no, that is not necessary. Thank you, but he is already paying me generously. I would not wish for him to think me ungrateful. His offer truly was a godsend."

Marianne nodded her understanding. She knew all too well a man's pride in wanting to provide for himself and for his family.

Her heart warmed at the level of trust he'd placed upon her, telling his employer's daughter that he was penniless. She would not betray that trust. But surely there was something she could do to help. Perhaps if she knew more of the story.

"Do you know why the work stopped when your father died?" she asked carefully. "Was it because you were spread too thinly with the workload?"

His voice fell quiet. "No, it was another matter entirely. Matters beyond my control frightened people away from accepting work from us any longer." He glanced in her direction. "You are not the only one whose life is dictated by Society's rules, Miss Coventry."

She waited for more, but he stopped, and she knew better than to press the issue further.

"So, there you have it," he said with a mirthless smile. "Now you see why it would not do to allow your sister to attach herself to someone who is so poor a prospect."

Wealthy or not, Marianne still could not agree that Mr. Steele was a poor prospect. He was as good a man as she had ever known.

"Now tell me, Miss Coventry, why are you out here all alone?"

She wasn't sure she was ready to turn the conversation back on her own problems, but she resigned herself with a shrug. "You must have heard the dinner party convening now at Daffley Park. I am out here because I am not welcome in *there*."

"So they do not allow you to even attend parties at your own home?"

"Only after dinner. I must remain at mother's side or at the edge of the room in silence. But I've found such a task horribly degrading."

Mr. Steele nodded, as if he agreed with her assessment. Honestly, she did not know who *wouldn't* agree with her, apart from Father, of course. And the Abbotts. Still, it was nice to be understood by Mr. Steele. Then again, she always felt understood by him.

"I'm sorry you feel so trapped," he said after a moment. "I do wish I could help."

Did this man's goodness have no end? "My trials are nothing compared to your own."

"It is not wise to compare trials or to claim that one's are more difficult than another's. After all, no one can understand fully what is occurring within another's heart. All we can do is strive for empathy. This way, we may better understand a person's needs, be that friendship or solitude, service or conversation." He stopped, leaning toward her. "That being said, I believe I may have just the thing to help ease your burden. If only for a moment."

Her heart grasped onto the hope he extended toward her as if it was a rope, saving her from drowning in the sea of sorrow she'd lowered herself into in the first place.

This man was in no way a poor prospect. "What is that?"

He sent her an enigmatic smile. "We must go in search of it."

CHAPTER SIXTEEN

Mr. Steele stood up from his spot on the grass, and Marianne averted her gaze from the wet patch that had soaked through his backside. She really should not be noticing such a thing.

He extended his hand toward her. "Come. We must hurry so we do not miss it."

Their hands met as he helped her up, his callused fingers on hers for but a moment before he released her and led the way forward.

"Where are you taking me?" she asked as he retrieved his jacket and her blanket and sketchbook from the ground.

She twisted her body around to avoid him noting her own wet skirts.

"You shall see soon enough." His mysterious smile grew as he led her forward past the pond and beech tree and out into the field bordering Daffley Park.

She glanced toward the house. Even though the dining and drawing rooms faced the other side of the estate, anxiety crept through her stomach. Then again, what could Father do if they were discovered? Prevent her entrance into Society even longer?

"It is just up here," Mr. Steele said.

She set aside her lingering worries and focused ahead.

Without the shelter of the large tree, the wind carried a stronger, brisker chill, seeming to penetrate her very skin. After a moment, they reached the stone wall that ran through the property and sectioned off fields of the grass still wet from the rain earlier that day.

Mr. Steele patted the top of the stone wall. "Sit here," he instructed.

She eyed the wall that reached well above her chest. "Do you expect me to scale it?"

He laughed, and Marianne's eyes swiftly met his. She'd never heard him laugh before. Heavens, she'd never even seen him *smile* so widely before. His whole countenance shifted, his brows raised, his jaw even more defined as he grinned.

He laid her blanket across the wall then turned to her, stretching out his arms. "Allow me to help."

Suddenly, the stone wall seemed ten feet tall instead of the five that it was. "You are to lift me up there?"

"That is precisely what I intend to do."

She looked at him with a wary eye. "Are you certain you can manage?"

He raised a daring brow, then in a swift movement, he grasped her around the waist and promptly placed her atop the wall. She barely had time to gasp in response.

"I've lifted wooden tables, trunks, and chairs that were heavier than you, Miss Coventry," he said.

There was that name again. How it taunted her. How she loved it on his lips.

He placed the flat of his hands on top of the wall next, then launched himself up, swiftly shifting around to land perfectly beside her. If only his sleeves had been rolled up. She wouldn't have minded observing the muscles in his forearms that had no doubt flexed with his movements.

She blinked away the lingering image and stared out at the moody surroundings, thick clouds still covering the skies. "So what are we here to see, Mr. Steele?"

He looked down at her, their shoulders a few inches apart. "With any luck, something that will bring you joy once again."

Hope knocked against her chest, begging to be let once more into her heart. But she was afraid, afraid to expect good things when her future looked so bleak. "But what is to be done if one cannot find joy?"

His smile faded away. "I know that notion all too well. When my father died, many months passed before I could even register the grief. It took a great deal of patience, but I was able to work through it, eventually finding joy in certain aspects of my life again."

The sorrow in his brown eyes, the slight raising of his brow, spoke measures of his anguish. How she longed to reach out and soothe the ache that was still there.

Before she could, he motioned in front of them with a tip of his head. Marianne followed his gaze forward, and she breathed an airy sigh. The clouds parted for the sun to make its final sweep across the countryside, brilliant shafts of white light bursting through in every direction. From her view atop the stone wall, she could better see the long stretches of grey stone and the sheep bleating softly in the endless fields, their white, woolen coats shimmering with remnants of rain.

"It is beautiful," she breathed. "How did you know such a sight would occur?"

He didn't respond for a moment, his eyes focused on the sunset. Then he leaned toward her until their shoulders touched.

"Sometimes, the brightest sunsets shine only after the longest rains."

Marianne did not know if his words or his proximity was what made her heart leap within her. But when she looked toward him again, his eyes already on her, her breathing became labored, and a strange sensation overcame her.

This. This was what she'd wanted all along. This was what she'd yearned for. A friend. Someone to speak to, someone with whom she felt heard. Someone with whom she felt *seen*.

How was it that this woodcarver from Bath whom she'd known for three weeks was the one to give her what she needed when her own family could not?

"Do not give up hope just yet, Miss Coventry," he whispered, the light from the waning sun lighting half his face. "Speak with your sister, with your parents. Be honest with them. If they are even as remotely as kind and generous as you are, they will listen to you."

Tears pricked the insides of her eyes, and the truth in his words filled her soul. She'd known all along that was what she'd needed to do, but the fear of being honest with her family, of facing possible rejection, had been too powerful.

But with Mr. Steele's supportive words, surely she could be brave enough to speak her mind.

A moment ticked by, and Marianne tried to thank him. But as his eyes searched hers, ultimately dropping to her lips, her words froze. Time stuttered to a halt, her chest overflowing with a powerful stirring to—

He looked away, and the spell was broken. Good heavens. What had she been thinking?

"It's growing dark," he said.

Marianne nodded at once to prove she was as unruffled as he seemed. Somehow, the sun had set without her knowledge, and the clouds had closed the gaps in the sky, promising more rain that night.

Mr. Steele jumped down from the wall then helped her next,

his hands encircling then releasing her waist so swiftly, she hardly had time to comprehend his touch.

"Will you allow me to walk you back to the house?"

She glanced over her shoulder, candles glowing from a few of the windows. "I think perhaps it is better if I go on alone. It is not far."

He nodded his understanding, taking a few steps back and swinging his jacket over his shoulder. "Then I shall leave you. Goodnight, Miss Coventry." He turned away, heading back in the direction of the beech tree and pond.

His foot kicked up a thick slab of a tree branch—about the length of his hand—that must have broken off during a recent storm. He paused a moment, bending down to retrieve the piece of wood then carried on. What was he to do with that?

A sudden longing to extend the evening, to extend their conversation, pushed her words forth. "Mr. Steele?"

He stopped, turning back to face her, the wood still in his hands. "Yes?"

"I...I just wished to thank you. Your words meant a great deal to me."

He gave a soft smile. "It was my pleasure, ma'am."

She tried with all her might to think of something else to say, but as a cold wind slipped past her neck and produced a shiver down her spine, he nodded toward the house. "You'd best hurry before you catch a cold."

He was right, of course. She was beginning to notice that he made a habit of being right. She nodded, delivering a curtsy, then turned toward the house.

Despair threatened to return, but she pushed it aside, recalling Mr. Steele's words, the sunset, and the way his eyes had searched hers. Just as he'd promised, the world—and her future—did not seem so very bleak, after all.

Edward stood near the beech tree, watching Miss Coventry until she disappeared within the house. Only then did he continue making his way back to the village.

He tapped the piece of wood against his leg and picked up his pace as the first drops of rain fell from the sky.

He was a fool. Not only for staying out so late and getting caught in the rain, but for speaking to Miss Coventry, for sharing things he ought not have, and for drawing closer to his employer's daughter—that wounded, aching, beautiful woman.

He replaced his jacket as a brisk wind blew against him, splashing raindrops against his cheeks. He'd been unable to stop himself from pursuing her when he'd first seen her seated beside that beech tree. He'd known she was injured, but he'd had no idea how greatly until she spoke, and his heart reached out to her.

Of course, he didn't regret helping her, but he could've done so without sharing that he was destitute. Not only was it humiliating for him to admit, but he was risking drawing closer by connecting with her. And for heaven's sake, he never should have looked at her pink lips.

He rubbed his thumb and forefinger against his closed eyes, willing the image to leave his mind. He had work to do, and he could not be distracted. Especially after receiving Mother's latest letter.

Pressure weighed down on his shoulders as he recalled the missive he'd received only that morning.

Son, I've debated about whether to write to you, but I know you'd wish to know. I'm sorry to tell you that Mr. Chapple has called in our debts. Apparently, he's heard word of the many commissions you've received of late. Coupled with you being hired by Lord Ryecombe and now Mr. Coventry, he believes we have more money to spare than we've let on. As such, he is requesting the rent in total that we owe him, to be delivered to him within a fortnight.

I take full responsibility for this, as I never should have been spreading word about your successes. Forgive your silly Mother, as proud as she is of you.

The first thing Edward would do upon arriving back at the Blue Boar was write his mother to ease her concerns. She was no doubt making herself sick with worry. Then he'd write to the landlord, explain the situation in full, and pray the man would have a change of heart.

Edward would be paid early next week, but that wouldn't cover the four months' worth of debt he'd accumulated. He also would never consider asking Mr. Coventry for an advance.

His only option was to finish the carving early and hope the man would give him the same amount they'd agreed upon. Indeed, that was the very reason he'd remained later at Daffley that evening—in an attempt to accomplish more work so he could return home sooner.

Of course, that meant bidding farewell to Miss Coventry sooner. Not that he took any issue with that. In fact, it would be better to sever his relationship with the woman now. The closer he drew to her, the more likely he would share more about his life, and inevitably, the rumors.

After all, how could he, in good conscience, allow her to befriend him further without her full knowledge of the facts around his family? No lady in her right mind would continue to spend time with a working-class man with a name of such ill-repute—false as it was.

He'd never keep his job at Daffley if word got out.

Curse his loosened tongue.

CHAPTER SEVENTEEN

Marianne stood outside the drawing room, biting her thumbnail. Beatrice had arrived only a few moments ago and now sat alone in the room. It was the perfect opportunity to speak with her, really. Yet, fear bound Marianne's feet to the floor with invisible chains.

Would Beatrice reject Marianne's feelings? Set her aside like days-old pudding?

With a firm shake of her head, she rid herself of the thoughts. She needed to do this now, or she never would.

Taking a deep breath, she stretched a cheery smile on her lips and entered the room. "Good evening, sister."

Beatrice looked up from where she sat near the fire, her eyes watery, the tip of her nose red.

Marianne's forced smile fell into a frown, all thoughts flying from her mind. "What is the matter?" she asked, moving to her side at once. Whatever she'd planned to say could wait.

Beatrice blinked, tilting her head to the side. "Whatever do you mean?"

"You appear as if you have been crying."

"Oh, heavens, no. I merely walked today, and I fear it is the typical reaction I receive in doing so."

Never had Marianne seen her sister cry due to a walk. What was Beatrice hiding?

"Did you visit Miss Clark again?"

She looked back to the fire, her voice flat. "No. Nor shall I any longer. She's far too busy with wedding preparations."

Was that why she was upset? Because she was losing a friend? Marianne sat down in the chair facing her. "She will be living in Ashwick still, even after she is married. You will get to visit her often, once she is not so occupied."

Beatrice didn't respond.

Their parents would be arriving any moment for the four of them to go into dinner together. If she was going to speak to her sister, now would be the time. But how could she, knowing Beatrice was already upset about something?

Mr. Steele's words slipped into her thoughts. *The brightest sunsets shine only after the longest rains.*

She would do this. Now.

"Beatrice," Marianne began carefully, "may we speak for a moment?"

Beatrice eyed her sidelong. "Are we not already?"

"Yes, but about something specific."

"I suppose." She lazily tipped her head to the side and averted her gaze.

Her lack of enthusiasm was certainly disconcerting. How in heaven's name could Marianne word this in a way that would show her subject to be beneficial to them both?

She wrung her hands together. "I do not know where to begin, so I suppose I ought to simply say it. I am—"

"This again?"

Marianne paused at Beatrice's hardened gaze. "What do you mean?"

Beatrice's jaw was set, her lips pressed so tightly together, they nearly disappeared. "I know what you are going to say. 'When will you marry, Beatrice? When will you settle down so I may enter Society?'" Her eyebrows raised. "Is that not accurate?"

Marianne held her tongue. After all, she didn't need to answer. The truth was apparent.

Beatrice shook her head. "Just as I suspected. That's all you and Mother and Father can speak to me about."

Marianne frowned. She'd tried to help Beatrice these last few years. She'd tried to bring back the frivolity to their lives and relationship. But Beatrice had been the one to leave Marianne at home and make other friends. Beatrice had been the one to flirt and dance and attend parties.

"How can you say such a thing, Beatrice? I have always expressed interest in every part of your life."

She scoffed. "You are taking an interest only because it pertains to your own benefit."

Her brash words pushed Marianne's vulnerable heart over the edge of the cliff on which it teetered. How could her sister be so cruel? "I suppose you of all people would know what it is to think only of oneself."

She regretted the words the moment they left her mouth. What was the matter with her? She never spoke so spitefully.

Beatrice's nostrils flared. "I am thinking of myself because I am not allowed to think of anyone else. All anyone asks me is whom I shall marry. When I shall marry. *If* I shall marry."

If? Since when was marriage an option for Beatrice? Did she not know what her staying single was doing to Marianne? "I did not know there was an *if*."

Beatrice shook her head, moving to stand beside the window. Rain tapped against the glass in soft patters. "You see? That is all you care about, too. I am exhausted from being questioned over and over again, having no value apart from my ability to wed an amiable gentleman." Her frown deepened. "Yes, it is an *if*. For I do not know if I ever shall marry. You ought to be thanking me, Marianne. You ought to be grateful you are not out in Society. You've no idea how tiresome my life is."

An ache greater than Marianne had ever known crushed against her chest. "*I* have no idea how tiresome life is?"

Beatrice turned away, but Marianne moved, ensuring her sister looked directly in her eyes. Marianne did not enjoy arguments. She despised feeling despair. But something had shifted within her at her sister's words. The need for justice, for understanding. The need for Beatrice to know just how her resistance to marry injured Marianne.

"You have no idea the life *I* lead, Beatrice. I am alone. Always. I am at home *always*. For years, I have patiently awaited my turn. I have listened to you speak of your prospects, and I comforted you when there were none. I have supported you through it all these last ten years, and now you say all I care about is myself?"

Her voice broke, angry tears welling in her eyes. "You've no idea how humiliating it is to sit in my chamber and hear music and laughter drifting through the windows as you, Mother, and Father delight in our neighbors' company. You've no idea how abandoned I feel when the three of you ride away to a ball. I have been patient, Beatrice. I wish for your happiness more than anything. But surely you must see that *I* am in need of happiness, too."

She ended her speech, her chest rising and falling as she awaited her sister's response.

Tears filled Beatrice's blue eyes, but her frown remained. "You are right, Marianne. You do lead a difficult life, and I am sorry for not realizing it sooner." She brushed past her then paused in the doorway. "But you will soon see that life in Society—whether you find love or not—is no better than the life you lead now."

With a final shake of her head, Beatrice turned and left the room.

Marianne stared at the empty doorway, fighting any urge to go after her, to force her to continue their conversation. But the words had already been spoken, and the damage to their relationship had been done.

Rather than feeling freed from finally speaking her piece, Marianne felt nothing but regret.

CHAPTER EIGHTEEN

Marianne had never experienced such a deafening dinner before, though no words were spoken. Only the clinking of silverware on plates and trays echoed about the space.

Beatrice had joined them late, her eyes no longer red, though her lips were still held in a firm line. Marianne avoided her gaze, though it was not necessary. Beatrice had yet to lift her eyes from her barely touched plate.

"My, but we are all silent this evening," Mother said.

Marianne responded with a silent smile.

"Indeed," Father said. "No doubt we are all enjoying the food. But let us discuss what is on our minds. Marianne?"

She blinked. What was on her mind? Everything was on her mind. Living at Daffley Park for the rest of her life. Being alone. Her sister not caring for her well-being.

Mr. Steele still working away upstairs. "Nothing at all, Papa."

She glanced at Beatrice, who pulled her eyes away.

"You are always so carefree, Marianne," he responded with approval. "Nothing ever brings you down."

Father was as obtuse as Beatrice, but she could not blame

him. After all, she was the one who held in her unhappiness. She was the one who chose to obey his wishes. She'd always thought she'd be rewarded one day for doing so, but her logic was flawed. She would not be rewarded. She would remain at Daffley Park until she was too old to be an amiable match for anyone.

"What about you, Beatrice?" Father asked next.

She stared at her plate. "Nothing at all."

"Hm, I do not believe that is the case." Father narrowed his eyes with a smile. "I wonder if you are thinking of a certain Mr. Wakefield."

Marianne tensed. Father's question only further proved Beatrice's earlier words. If only she could warn him off to avoid another escalated conversation. Obviously, he knew nothing of Beatrice's decision to remain unmarried.

Beatrice took a bite of her potato, no doubt to avoid responding.

Father hardly seemed to notice. "I do think he will make for a fine son-in-law. And a fine husband, of course. What do you think of an autumn wedding, Beatrice? Unless you and Mr. Wakefield are eager to begin your lives together, of course. If that is the case, perhaps the end of summer will be better."

Beatrice's cheeks reddened, and Marianne's chest constricted. As much as she disagreed with Beatrice, as much as she was frustrated with her sister for not caring about her, Marianne could not prevent her heart from reaching out to her. Both of them were mere pawns in Father's plans. As much as Papa loved them, he had very little sense when it came to their happiness.

"Perhaps she merely wishes to make plans later," Marianne said, hoping to pull the attention away from Beatrice. "Mama, I am eager to taste what you've ordered for dessert tonight."

Papa spoke before Mother had a chance. "Oh, we may speak

of dessert later, Marianne. There are far more pressing matters than your sweet tooth."

"I think I would prefer speaking of dessert," Beatrice said.

"Nonsense. Plans must be made. We mustn't wait, or we shall be all aflutter when the wedding comes. Now, Marianne, what do you think? Won't our Beatrice look lovely as an autumnal bride?"

Autumnal bride, spring bride, any bride would do, so long as Beatrice *would* be a bride. But she could not betray her sister's trust by saying that.

"I hardly think my opinion matters on the subject."

Beatrice watched her with a calculated gaze, Mother glancing between the two girls with a wary eye.

Father merely shrugged. "I suppose it is Beatrice's opinion we ought to take into account more than anyone's. So tell us, Beatrice, when do you prefer the wedding to be held?"

All eyes fell on Beatrice. Would she deliver a response simply to appease Father?

Slowly, she placed her fork and knife together on her plate, straightened her back, then looked at Father directly. "I would prefer a spring wedding, Father. But, I'm sorry to say, not with Mr. Wakefield."

If the silence had been loud before, it was now thunderous.

"Excuse me?" Father replied, lowering his own fork and knife.

"I will not be marrying Mr. Wakefield."

Marianne looked between her sister and father, the tension between them visible in their stares and rigid shoulders.

"Why is that?" Father asked, his joviality gone, replaced with flared nostrils and a furrowed brow.

"Because we have nothing in common," Beatrice responded. "Because I do not love *him*."

Was Marianne imagining things, or did she hear a slight

emphasis on the word 'him'? But then, of whom else could Beatrice be speaking?

Father obviously hadn't heard anything of the sort, a small vein beginning to pulse down his temple. "Mr. Wakefield is quite taken with you, Beatrice."

"After seeing me twice? I'm certain he will be able to overcome the infatuation."

Father let out an aggravated huff. "Beatrice, your arrogance is—"

"Just like yours?"

"Do not disrespect me."

Marianne shifted uncomfortably in her seat. She glanced at Mother, whose worried expression matched Marianne's. "My dear," Mother said to Father, "perhaps we might discuss this another time."

"No, I'd like to have this discussion now," he stated firmly. Then he faced Beatrice once more. "I will not allow you to make such swift judgment upon the man. He is your perfect match in every way, and you will come to see this for yourself."

"And if I do not?"

"You will."

"Why?" Beatrice stood, her napkin falling to the floor, her own nostrils flared so much like Father's. "Why must I marry a man I do not love? To satisfy your own ends? To raise you up in Society's eyes? To prove that you are better than every member of each lower class?" She leaned forward, spitting out her words. "I am sorry to be the one to inform you of this, Father. But you are not better than they. None of us are."

"Beatrice," Mother said, gasping under her breath.

But Beatrice was already walking from the room, ignoring the calls of both her parents. When it was just the three of them in the dining room, silence returned.

Marianne reeled. Since when had Beatrice not believed they were better than the working class?

"What was that?" Father asked after a moment. He turned to Marianne. "Were you aware of her lack of feelings toward Mr. Wakefield?"

Thankfully, Marianne could answer honestly. "No, Father. I did not know."

"Well, I will not stand for it." He sat down in a huff. "She has had long enough to choose a husband. I am through with waiting."

"So you will force her to wed a man she does not love?" came Mother's quiet voice before him.

He exhaled once more. "Well, something must be done. She can wait no longer. Marianne must be allowed to wed, and she will *not* enter Society until Beatrice has married."

The blow his words dealt to her hope was catastrophic, obliterating the pieces into shards smaller than shattered glass. There was her answer.

She stood, mumbling, "Excuse me," before walking from the room without a glance back at her staring parents.

Beatrice would not change her mind, and Father would not yield.

So Marianne would take her future into her own hands. She was finished waiting for her sunset. She was finished with the rain.

She was ready to shine.

CHAPTER NINETEEN

E dward woke at the crack of dawn. How he longed to stay in bed. No matter the lumps protruding into his spine, the mattress called his name in soothing whispers, beckoning him to receive more sleep.

The novelty of carving the bookshelves had worn off, his exhaustion stiffening his limbs and weighing down his mood, but he could not give up now. He needed to finish the library. He needed to return to Mother. He needed to receive word from Mr. Chapple. Would the man accept his request to postpone payment for longer? Or would Edward return to Bath to find an empty shop and no home?

Rolling out of bed, he made ready for the morning, tucking the small piece of beechwood he'd collected with Miss Coventry into his satchel. He brought the wood with him each day to Daffley, working on a side carving every spare moment he received. He was almost finished, even though he was not sure anything would ever come from carving it.

With his satchel over his shoulder, he left the Blue Boar and headed straight for the bakery. Mrs. Hill did not open her shop until much later, but over the last week, she'd generously offered to give Edward his usual pastries earlier so he'd still have the option to collect them.

"I've made queen currant cakes for you today, Mr. Steele," Mrs. Hill said with her customary warm smile. "I've added a few more than usual, too, to help you last the day out."

After retrieving the parcel of pastries and professing his great appreciation to Mrs. Hill, Edward continued down the quiet street. The area around him was empty, excepting a gentleman striding down the other side of the street, a single carriage rattling by, and a woman walking in the opposite direction of him with a cloak drawn over her face, trailed closely by her female servant carrying a full portmanteau.

He tucked the pastries securely into his satchel as he passed by the woman, ignoring the scent of cherry tarts that wafted toward him from his package.

His brow puckered. Cherry tarts? Had Mrs. Hill not said they were queen currant cakes today?

"Mr. Steele?"

He nearly jumped at the whisper spoken just behind him. Stopping his progression down the street, he turned to see who had called for him. But the only person was the cloaked woman he'd passed by before.

Her head shifted left and right then raised just a fraction. Edward knew at once who she was. There was no mistaking those perfectly curved lips.

"Miss Coventry?" he said aloud. He hadn't seen her since they'd spoken at sunset four days past. Had his words and suggestions managed to help? Or was she still just as forlorn?

She winced at her name on his lips. She held up her hands, a bonnet in one of them as she looked swiftly around them. "Heavens, Mr. Steele, do take care."

He looked around, as well, but no one was in sight. "Why must I take care?" he asked in a far lower tone. What the devil was she doing in town so early and with only a maid to chaperone?

A smile curved her lips, and she moved closer to him. "Because I mustn't be discovered."

"Why mustn't you be discovered?"

Her eyes sparkled, but she remained silent. He glanced at the maid standing off to the side, her face also covered by a wide-brimmed cloak, hands poking out from the folds of fabric where she held the large portmanteau.

A portmanteau. Why would they...

He looked back to Miss Coventry. "Do not tell me," he began.

She nodded. "I am leaving Ashwick."

"Miss Coventry—"

She shushed him again with another look around. "You will certainly be the death of me, sir. Please, refrain from using my name."

He drew a deep breath. "My apologies. I'm simply astonished to see you here. What do you mean, you're leaving Ashwick? Why?"

Her eyes dimmed. "Beatrice has no intention of marrying, and Father has no intention of allowing me out in Society until she does. Instead of waiting for my turn to be out, I am seizing the opportunity for myself."

His heart reached out to her, but honestly, the woman was absolutely mad. "But, Miss—" He stopped as she raised her hand to silence him again. He restarted. "Your family will surely notice your absence."

She sniffed out in disbelief. "They will not even notice I am gone, I assure you. They are to attend a private ball this evening here in Ashwick. When Beatrice is set to parade before gentlemen, I am left to my own devices. At any rate, I've another servant I'm paying at Daffley to ensure my absence remains unnoticed for a time."

That hardly resolved his concerns. "Surely you are aware of

the possible repercussions should you see this through. Your reputation will be ruined, as will your family's."

"I care not about reputation," she said with a raised chin.

The words pinched a nerve. "You only say that because you do not know what it is to suffer with a poor one."

She paused, narrowing her eyes. This was not the conversation he ought to be having right now. He needed to be at Daffley Park, working for Mr. Coventry. Not in Ashwick, trying to bring his employer's daughter home.

"You cannot simply leave without thinking of the dangers of traveling alone," he continued. "Where in heaven's name do you plan to stay? And with whom?"

She raised a flippant shoulder. "I've an aunt in Cornwall. Or an uncle who lives in Scotland."

"Scotland?" His eyes widened. She was planning to take the stagecoach all the way to Scotland? "You cannot be serious."

She sighed. "Very well, then I shall travel to Cornwall. I hear it's lovely. The sea, the lighthouses, the mines. What a beautiful place to live."

She'd clearly taken leave of her senses, and it was all his fault. He never should have persuaded her to take courage. "Please," he continued, forcing himself to remain calm, "you must think this through. You cannot travel the entire way to Cornwall alone."

"I'm not alone." She gave him a knowing smile. "I have Jane here with me."

He glanced at the maid who was smaller in stature and height than even Miss Coventry. Oh, yes, she would provide a great deal of protection.

He rubbed a hand across his brow. What could he say to speak sense to the woman? Clearly, logic was not working. But when he looked at her again, he noticed a forced innocence in her raised brows and an amused glint in her green eyes.

"Are you...are you in earnest?" he questioned. She grinned

from ear to ear, and relief flooded through his person. "Oh, thank heavens. I did not believe you could be so daft as to leave your home." He paused. "But then, why the portmanteau?"

"Oh, I am still leaving Ashwick, but only for the day—and not to Cornwall or Scotland." She leaned in closer with a conspiratorial whisper. "You see, there is an assembly I am inclined to attend at the inn in Wells this evening. It is but eight miles southwest of here. That is why I am here so early—to catch the only coach through the town. I shall be delivered there in safety in but a little over an hour."

For a brief moment, all his fears had been laid to rest at the notion of her remaining in Ashwick. Now, however, knowing Miss Coventry had a plan and a way to see about said plan, his concern only grew.

"A coach will not ensure your safe deliverance," he said slowly, hoping the words would speak directly to her judgment. "Any number of accidents could befall you, not to mention the very real possibility that you will be recognized at one point or another during your travels."

She simply waved a passive hand. "I'm sure an accident will hardly be likely. And as luck would have it, being held captive at Daffley is my one saving grace. No one will recognize me, for I have never been there. As for the stagecoach, my dependable hood shall do the trick." She pulled it closer as if to emphasize her point.

He scoffed. The woman really was mad. There was no other explanation for her flawed logic. "I am sorry, but I cannot, in good conscience, allow you to do something so reckless."

She gave a little smile and a shake of her head, as if she thought his attempt to stop her was laughable. "Well, *I* am sorry, but I cannot, in good conscience, remain here. Goodbye, Mr. Steele. I wish you luck with your work in the library today."

She curtsied then made her way down the street.

Edward's jaw went slack. Confound it. She was in earnest.

Swiftly, he stepped toward her, holding her arm softly until she turned toward him again. "If you insist on going right now, I shall…" He opened and closed his mouth twice, attempting to concoct a threat. "I shall tell your father."

She laughed airily, walking ahead. "You threaten poorly, sir. I know you are far too kind to out me in such a way."

Blast. She knew him too well. He took a few steps then moved in front of her to stop her progression again. "Well, I am also far too kind to allow you to throw your future away by leaving Ashwick unaccompanied."

She studied him carefully for a moment. "It appears we are at an impasse then, sir."

He folded his arms. "Indeed."

They stood in silence, both waiting for the other to cave, both refusing to be the first to do so.

Finally, she sighed. "As I see it, you have three options." She raised a gloved finger. "The first, you allow me to go on my own and keep silent about it, offering me the chance to live out my life the way I wish to. The second"—she held up another finger—"you make for Daffley and tell my father my plan, thereby ruining my chance at freedom. This may sound the obvious solution, but you see, I shall already be gone on the coach before either of you have the chance to stop me, and my reputation will already be at risk."

Edward listened with growing unease. Perhaps Miss Coventry was not so daft as he'd thought. She certainly knew how to play his own logic against her senselessness, for her words were beginning to sound sensible to him.

She drew a deep breath and continued with three fingers raised. "Finally, your third option is to accompany me to Wells."

Well, she had certainly lost him there. He barked out a disbelieving laugh. "You cannot be serious, Miss Coventry. How could—"

She reached up, holding a finger against his lips and looking around. Fortunately, the street was still vacant. Unfortunately, her touch had rendered him as useless as an unsharpened hatchet. His heart stopped, resuming a second later with slow, irregular taps against his swelling chest.

She turned back to look at him, stared at her finger touching his lips, then swiftly pulled away. The warmth lingered like hot tea on his lips.

"You mustn't say my name," she murmured.

He nodded, still unable to push a word from his mouth, though his thoughts continued. Was she entirely unaware of the risks to both of them should they be discovered at any point during their absence? They'd be accused of horrible things. Her reputation would be destroyed. He'd be released from his job. He'd lose his one source of income, his chance to finally escape poverty.

"I take it you did not appreciate my third suggestion," she said, smoothing the outside of her cloak.

Finally, he forced out his words. "Only because such an idea could never work. I could keep you from danger, yes. But all the risks would remain the same—being discovered, your reputation, my work at Daffley—"

"I would ensure that will not change," she blurted out.

He regarded her skeptically, and she hid the flicker of doubt in her eyes. "You can promise no such thing," he said. Then he glanced to the maid who stood a distance away. He and Miss Coventry had been speaking softly enough for the young woman to hear only pieces of their conversation, but he lowered his tone even more. "What if someone else informs your father of your departure from Daffley?"

Miss Coventry picked up on his insinuation in an instant. "I've paid her for her silence, as well."

That meant very little to Edward. Money only went so far when a person's livelihood was at stake.

"Your presence would help me," Miss Coventry's soft voice

drifted toward him, her expression vulnerable. "Especially at the assembly. You could be my chaperone."

"You know that would not be proper. I am not your brother, nor am I married myself."

She wrung her hands together. "No...but you could pretend to be my husband for the evening."

His mouth dropped open. Just when he thought she could not surprise him further. "Do you know what it is you are even asking me to do?"

Finally, she sobered, looking up at him with rounded eyes akin to a lost child. "Yes, Mr. Steele. I am asking you to help me live for just one evening."

Her words struck his conscience. He wanted to help her. Truly, he did. But there were things that could not be solved, matters that could not be ignored.

"How would I explain my own absence to your father and the rest of the household who expect to see me?" He did not wish to encourage hope by asking such a question, but perhaps she would cease her endeavors if she realized how difficult the task was that she asked of him.

She thought for a moment. "My father is not entirely unreasonable. Send a note requesting the day to recoup from your early mornings and late evenings. He will understand."

Perhaps. But Mr. Coventry would *not* understand Edward taking time away from work to gallivant around Wells with the man's daughter.

"I will compensate you for your efforts," Miss Coventry offered next, clearly attempting to sweeten the offer.

He cringed at the very notion. "I would never accept your money, especially when there is potential for ruining your reputation. Heavens, the risk involved..." He ended with a shake of his head.

"I am well aware of the risks in regard to myself, sir. And I am willing to subject myself to such."

She certainly did not know of the greatest risk of all—the risk of her reputation being tainted simply by *conversing* with a Steele. Being alone in a different town with one would be catastrophic. How could he subject her to that? How could he risk everything for *that*?

"I do not wish to injure you," he said softly, unable to share the gravity of the rumors surrounding his father, the rumors they'd all tried so hard to leave behind.

Miss Coventry's shoulders fell forward, and she nodded contritely. "I understand why that is your answer, sir, and I accept that your mind has been made up. But then, so has mine. Good day, Mr. Steele."

She moved down the street, her maid following closely at her heels.

Mr. Steele shook his head. She was still going, even knowing he might alert her father—thereby ending her chances at attending the assembly at all? This woman's stubborn madness would be the death of them both.

If only she was teasing him once again. And yet, was it worth the risk of waiting to find out if she was?

He rubbed the back of his neck, a rod of worry lodged down his spine. How had he ever found himself between two decisions such as these—risk Miss Coventry's life or risk his and Mother's livelihood?

Still torn to pieces like an inconsequential piece of paper, he made his decision. If he accompanied Miss Coventry, at least he knew he could keep her safe.

"Wait," he said, moving swiftly down the street, catching up to Miss Coventry and her awaiting maid. "I will go with you."

Miss Coventry turned to face him with wide eyes. "You will?"

He nodded. "If only to keep you out of trouble."

"You are certain?"

"Yes."

She placed her hands over her mouth with excitement. "Thank you, Mr. Steele!" Then she waved him toward the Blue Boar. "Now you must move swiftly. The coach will arrive in just a few moments. Find something to wear to the assembly this evening and bring whatever else you might need. Oh, and do not forget to write the note to Father. Swiftly, Mr. Steele. Make haste, make haste!"

He shook his head at her urging, moving toward the inn in a daze. What had he just agreed to do?

CHAPTER TWENTY

Marianne was fairly certain she was going to a place after she died that did not involve eternal peace and rest. How could she have pressed Mr. Steele into doing something that involved so great a risk?

She knew he could have easily refused to accompany her, told father, and she would have been discovered in Wells within a few hours—stopping her chance at attending the assembly. It would have been the ultimate blow, being so close to freedom but only receiving a small bite as opposed to the feast she so desired.

Instead of allowing that to occur, she had absolutely played with Mr. Steele's emotions in her coercion, and she really had given him no choice but to join her.

Yes, fire and brimstone were certainly in her future.

Mr. Steele returned shortly with his own portmanteau, and she stood in silence with him and Jane until the coach came moments later.

Fortunately, they were the only passengers who boarded the coach, otherwise their hour-long journey would have been fraught with even more misery as they hid their faces in the hoods of their cloaks.

As they situated themselves onto their respective seats—Marianne settling beside Jane with Mr. Steele across from them—Marianne finally removed her hood, leaning far back from the window to avoid any unsuspecting stares.

The horses were changed over, then the coachman boarded the stagecoach, and they were off.

She looked to Mr. Steele with a sigh of relief, but he simply stared out of the window, his leg bouncing up and down, a scowl on his brow.

She'd upset him, that much was clear.

She turned to Jane, the maid's brow crumpled in worry as she also stared out of her window. There was yet another prime example as to why Marianne was a terrible person. She had coerced Jane—the maid tasked to care for Marianne's dressing and hair, since Marianne wasn't quite in need of a lady's maid—and Jane's sister to help her with her plan. The sisters were being compensated, but was it worth the risk?

She could not blame them for their anxiousness when her own nerves were as taut as Mr. Steele's jacket stretching across his broad shoulders. She feared so much. Her reputation being ruined, offending her family, jeopardizing the maids' and Mr. Steele's employment.

But she also feared remaining at Daffley Park for the rest of her life without the chance for freedom. Without the chance to dance, socialize, and live.

No matter how her guilt felt seared into her conscience as if with a branding iron, she had come too far and involved too many people to turn back now, hadn't she? Or did she simply need to find a way to coax Mr. Steele and Jane to be on her side?

"Have you everything you need, Mr. Steele?" she asked.

He nodded, still staring out of the window. "I do, and I've

had more time to think, so I would like to say that I still heartily disapprove of what we are doing right now."

The pout of his chiseled lips made him, dare she think it, adorable.

"I am well aware of how you feel, Mr. Steele. Perhaps you ought to sleep on our journey there? You might feel better afterwards."

"I am not tired," he said with a sidelong glance. "I am worried."

Weren't they all? "You mustn't be. All will be well."

"You can promise no such thing."

Well, that was certainly true. "But is it not better to be positive and seek the sunset through the rain?"

He stared at her, still frowning, though the severity of his stern brow had lessened to a degree. "I never should have told you such a thing."

She smiled, the air instantly lightening around them. "I am sorry for coercing you into all of this. But I have something that may make up for it."

She reached into her reticule and produced a small parcel, which she untied to reveal three cherry tartlets. She extended it to Mr. Steele with raised eyebrows and a smile. "They're a bit crumpled," she said apologetically. "But what say you now about our little journey? It has been made instantly better, has it not?"

He eyed the tartlets with hesitation, then he accepted the offering with a sigh. "I suppose," he said gruffly, but his brown eyes shone brighter already.

"What about the two of you?" he asked after taking his first bite, motioning to the remaining tartlets.

"Jane has her own already," Marianne replied with a motion to Jane's reticule. Then she placed a hand over her stomach with tight lips. "I already devoured three on our walk from Daffley Park."

His frown fully disappeared. "I should've known."

She smiled as he chewed his second tartlet. She'd never really thought that a man eating food could be attractive. But then, Mr. Steele apparently made everything alluring—carving, swallowing, chewing... Breathing.

His eyes met hers, and she swiftly looked away. She needed to get ahold of her thoughts and keep her wits about her. She couldn't afford any distractions today.

When Mr. Steele's tartlets were gone, he carefully folded the brown wrapping to avoid spilling any of the crumbs left behind. "How did you come to find out about an assembly in Wells anyway?"

This was good. He was in far better a mood now. Though, she shouldn't have been surprised. Pastries always made one's day better.

"Jane's friend is a lady's maid for a woman who lives there," she explained. "Isn't that right, Jane?"

The maid ducked her head even more—which Marianne had not thought was possible—and nodded her head in silence.

Marianne would have to pay the girl more to make up for the trauma she was putting her through.

"You're certain no one will recognize you if you attend?"

His eyes were wary, but he no longer looked upset. Thank heavens.

"Yes," she stated firmly. "Anyone who would have attended the assembly will be at the ball in Ashwick. As I said before, I know no one in Wells. The assembly will certainly be large enough for me to blend in perfectly with the crowds, though small enough to not attract many outsiders."

The entire way the plan had come about was so coincidental, Marianne believed it to be providential. When she'd overheard Jane and her sister discussing the assembly, everything had fallen into place. Marianne's desperation had taken hold of the reins and brought them to where they were now—in a carriage, running away from Daffley Park.

Mr. Steele merely nodded, then he took to staring at the green fields they passed by.

The coach fell into silence once again. Unfortunately, with that silence, Marianne's thoughts began to wander, and her conscience came knocking once more.

How could she have done this? Did she not care what repercussions could come? It was true, she had accounted for every possible thing that could go wrong. But then, there were no guarantees. Suppose she was discovered and her family disgraced? She and Beatrice would never have the chance to marry gentlemen, then. Their parents would be so disappointed, not to mention heartbroken.

The worst of it all was what she'd tried to ignore from the beginning. If she was discovered with Mr. Steele, what would become of him? She, of course, would vouch for his personal character, and she would go down fighting to the end to have him keep his work at Daffley. But...would Father really keep him on?

By the time they reached Wells more than an hour later, Marianne was fairly certain she was going to relieve the contents of her stomach. Never mind that they'd already made it to Wells and that she'd already risked so much to get there. She was finished. She'd put too many people's livelihoods at risk, and she could not be selfish any longer.

They exited the coach, Marianne and Jane once more hiding within their cloaks as Mr. Steele thanked the coachman and guard then carried both portmanteaus himself. Before they made it two steps toward the inn, Marianne paused, wringing her hands together.

"Mr. Steele."

But he raised a hand to stop her. "Worry not, I've already thought this through. I'll simply reserve two rooms so we may dress separately tonight. You may both wait out here to avoid us being seen together at the inn."

He walked forward, but she called out for him. "Wait a moment, Mr. Steele."

He turned, frowning with exaggeration. "Excuse me, but if I cannot say your name, I'd prefer if you would not use mine, either. We are in this together now, you and I."

He faced forward.

"Mr. Steele—"

He whirled around with his finger to his lips and a barely refrained smile then made for the inn again.

Marianne would have grinned at his playful behavior, were it not for her continued guilt. Was he truly all right going along with her plan, then? Or was he simply doing so because he had no other option?

She looked away from his masculine stride, moving to the side of the inn where they were further removed from the busying street.

"Are you well, Jane?" Marianne asked.

Jane nodded. "Yes, miss." Her eyes darted around anxiously.

"You mustn't worry. Even if we are discovered—which we will not be—you will not be removed from your position at Daffley Park. I will make certain they know that I forced you into this."

Jane's shoulders lowered a fraction, and she smiled with gratitude, though the worry in her eyes remained.

Marianne's worry persisted, as well. If she could not even control her own life, how could she convince Father to not remove the maids from their positions at Daffley? And how could she convince him to keep Mr. Steele on?

Mr. Steele returned with two keys only a moment later, extending one to Marianne. "I've placed the portmanteaus in our respective rooms and requested a meal to be sent up for us midday. I would advise you to remain in your room from this point forth to avoid anyone happening on us until the assembly this evening."

Marianne fiddled with the key between her fingers. Mr. Steele motioned them forward toward the inn, but she hesitated.

"What is it?" he asked. "Do not tell me you've lost your nerve now."

"No." She paused, pulling her cloak further over her eyes as a couple walked past them. "No, it is not that at all. I'm afraid I've developed a conscience."

He watched her in silence.

"I'm so sorry," she said, grimacing. "I never should have done this. I put so much at risk. That alone would not be so terrible if I was not also endangering your own reputation and livelihood."

He huffed a mirthless laugh. "My reputation is not at stake from *this*, I assure you. You ought to be more concerned with your own reputation by being with me."

She paused. What on earth did he mean by that? She brushed the comment aside and moved forward.

"I should not have coerced you into such a thing. I will retrieve my belongings now and reimburse you for the rooms and for your troubles. Then we may leave for Ashwick the moment the next coach arrives."

"At midnight tonight?"

Her heart sank. "The coach does not return until then?"

He shook his head, a small smile lifting the corner of his lips. How was this in any way humorous?

She pressed a hand to her brow. "Then I suppose I shall simply heed your advice and remain in my room until the coach arrives."

She made to walk past him, but he held out an arm to stop her. "Just a moment. After all you went through to get here, after traveling and scheming and plotting, you mean *not* to attend the assembly after all?"

She stopped. "I hardly deserve to, especially with the man

I've deceived."

He dropped his chin and raised his eyebrows in a dubious look. "Miss Cov—" He stopped, looking around to ensure his blunder hadn't been heard. "I was aware that you were playing to my conscience earlier. But I assure you, I came of my own accord."

She shook her head. "You couldn't possibly have. You never would have come had you not been determined to protect me."

As she said the words aloud, a bud of warmth grew in her heart. He was trying to protect her. This man, this woodcarver, whom she'd known for a mere few weeks, had sacrificed his well-being, his livelihood, his future...for her. But, why?

She stared up at him, studying his face. He must have sensed her question, as he shrugged and looked away.

"I did what I needed to do. Besides, what would your father have said had I allowed you to go off on your own?" His words were weak, a mask to hide the real reason why he had gone along with her, but Marianne allowed him to keep his knowledge secret.

"Even so," she said, "I cannot allow you to risk anything further by forcing you to attend the assembly this evening."

He was silent for a moment, pursing his lips. "What if you weren't the one asking me to risk everything, and I was simply offering?"

She paused, hope spreading its wings within her heart. But she could not allow the wind to take them. "No, I cannot. What if you lose your work at Daffley because of me?"

A shadow passed over his eyes, but it was gone in an instant. "All is taken care of."

Was that true? Had Father paid Edward enough to satisfy his debts?

Mr. Steele peered down at her, his gaze stalwart. "You've come so far, Miss Coventry. Be brave and take the opportunity for which you've worked so hard."

The urging in his tone and the smile on his lips finally pushed her forward. "You are certain?"

"Absolutely."

Her chest rose and fell, excitement flooding her senses. "Very well, Mr. Steele. Let us follow through with our plan."

He grinned. "Excellent. Now, before we do anything else, let us first decide on what we shall call each other."

"Oh." Yet another thing she hadn't taken into account. "But we do not have to worry about such a thing until the assembly."

"Not if we walk about Wells."

"But I thought you said..."

He raised a careless shoulder. "Perhaps I was a bit hasty before. We do not need to stay in our rooms for the entirety of the day. Unless you wish it, of course."

"But will we not be leaving more opportunities for us to be discovered?"

"Your cloak or bonnet will cover you more than enough." He tugged the hood forward to better cover her face. "We shall be on close alert. Besides, are you here to hide, Miss Coventry, or are you here to live?"

With a shake of her head, she beamed. "You are a terrible influence, Mr. Steele."

He smiled right back. "As are you. But perhaps that is why we make such an excellent married couple."

Her heart stuttered, though she did not know why. He was teasing, after all. "Yes, what *shall* we call each other then?"

"I've just the name. The Hickenbottoms."

She pulled back. "The Hickenbottoms?"

"Oh, yes. They were a very respectable family in Bath when I was growing up."

She laughed. "Very well, I suppose that will do."

"It will do *nicely*." He offered her his arm. "Come along then, Mrs. Hickenbottom. We've a town to explore."

CHAPTER TWENTY-ONE

E dward had never seen Miss Coventry so happy. In truth, he'd never seen *anyone* so happy.

After a brief walk around the town, the two of them had decided it would be best to take a moment to rest from their early morning—especially because it was sure to be a late night for them both.

They'd slept in their separate rooms then woke up to luncheon. After eating, Edward had met Miss Coventry and Jane outside of the inn, where they began their exploration of Wells.

Miss Coventry had dared to replace her heavy cloak and hood with a simple spencer and bonnet adorned with those same small blue flowers he'd first noticed at the cricket match four weeks before. "Will this be enough cover, do you think?" she asked, motioning to the bonnet.

He nodded. "I believe so." Then he looked away before he could admire the way her green eyes brightened against the light blue of her spencer.

Their first stop was to purchase a ribbon, and after ensuring the shop was vacant apart from the owner, Edward held the door open for Miss Coventry and Jane. But Miss Coventry paused, her brow wrinkled.

"What is it?" He looked over her shoulder in the shop. "Do you recognize someone?"

She shook her head. "I have never been within a shop before without my sister or mother. I know there is nothing to be anxious about, and yet...I am."

Her father certainly had been dedicated to keeping up appearances. Would the man ever regret the toll his efforts had taken on his daughters?

With an encouraging smile, he offered his arm to her again. "Well, you shan't be alone, if that's what concerns you."

She gingerly took his arm then gripped it tightly as they moved about the shop.

The owner, a short man with hair falling forward from behind his ears, came to stand before them. "Good morning. May I help you find a certain color, Mr. and Mrs....?"

Miss Coventry's grip tightened on his arm.

Edward smiled comfortably. "Hickenbottom."

The man paused then nodded with a comfortable smile. "What can I help you find?"

Edward looked down at Miss Coventry. "What color are you in need of, Mrs. Higgenbottom?"

The shop owner's sharp eyes focused on him in an instant. What had Edward said?

Miss Coventry squeezed his arm. "Hickenbottom," she whispered in correction.

Heavens above, he'd said the wrong name. A bubble of laughter moved up his chest, but he barely managed to keep it down.

"Light blue, please," she responded, her twinkling eyes matching the humor laced through her tone.

The man eyed them with suspicion then showed them to the blue ribbons. Miss Coventry picked two long strands and purchased them both before the owner wrapped them up and extended the package toward them.

"There you are, Mrs...." He paused, having clearly forgotten the name again.

Edward could not blame him, nor could he help himself from saying, "Higgenbottom."

"Hickenbottom," Miss Coventry corrected swiftly.

This time, his laughter could not be warded off, and a short chuckle escaped Edward's lips. "Not long married, you see. We both keep forgetting the name."

A barely stifled giggle came from Miss Coventry, then she tugged on his arm, and they swiftly left the befuddled man's shop.

Their laughter fully erupted once they were safely on the street, Jane following close behind with a smile of her own.

"What on earth were you thinking, Mr. Steele?" Miss Coventry whispered, tears of mirth filling her eyes as their laughter settled. "Why would you forget your own last name if *you* were newly married?"

He chuckled along with her. "I figured I may as well confuse the man more than he already was."

"Well, you managed to succeed in that regard."

Their laughter continued, and they carried on to the next shop. After that, Miss Coventry's hesitance melted swiftly away, and she entered the next three shops without an ounce of reluctance.

As for Edward, keeping up the façade that they were, indeed, husband and wife, became more and more enjoyable. He'd always wanted to marry. But once the rumors began and business waned, marriage became a distant dream. To pretend now that his dream had come true, it was both happy and unsettling. In reality, it could never come to fruition, especially with such a woman.

As they moved from shop to shop and stall to stall, their

anxieties about being discovered faded, and Miss Coventry's joy grew and expanded to each person she spoke to or even so little as smiled at.

She found joy in everything, whether that was pointing out various trinkets for sale at one stall, a street performer making adults and children laugh, or the way the trees created spotted shadows against the cobblestones.

Near the end of the afternoon, the three of them made their final stop at the town's bakery. Edward purchased a few cheesecakes for the three of them, and they meandered slowly down the street as they ate, speaking of their parents and growing up, until the conversation shifted to their time in the town.

"Have you truly never been to any shop before in Ashwick without your family?" he asked.

She nodded, taking a bite of the cheesecake. A piece of the pastry clung to her lower lip before it fell to the ground. It was unfortunate he could not have wiped it off himself.

"You never went with your friends?"

She sniffed with derision. "What friends?"

"Ashwick is not so very small. There is not a single woman your age?"

She sighed, swallowing the last of her cheesecake and rubbing her hands together. "I did have friends when we first moved there, when I was ten years of age." She retrieved her gloves from her reticule and put them on one by one. "I enjoyed their company, especially when Beatrice grew busy with her own friends and courtships, but eventually, they all entered Society and married, starting families of their own." She looked away. "It became too difficult to find things in common, and our friendships faded fast."

His heart reached out to her. What a lonely life to have been dealt. "Did your relationship with your elder sister help you in any degree?"

"Unfortunately, no. Once we moved to Ashwick, our relationship faltered, as well."

Edward had always wanted a sibling, though he only now realized how infinitely more sorrowful it was to have had a sibling and lost one, than to have never had one at all.

"Do you remember much of life, before your father made his fortune?" he asked next.

"Yes. It was far simpler in many ways. In truth, there are times I long for that life to return." Her eyes took on a distant look. "Now, my family is always separated. Father is preoccupied with business matters, Mother is taken with Beatrice marrying, and Beatrice, well, she has become disenchanted with life. She is a mere shell of whom she once was. We may have had very little before, but at least we had each other."

Edward frowned. Even with his business failing, he still had friends who wished to see him and a mother who loved him. With a controlling father, an obedient mother, and an absent sister, Miss Coventry truly had very little. No wonder she'd wished to escape the confines of Daffley Park.

His mind was brought back to what she'd said earlier that morning in Ashwick. "You mentioned that your sister has no intention of marrying. She told you this?"

She nodded. "After my conversation with you in the fields, I decided to share with her how difficult the last few years have been for me. I had every intention of helping her so we'd both be happy, but I'm afraid our conversation shifted. She told Father that she would never marry, and it was then that I learned that Father still had no intention of allowing me out in Society. I was tired of waiting, so I decided to take matters into my own hands."

They reached the outside of the inn and paused off to the side, standing in front of an alleyway that led between the inn and another shop.

Miss Coventry turned to Jane. "Will you continue to the inn

to ensure my dress is made ready for the evening? I will be up shortly."

Jane glanced between her and Edward, then with a barely contained smile, she nodded. "Yes, ma'am."

She scurried away, and once they were alone, he faced Miss Coventry. "I'm sorry that speaking with your family was not successful. I cannot help but blame myself for giving you such poor advice."

"It is no one's fault but their own. Besides, I am finished waiting. I simply decided to create my own happiness."

"A wise decision," he responded. "So long as you do not do anything reckless, such as fleeing from your home."

He gave her a pointed look, and she smiled. "May I ask you a question next?"

His stomach shifted. Given the questions she'd asked him in the past, she could throw anything at him. But it was only fair for him to answer after the questions he'd sailed at her. "Of course."

"What was it that made your business no longer profitable?"

He had been expecting this question for some time. It was only natural to wonder. But he could not tell her the truth. Not now.

"A misunderstanding occurred between my father and a gentleman who'd hired him," he explained briefly. "Words were exchanged, and false accusations were made. Horrible accusations."

Solemnity crowded around him as it did every time he thought of that period of his life, sitting with his parents, listening to Father as he described the lies said about him.

Such darkness, such sorrow, could not be imagined, nor could any of them truly comprehend what had occurred. It had taken its toll on them all, especially Father.

"Those accusations, despite having been proven false, were spread throughout the community. One by one, our friends and customers, gentlemen who had been working with us for years, no longer commissioned our work, and our business fell apart."

Her eyebrows drew close together, pain reflected in her eyes. "And your father died shortly after that?"

"He died *because* of that."

Edward would never forget how Father had stopped eating and sleeping due to his sorrow, how the weariness in his eyes had increased daily until no light was left within him.

"How did you manage to move past it?" she asked, her voice barely above a whisper.

He blinked away the image. "I do not know if I have fully. But each day, I must remind myself to forgive and move on. For if I do not, bitterness and anger will consume me until there is no longer light within *me*. I know that is not what Father would have wanted."

She nodded, compassion veritably spilling forth from her eyes. "Wise words to live by," she whispered. "Ones I would do well to remember, too."

Then her gaze dropped as she looked past his shoulder, and her eyes rounded. She launched her hand forward and clutched his arm. "I know her."

CHAPTER TWENTY-TWO

Marianne clutched Mr. Steele's arm harder, repeating her words and confirming her worst fears.

"I know her!" she whispered again.

Instinctively, she stepped closer to Mr. Steele, hoping to shield herself from the woman approaching.

"From Ashwick?" he asked.

"Yes, she is one of my mother's closest friends." The woman, Mrs. Perkins, drew closer, her voice getting louder and louder. What was she doing in Wells? Would she be at the assembly that night? Marianne's heart sunk lower and lower. "I need to go back to the inn," she whispered. "I must hide!"

She turned around, about to dart farther out onto the street to make for the inn, but Mr. Steele wrapped his hand around her wrist and pulled her back.

"There isn't time," he said.

Swiftly, he led her deeper into the alleyway, turning his body toward her so his back faced the street. He pulled her near him, resting his hands on her arms just below her shoulders. In response, she tucked in her elbows, holding her fisted hands against his chest to hide behind his large frame.

If the woman saw them, the position they were in would be more than compromising—it would be detrimental.

Mrs. Perkins's voice sounded right at the opening of the alleyway, and Marianne's legs turned to jelly. The woman's words were unintelligible, but her voice was unmistakable.

Only, it was not Mrs. Perkins's.

Marianne paused. Carefully, she peered around Mr. Steele's shoulder quick enough to see the woman walking by. Sure enough, it was another woman entirely.

Marianne's shoulders fell with relief. Her eyes must have tricked her, convinced her of her greatest fear.

She leaned back to inform Mr. Steele of her blunder, but when she looked up at him, she became acutely aware of just how closely she stood before him. Her hands were still against his chest, his fingers around her arms.

He watched her, his brow creasing as he frowned. Was he upset with her for almost having been discovered? For bringing them both to Wells and risking everything?

"Is she gone?" he asked, his voice gruff.

She nodded, her words wavering. "Forgive me. It was not her after all. I thought…"

She couldn't finish her words, her eyes taken with his mouth as his lips parted. A moment passed by in silence, their proximity pushing her heart to race harder and harder until finally, his hands dropped, and he took a step back.

"You are certain it wasn't anyone you recognized?"

She nodded, unable to say a word.

"Thank heavens," he said, looking anything but relieved as he averted his gaze. What had troubled him so greatly to cause that frown of his to return? "We had better return to the inn. You must have time to make ready for the assembly."

He stepped aside, allowing her a wide berth. "You may go first. I'll follow shortly after."

She nodded in silence, stepping past him and making for the inn alone.

It did not take long for Edward to dress for the assembly that evening, yet still, he lingered as much as possible in his room, pacing back and forth and whittling away at the beechwood—the way he usually cleared his mind.

Except this time, the piece he carved did nothing but clutter his thoughts, adding another opportunity for his attention to dwell on Miss Coventry.

He wasn't blind to the fact that he'd been attracted to her ever since the cricket match. But now, he had feelings for her, and he shouldn't. He cared for her, and he *shouldn't*.

He wanted to protect her, to shelter her from the cruelties of the world so she could maintain her happy spirit. Spending the day with her, pulling her against him in the alleyway—that had done nothing but dump kindling onto a fire errantly lapping toward Miss Coventry.

That same fire edged dangerously close to his heart.

With an aggravated sigh, he set the whittling down and retied his cravat, then he left the beechwood behind. The carving was frustrating him anyway. Something was missing in the design, but he couldn't quite put his finger on what.

No doubt because he was far too distracted with a certain lady making ready for the ball in the room across from his.

He ran his fingers through his hair as he descended the staircase of the inn. What was he going to do with himself? How had he even allowed this to happen? How in heaven's name was he to remain unaffected, all while pretending to be married to the woman?

The assembly's raucous noise grew louder as he neared the

large hall, laughter and conversation drifting down the corridor to where he stood awaiting Miss Coventry.

Where was she? Had she finally lost her nerve, with this being her first dance? He wouldn't blame her. He'd attended quite a few assemblies when he was younger, and butterflies still fluttered in his stomach tonight.

He paced back and forth at the bottom of the stairs, his footsteps sliding against the wood floor as he attempted to talk sense to his mind.

He and Miss Coventry would never work. Their lives were too different. She was wealthy, he wasn't even making ends meet. Her father heartily disapproved of his daughters marrying working-class men, and his mother had very little to her name because of Edward's failing business.

And then there was the matter of the rumors...

No, having a relationship with the woman—even a friendship—would prove detrimental to them both, and tonight, he would no longer allow himself to entertain thoughts of the two of them being together.

Then she descended the stairs.

The very sight robbed him of his breath, stripped him of his senses, and rendered him utterly hopeless.

At the cricket match and later at Daffley Park, Miss Coventry had been odd, though undeniably pretty. As she'd explored Wells earlier today, she had been lively, enthusiastic, and beautiful, smiling and skipping from shop to shop.

But now, as Miss Coventry slowly moved down the stairs step-by-step, confident and calm, she was stunning. Her chin was level, not raised to her sister's superior height, and her shoulders were squared with confidence and regality. Her light-blue gown accentuated her feminine curves in a modest manner, the soft fabric cascading down from the ribbon around her bodice like a crystal blue waterfall.

White gloves extended up her arms and past her elbows, and

a simple pearl bracelet matched her necklace and drop-pearl earrings.

She was the portrait of perfection, and Edward was lost.

"Good evening," she greeted, looking past him to the doorway down the corridor. The first dance had already begun, the music sailing toward them as dancers swirled past the side entrance they stood nearby. "I'm sorry I took so very long. I'm afraid Jane is not entirely practiced for such elegant hairstyles. She was a little anxious due to the pressure of the evening."

Edward could only nod.

"Does the ribbon look terrible?" she asked next. "Jane assured me it did not, but I had no mirror large enough to know for certain."

She turned her head to the side, angling her neck to provide him a better view of the ribbon.

All he could see was the smooth skin of her neck.

He swallowed, willing his gaze to follow the ribbon laced perfectly through her dark curls. "It looks..." His voice cracked. Cursed, wretched...He cleared his throat and lowered his tone. "It looks very fine, indeed."

She remained where she was, still speaking away from him. "And the flowers?"

Small blue flowers adorned the top of the hairstyle, as if the petals had sprouted from the ribbon woven throughout. They were the very flower she'd worn at the cricket match.

"They are perfect," he stated simply, afraid his voice would give way once more.

"Thank heavens." She breathed a sigh of relief, facing him. "They are my favorite flower, forget-me-nots. I plucked them from my bonnet."

Her favorite flower. Of course. With a small smile, he tucked away the information then nodded. "They match very well."

"I hoped so." Finally, she turned to face him, her eyes scaling him up and down. His back straightened of its own accord. "You look quite dashing yourself, sir."

For a moment, he thought she was simply saying such to be polite, but when her eyes lingered on his, her warm gaze filled every inch of his soul with heat.

He looked away, drawing in a deep breath. "Well, Mrs. Hickenbottom, are you ready to attend your first dance?"

CHAPTER TWENTY-THREE

Marianne's smile disappeared. Her nerves had continued to mount from the very moment she'd begun to dress, but now, with her dream right before her, she could hardly breathe. "I feel as if I might be sick."

She backed away from Mr. Steele, and he lowered his arm.

"I do not think I can go through with this after all."

He approached her with a kind smile. "I'm sure it is only a bout of nerves."

She pressed a hand to her stomach, shaking her head. "What if it isn't? What if this is a sign from Heaven?"

Mr. Steele was silent as she continued.

"Suppose I am recognized? Or that I draw attention to myself because I do not remember any of the dance steps? Suppose I lose my freedom even more, or you lose your work? What then?"

Her stomach twisted and pulled apart until Mr. Steele reached forward, resting his hand just above her elbow and ending the storm raging within.

"What are you really afraid of, Miss Coventry?"

Marianne *was* worried that someone would discover them,

but they had taken every precaution—even to the effort of watching from the window to observe the guests entering the assembly. She'd also practiced countless dances over the years in her chamber at night, so that was not where her concern truly lay either.

But how had Mr. Steele known that there was something more, some deeper turmoil inside her heart?

She blinked away unexpected tears and watched the dancers moving past the doorway before them, her voice coming out in a whisper. "I've been waiting for this moment for so long, building it up within my mind to be a glorious affair. But what if it fails to live up to the ideal I've created? What if I've spent my entire life living for this moment that ends up a disappointment?"

As she voiced her concerns, her heart contorted. She backed away, ready to flee upstairs, unwilling to face the disillusionment that would inevitably follow attending the dance.

But Mr. Steele reached forward, crooking a finger to raise her chin. "How could anything ever be a disappointment when *you* are involved?" His eyes softened, and the tightness in her chest dispelled as he continued. "I know you well enough to say that in everything you do, your passion for life and your ability to see joy and splendor in the ordinary, makes every experience with you a memorable, unforgettable delight."

Marianne had always prided her optimism, but lately, her positivity was flailing, lost at sea, dimming within the darkness. To have Mr. Steele say such kind words, to have him still see the hopefulness within her, meant more than he could ever know.

She blinked away her welling tears with an embarrassed smile. "Thank you. That means a great deal to me."

He reached within his jacket and produced a handkerchief for her, which she readily accepted.

When she had composed herself—honestly, she'd never cried

so much than with this man—she drew a settling breath and looked toward the dance hall.

"Well then, shall we? Before I lose my nerve once again?"

He offered his arm once more, and she tucked her gloved hand around his forearm before they made for the side door of the hall. He placed his free hand to rest atop hers, a simple gesture, though it pulsed comfort throughout her soul.

The hall was not as grand as Daffley Park's ballroom, but it was clean, bright, and decorated in a way that welcomed Marianne to the quaint, comfortable environment.

Fresh flowers hung near the sconces in baskets, light flickering against them and spreading their scent throughout the crowded room to shroud out the many moving bodies. The chandelier extended even more light, bouncing against the diamond-paned windows situated low in the walls.

At one end of the room, a tapestry hung from the ceiling, covering the entire length of the wall in a depiction of a hunter riding atop a rearing stallion. In the center of the hall, the set of dancers moved about in synchronized movements, airy gowns and coattails gliding behind elegant women and dashing men, smiles and sparkling eyes abounding.

"Whom will you dance with first?" Mr. Steele asked, his gaze averted.

Marianne glanced up at him. Did he not wish to dance with her? "I suppose I must wait until I am introduced to someone."

He nodded, his jaw twitching. He chewed his lower lip as if hesitating. "I know it is not considered so very polite to dance with one's spouse, but as we are not truly wedded, and if...if you'd prefer to have the first with me, that may provide you with more confidence, perhaps. If you'd like."

A smile inched across her lips. When had Mr. Steele ever been so *vulnerable*? Did he really think she'd choose to dance with anyone but him?

"The way I see it," she began, "we've already broken so many of Society's rules, why not break another?"

Finally, his eyes met hers. "I do enjoy your logic."

The music ended, then the next dance was announced.

"The Hopeless!" cried a voice from the front of the set.

Marianne breathed a sigh of relief. She knew the dance well, as it was one of her favorites.

Mr. Steele raised his hand to hers, and she accepted it, placing her gloved fingers atop his as they walked toward the dance floor.

"Are you ready, Mrs. Hickenbottom?"

"Absolutely." Marianne beamed. How she enjoyed playing his wife.

They faced each other in the middle of the set, taking a quick glance around them. There were so many people, so many chances for them to be found out, but as Marianne recognized not a soul, the tension in her shoulders eased.

Instead of watching for faces she'd recognize, she began to admire fluffy feathers and the ribbons in women's hair. Instead of fearing discovery, she smiled at those around her.

This dance, it had hardly begun, and yet, it was exactly as she'd imagined it would be. No, it was better. For instead of being with her parents, walking one step behind them and dancing with whomever *they* wished, she was dancing with whom she wished—no one else but the handsome woodcarver before her.

Father and Beatrice both had it wrong. They believed Marianne wished for her turn to be at the center of all the attention. But this was what Marianne wanted—to simply be seen and heard. She wanted the freedom to dance, to socialize, to be a part of something exciting and memorable. With Mr. Steele, she was given all of that.

The strings at the top of the dance hall sounded loudly above the conversation around them, and Marianne glanced at Mr. Steele, his bright eyes already on her.

The dance began, and they moved from side to side in slow steps. For the next movement, Mr. Steele reached out toward her, and Marianne's stomach jolted forward, as if her body was just as eager to be closer to the man. They held softly onto each other's fingers, Mr. Steele giving her hand a slight squeeze, though she was not sure if it had been intentional.

Their contact broke with the next few movements, but they returned soon to hold one another's hands. This time, his eyes watched her with such intensity, she could hardly breathe. What he was thinking of, she had no idea, but she knew exactly where her thoughts strayed.

She'd imagined for so long what it would be like to dance with a gentleman. To have his perfectly tailored suit, pressed and nearly shining because it was so black. His crisp, white cravat would be perfectly tied, and his collar would be worn fashionably high.

In contrast, Mr. Steele wore a blue jacket she'd seen twice before, his cravat was simply tied, and his collar was of a sensible height.

And he was not a gentleman.

Yet, Marianne found it very difficult to be bothered at all. Mr. Steele could rival any gentleman there that evening tenfold, not only with his manners and conversation, but also with his kindness and selfless behavior.

When the dance ended, she clapped toward the musicians, then she and Mr. Steele left the floor.

"Did you enjoy yourself?" he questioned.

"As if you need to ask, Mr. Hickenbottom," she said with a knowing smile.

They hardly had a moment to themselves off the floor before an older gentleman with thick brows introduced himself as Mr. Wilson, the Master of Ceremonies.

"Mr. and Mrs. Hickenbottom," Mr. Steele introduced next.

"I've a gentleman who wishes to dance with you, Mrs. Hickenbottom, if you are so inclined this evening."

Instead of the excitement she'd expected at being sought out, an odd emptiness filled her chest, as if she lost something but didn't know exactly what.

"Of course," she said, forcing a smile with a glance in Mr. Steele's direction.

He was looking around the crowds himself. Was he attempting to find his next prospective partner?

The angry heat of jealousy replaced the regret she felt for accepting another man's pursual of her, but she quickly checked her emotions. She and Mr. Steele were not attached in any regard other than friendship—despite feigning marriage for the evening. She had no right to feel such a way.

A moment later, Mr. Wilson returned with a tall, handsome man named Mr. Robins.

Black jacket, sleek collar, crisp cravat. A gentleman. Father would be impressed. So why was Marianne not?

"Enjoy yourself, my dear," Mr. Steele said as Mr. Robins led Marianne to the dance floor.

She glanced back at her fictitious husband, knowing the endearment had simply been for show. But then, why did his eyes say otherwise?

Her dance with Mr. Robins was pleasant, if not a little long. Her eyes continually strayed around her, taking note of the fact that Mr. Steele did not dance with another.

But such a thought should have never made her so happy.

CHAPTER TWENTY-FOUR

When the dance finally ended, Marianne expressed her gratitude to Mr. Robins, who left straight away to find another partner, then she turned to find Mr. Steele. After a moment, she spotted him standing by the refreshment table, raising his head above the crowd for her to see him.

Their eyes met, and his smile brightened.

She walked straight toward him, noticing only then that he spoke to another couple, a middle-aged man and woman with bright smiles of their own.

Her footing faltered. How could she keep up the façade that she and Mr. Steele were married?

"Mrs. Hickenbottom," he greeted when she arrived at his side. He reached out toward her, his hand resting softly against the small of her back. "Allow me to introduce to you two new friends I've made. Mr. and Mrs. Parson, this is my lovely wife."

The Parsons greeted her with a bow and a curtsy, which Marianne nearly forgot to return as she struggled to focus on anything beyond Mr. Steele's hand at her back.

"Oh, Mrs. Hickenbottom," Mrs. Parson said, "you are as lovely as your husband described you."

Marianne glanced at Mr. Steele, who removed his hand and cleared his throat. Lovely? Mr. Steele thought she was lovely? He'd called her that word before, hadn't he?

She smiled, her energy returning after the dance with Mr. Robins had almost sapped her dry. "How lovely it is to make your acquaintance."

Mrs. Parson's turban wrapped up nearly all of her dark brown hair. "Your husband was just telling us that you are visiting from Bath."

Marianne nodded, unable to say anything for fear of contradicting whatever Mr. Steele had said before she'd arrived.

"What brings you to Wells?" Mr. Parson asked, his smile friendly.

Marianne blinked, looking to Mr. Steele. They hadn't prepared for this—small conversations with others where they would be required to share falsehoods.

Mr. Steele merely smiled comfortably. "We enjoy public assemblies, so when we heard of the one here, we couldn't pass on the opportunity to attend it. Isn't that right, my dear?"

She smiled. He certainly hadn't told a full lie.

"To travel so far, though, for a public assembly?" Mrs. Parson tapped on her chin and narrowed her eyes. "You two have only recently been married, I assume?"

Marianne's cheeks burned.

"Very newly married, yes," Mr. Steele replied.

"I knew it." Mrs. Parson turned to her husband. "Did I not say such a thing, Mr. Parson? Yes, I knew the both of you were. For only young, newly marrieds would ever think of traveling such a distance for a simple dance." She gave a laugh. "Do tell me how long you've been wedded."

A day? Less than twelve hours?

"But a few weeks," Mr. Steele replied much more sensibly.

Thank goodness for the man. Marianne was still tongue-tied from the fact that he'd called her 'lovely.'

What did *lovely* mean, exactly? Attractive? Beautiful? A word to describe an aunt or a sister?

"Ah, to be young and in love," Mrs. Parson said, looking up to her husband with a smile. "But I must confess, being older and in love is just as wonderful." She turned back to Mr. Steele and Marianne. "You two will certainly discover that all too soon. Once children come, oh, your love will magnify tenfold—for each other, as well as for your children!"

Marianne smiled weakly. Her whole face was aflame. Love? Children? She longed to see Mr. Steele's reaction, but her embarrassment prevented her from looking anywhere but the marked, wooden floor beneath her slippers.

"Well, we wouldn't wish to take up any more of your time," Mr. Parson said. "I am certain you are both eager to continue dancing."

The couple moved on after a departing curtsy and bow, but Marianne felt a bit like she'd just experienced a torrential downpour and was now left to deal with the aftermath. How many more times could her mood shift?

"They seemed very kind," she said, awkwardly attempting to start a conversation.

"Indeed."

Obviously, Mr. Steele had been rendered just as uncomfortable as Marianne. She longed to ease his discomfiture. After all, it was unneeded. They both knew they were unavailable to each other. Marianne had to marry a gentleman, and Mr. Steele couldn't afford to take on a wife.

"Shall we enter the dance hall again?" he suggested.

Her heart picked up as she anticipated him asking her once more. To partner twice with one's husband would be terribly impolite, even if he was imaginary. But could she ever say no to such an opportunity?

"You ought to be where others can see you so they may ask you to dance," he finished.

Her heart plummeted as swiftly as a fallen star. "I suppose that would be the wise thing to do."

She took his arm, his other hand remaining at his side, rigid and stiff. Uncomfortable.

Of course he would feel such a way. He was affirming with no uncertainty that his being there that evening was out of duty and duty alone. He had to protect his employer's daughter. He'd joined her that evening, had danced with her that evening, for no other reason.

The next two hours crept by. Even though she'd had a partner for nearly every other set, Mr. Steele did not dance with her again. He maintained his kind behavior, but Marianne was relieved when the time came to make ready for the coach—though the assembly continued on.

The two of them departed to their respective rooms to change and gather their belongings.

"Did you enjoy your evening, miss?" Jane asked as she helped Marianne into her habit.

"I did," Marianne said, feigning a yawn, "but I am ready to sleep, I think."

Fortunately, Jane had taken the hint and ended her questioning before it could really begin.

Once they were ready, they hid under their cloaks and slipped down the stairs and out of the inn, finding Mr. Steele awaiting them near the side of the building.

"Ready to return home?" he asked.

Marianne nodded, though she felt anything but ready. All day, she'd struggled to push from her mind their inevitable return home, the prospect of sneaking through Daffley Park not terribly appealing. But now, there was something more potent creating a yearning within her to prolong the day.

Reality was approaching, and she could not prevent it. Tomorrow, she would return to her schedule and her loneliness.

Tomorrow, Mr. Steele would go back to carving for her father. Tomorrow, they would no longer be together.

As the stagecoach rattled closer, Marianne resigned herself to the fact that things were better this way. She needed to be away from Mr. Steele to stop her feelings from growing even stronger.

The stagecoach emptied of its few passengers, and the three of them were once again alone on their journey from Wells. Marianne's thoughts continued to sprint so swiftly through her mind, she did not think she would ever fall asleep.

But moments later, when the carriage stopped, she jolted awake, her eyes flying open as she realized she had, indeed, fallen into a dreamless slumber.

She glanced around her in the darkness, confused. Jane still lay fast asleep against the side of the coach, her cloak fully covering her face.

"Have we arrived already?" Marianne asked in a groggy whisper, blinking as she stared out the coach's window.

Mr. Steele's response came from before her in the darkness. "No, this is Masbury, I believe. Ashwick is next."

She blinked, eying his darkened profile as he stared out of the window. With a slow nod, she leaned her head back against the coach and stared through the glass herself.

A man walked by with a lantern, and she winced at the jarring light in the darkness. Blinking, she allowed her eyes to adjust, looking past the guard who stood at the side of the coach.

"Are those men approaching passengers?" Mr. Steele whispered.

Marianne had already seen the two men coming toward them. She narrowed her eyes. One looked like...No. No, she would not make that mistake again.

Yet, as he drew closer, her heart thumped painfully against

her chest. "Mr. Barton," she breathed. "That is one of Father's business acquaintances. I'm certain this time."

Mr. Steele was already nodding. "I recognize him from the Blue Boar."

"Is he coming on the coach?" she asked, her mind spinning.

What was the man doing there so late at night? A distant memory of Father saying Mr. Barton's place of residence was in Masbury flashed through her mind, but she could not be sure.

She pushed the thought aside as he drew closer with another man she did not recognize. She prayed they would walk straight past the coach, but as he continued forward, she knew the worst was to occur.

If they were discovered, he was sure to tell Father. Mr. Steele would lose his job, and Marianne would lose her father's trust.

"They're coming aboard," Mr. Steele said. "Shift closer to Jane."

"What?" she asked in a daze.

"Shift closer to Jane," he commanded again.

He stood from his seat, hunched over beneath the shortened height of the carriage roof. Swiftly, she obeyed, sliding closer to Jane as Mr. Steele whirled around to sit beside Marianne.

He patted his shoulder. "Rest your head here."

She stared at his shoulder in alarm. If they were found in that manner, surely…

"It will be easier for the two of us to hide together," he explained with hurried words. "Quickly now. They are coming."

With stilted breaths, she did as she was told, bending her neck at a rigid angle to rest the slightest of touches against his shoulder.

"You must be more convincing than that, Miss Coventry."

He brought his hand against the side of her head, gently coaxing her closer until her cheek and temple rested fully against the side of his arm and lower shoulder. He reached over, pulling her cloak to cover her face, his fingertips brushing against her cheek in the process. "Can you breathe?"

No, no, she could not. But she nodded all the same.

Her heart beat wildly, though she was no longer sure it was because of Mr. Barton's approach. Mr. Steele's cologne tickled her nose, and his broad shoulder pressed hard against her temple.

He shifted once, then the door opened, and he grew still, steadying his breathing to feign sleep.

She attempted to do the same, squeezing her eyes closed, despite her face not being visible to others.

The coach shifted back and forth under the weight of the two gentlemen entering the carriage. Their voices were loud before they no doubt noticed the other three supposedly sleeping passengers, then their whispered tones followed.

Marianne was certain she had never prayed so greatly before in all her life. They could not be discovered. Not now, when they were so close to escape.

The door closed, the crack of the whip sounded, and the coach jerked forward. Before long, the gentlemen's conversation ended, and a soft snoring exuded from the mouth of one.

Marianne attempted to count down the moments that ticked by, but in the slower-moving coach—due to the darkness of the night—it was impossible to measure. Not to mention the fact that she was utterly and thoroughly distracted by the man whose arm she lay against.

His breathing was steady, too steady to be feigned. Had he fallen asleep? Carefully, she leaned back and stole a glance at him. His hat covered most of his face, his hand resting against the brim of it to keep it up.

Thank goodness the coach was so dark. One large jostle and the hat would certainly slip from his grasp, revealing his presence to the gentlemen.

Despite the darkness, she could still see his chest rising and falling as he drew deep breaths. He *was* asleep, then.

The knowledge instantly soothed her concerns. Mr. Steele felt nothing for her. He'd done his best to inform her of such at the assembly. But now that he slept, Marianne could finally be at ease, for Mr. Steele would be entirely unaware of just how greatly she enjoyed their proximity.

With a slow sigh, her shoulders fell, and her head sank into his shoulder as if it were a feather pillow. The coach continued to jostle back and forth, seeming to hit every hole in the road, but Marianne hardly cared. With each bounce, her cloak slipped to reveal more of her face, but instead of pulling the hood closer around her, she nuzzled deeper into Mr. Steele's arm, burying her face in the folds of his jacket.

She may as well take advantage of the opportunity she had to memorize his scent. It would certainly be the only time she'd ever be able to.

Despite that discouraging thought, she soon drifted off to sleep, and the smell of musky cologne and carved mahogany filled her senses.

CHAPTER TWENTY-FIVE

E dward could not sleep. He lay with his head back against
the coach wall, bouncing uncomfortably against it with
each hole in the road the coach did not miss, which he was
fairly certain was all of them.

But that wasn't what pained him. It was his heart pounding
against his chest, squeezing tightly and twisting around to the
point that he felt like a dry rag being rung of water that was not
there.

Miss Coventry's head against his shoulder would be the
death of him. At least *she'd* managed to fall asleep. There was no
other explanation for how she continued to nuzzle against
his arm.

He could not believe his own resolve, for he wished to do
nothing more than to wrap her in his embrace, not to protect
her, but simply to hold her, to pretend that this remarkable
woman was really his wife.

Another bounce of the stagecoach, and Miss Coventry
brought her hand up to rest in the crook of his arm, her fingers
encircling it.

His eyes flew wide open, and he stared at the blackness that was the inside of his hat.

He'd lost his senses at the ball, allowing himself to get wrapped up in the woman's beauty and her vivacity for life. Thank goodness the older couple had shocked him back to reality, reminding him that he could never love Miss Coventry—no matter how naturally it came. He could not afford to.

Finally, after what seemed an eternity, the stagecoach pulled to a stop before the Blue Boar. He waited for the two gentlemen to unload and make for the inn before Edward even stirred.

He shifted against his seat, but Miss Coventry didn't budge. How he longed to keep her there.

He moved again, but still she did not move.

Hesitating, he hovered his hand above her own for a moment before rubbing his thumb against the back of her glove. She sighed, leaning closer against his arm.

He ground his teeth together, his aching heart unable to take her sweet caress any longer. This woman was destroying him, one soft touch at a time.

"Miss Coventry," he whispered.

"Hmm?"

"We're in Ashwick."

"Hmm."

He smiled despite himself. The poor woman must be exhausted.

He rubbed his hand against the back of hers again until she stiffened, leaning up with rounded eyes.

"Forgive me," she mumbled. "I did not realize I'd fallen asleep." She roused Jane next without awaiting a response, then the three of them exited the carriage, ducking their heads and averting their eyes, though the street was veritably empty at more than an hour past midnight.

"I will see you both home," Edward offered, and he was met

with very little protest as Miss Coventry and Jane stared down the darkened street with a wary eye.

They opted out of using lanterns from the inn, for fear of alerting anyone to their presence as they continued on foot. Edward knew the way to Daffley Park by heart now, though the moon lit their pathway just enough for the three of them to travel safely side-by-side.

The walk was accomplished in silence, Miss Coventry and Jane no doubt half asleep as they traversed the darkened ground. By the time Daffley's lights shone in the distance, Edward was fairly certain he had been walking in his sleep, too.

They paused beside a few oversized hedges near the house, close enough to see the door but far enough away for them to remain unseen.

Miss Coventry dismissed a weary looking Jane then turned to face Edward. "Thank you for seeing us home."

He nodded. "You're certain you shall be able to sneak in without notice?"

"My family will be at the ball for another hour or two. Papa always encourages them to stay late to maximize the chances of Beatrice making a match."

Edward nodded. At least she appeared confident in her ability to predict where her family would be. He himself was unsure that he would arrive the next morning *without* Mr. Coventry awaiting him with a pitchfork and flaming torch. What would Edward say to his mother if he returned home without the finances to secure their future?

"Mr. Steele," Miss Coventry said, breaking through his troubling thoughts, "I wish to thank you for what you've done for me today. I know how much you risked in doing so, and I wish I could tell you..." She broke off, shaking her head. "Your kindness will never be forgotten."

He stared down at her, only the shadows on her face visible. How he longed to share what the day had meant to him as well, how he'd loved every moment he'd spent with her. Despite the risks, despite his fears of what may come…how could he regret the moments they'd shared?

But he could not complicate matters further with words. Instead, he reached for her hand and brought it to his lips, placing a lingering kiss to the back of her glove. "It was my pleasure, Mrs. Hickenbottom."

Even in the darkness, her smile lit her face. "Goodnight, Mr. *Higgenbottom*."

Edward reluctantly released her hand. He motioned toward the house. "I'll wait until you are safely inside."

She nodded her gratitude then made for her home.

Edward did as he said, standing watch until the front door closed behind her.

Then reality sprawled its imposing figure once more across his shoulders. That woman deserved the world. Her father truly was a fool to keep her in.

And Edward was a fool for taking her out.

CHAPTER TWENTY-SIX

E dward Steele had kissed her hand.

Marianne had lain awake in bed that night, revisiting the moment over and over until she'd fallen asleep, only to awaken at dawn to the very same image bidding her good morning.

She knew not to dwell on Mr. Steele's affection, nor to place too much meaning onto his lingering kiss, but she could not help herself. Yesterday had been perfection, and it was all because of Mr. Steele.

Before long, she rose from bed, ready to begin her schedule. Then she stopped. What reason had she to follow her routine? She had no unpleasant thoughts from which to distract herself, nor was she seeking busyness. Perhaps a little walk would do her good, though. Somewhere spontaneous. Like the library.

With a veiled smile, she tugged on the bell pull, Jane arriving only moments later.

"You are here already?" she asked as the maid entered the room.

Jane didn't respond, a wary crease in her brow. "Your father wishes to speak with you, miss, in his study."

Marianne's heart dropped, a chill filling her to the core. She had been right the night before. Her family had still been at the ball when she'd arrived home, and she and Jane had fortunately been able to sneak into Daffley without notice. Or at least, so she'd thought. "Does he know?"

"I can't say for certain, miss. According to Mr. Morley, Mr. Coventry hasn't been happy of late, this morning included."

"Did anyone see you last night when you entered?"

"No, miss. My sister covered for the both of us."

Marianne nodded solemnly. Of course Father knew. Why else would he be calling her to his study when he'd never once done so before? She'd been naïve to think she could do something so reckless without notice. It mattered not how he had discovered the truth. What mattered was the repercussions that would surely follow.

"Worry not, Jane. I will ensure your situation at Daffley does not change, nor that of your sister." Mr. Steele's, too.

Jane nodded, though her brow remained wrinkled.

After helping her dress, Jane left the room with a sympathetic grimace, and Marianne followed shortly after, moving as slowly as possible through the corridors toward Father's study.

She would graciously accept whatever consequences Father deemed fair. But in regard to those who helped her, she would not rest until she was certain they would not be punished for their involvement. She'd never forgive herself if they were, for clearly, no one was at fault for this masquerade but herself.

When she reached his door, she lingered outside for a moment. Could she run away again, this time for good? No, she had made the mistake, and now she needed to pay for it.

With a raised chin, she knocked on the door, entering when Father invited her in. Her eyes focused on his instantly. Jane was right, he *wasn't* pleased. His brow furrowed as deep as the divots in the road last night. Mother sat off to the side in a chair by the window, a somber smile on her lips in greeting. No doubt she was bestowing on Marianne the only comfort her daughter would receive that morning.

Marianne approached the desk as if approaching the judgment seat of Heaven, blood rushing from her head and legs trembling. "You wished to speak with me, Father?"

"Yes, we did." Father glanced at Mama with a deep breath, then he faced Marianne once more.

This was it. This was her end. But it would not be Mr. Steele's. She would say anything, tell any lie, take any bribery, for that man not to lose his position at Daffley Park.

"Please, take a seat." Father motioned to the chair before his desk.

Marianne did as she was told, just as she always did. *Almost* always.

"I'm sure you have already guessed what we wish to discuss with you," Father said.

She swallowed. "I've an idea."

He nodded, lacing his fingers together and resting his hands atop his desk. "First, I will say, I've been deeply hurt by the mistrust that has occurred within our family. Such deceptive behavior, we never thought possible."

Heat crawled up the back of her neck.

"But, as usual, the trust we have in you is unwavering."

She blinked. Trust? They trusted *her*? Was this some sort of trick?

"Therefore," he continued, "we hope that, even with more freedom, you will still do what is expected of you." He turned to Mama. "Would you like to tell her, or shall I?"

Mother pressed her lips together, turning to Marianne with a brighter smile. "Marianne, your father and I have decided it is now time to allow you into Society."

A ringing occurred in Marianne's ears, and she darted her eyes between her parents. "I don't understand," she breathed. "Why?"

Mother and Father shared a wary look before Father spoke. "We've been made aware of a few concerning matters in regard to your sister. As such, we believe it is time for you to have your turn in Society."

Concerning matters? What in heaven's name did that mean? "Is Beatrice well?"

Father grimaced. "Yes, she is. She…" He hesitated. "She has informed us that she will not be marrying after all."

The words were not surprising to Marianne. Beatrice had already said as much, had she not? But there was one thing she did not know. "Has she said why she will not?"

Father looked away. "Her reasoning is unimportant. What *is* important, however, is that we wish for you to have the same opportunity to find a spouse as we so graciously gave Beatrice."

Marianne could not agree less. Of course Beatrice's reasoning was important. What on earth could happen to have made her sister so despise the very notion of marrying?

Would that they were still as close as they had once been. Marianne could have helped Beatrice with whatever trial she was clearly suffering through.

"Are you pleased, Marianne?" Mother asked.

Pleased? She really ought to be. To be out in Society, attend dances and parties and socialize whenever she wished—it was a dream come true.

So why did dread accompany her like an overbearing, unwelcome acquaintance?

"You've been so patient throughout this whole endeavor, Marianne," Father said, "and always obedient. We are pleased to finally give you this opportunity. Neither of us ever wanted you to struggle. But we realize that you have. For that, we are sorry."

This had to be some plan her parents had concocted to see if she would be honest about traveling to Wells. There was no other explanation for it.

Mother stood from her seat and approached her side. "We

hope to make it up to you, as well. What would you say to attending the Clark's dinner party this evening?"

They *were* in earnest. Her parents truly did not know. They were letting her out in Society—encouraging her to attend a party that very evening? Had this occurred before yesterday, Marianne would have leapt from her seat and embraced them both. Now, guilt strapped her excitement tightly to her conscience.

She had to be honest with them. She could not keep up the charade any longer. She had to tell them what she and Mr. Steele had done.

Mr. Steele.

Her chest stiffened. If she told Mother and Father the truth, Mr. Steele would once more be at risk. Marianne would fight for his innocence, but truly, what power did her word hold when she'd already deceived them so greatly? No, she could not risk the man's well-being, she could not make him suffer more.

Oh, why had she been so reckless the day before? Why could she not have just waited?

"Marianne, did you hear me?"

Mother's voice cut through her thoughts. Marianne dragged her attention to the present and nodded. "Yes, I-I am simply thinking through this new state of affairs. Of course, I am delighted."

Disbelief etched across Mother's expression, but Father smiled. "We thought you would be surprised."

"Indeed." Marianne forced a smile of her own. "Are you certain the Clarks can accommodate for me?"

"I've already written them to let them know it will be you instead of Beatrice who shall be attending," Mother replied.

Marianne pulled back. "Beatrice will not be coming? If it is the matter of having no room, I will gladly remain at home for her to attend." If only to appease her own conscience.

Her parents exchanged glances again. "No," Mother

responded, "that is not the reason. Beatrice has requested not to attend this evening."

Marianne frowned. Not only was Beatrice refusing to marry, now she was refusing to attend social gatherings? What in heaven's name was going on with her?

"You mustn't worry about your sister, Marianne," Father said, as if reading her thoughts. "All will be well in future."

"Yes," Mother agreed, "and we've some tasks to see to before we leave tonight. Would you care to go into the village today and purchase a ribbon or two? Perhaps we could even order a new gown for the Abbott's approaching ball."

Marianne's forced smile fell more and more into a grimace. "That would be lovely, Mama. Thank you."

"Excellent idea," Father agreed. "We must have you looking your best for the gentlemen who will be in attendance."

Marianne had dreamt of this day for so long. To go to a party, to be out in Society, to shop for herself with Mother. But now, they were tainted. Tainted with her dishonesty, with her fear of ruining Mr. Steele, with her concern for Beatrice—and with her worry that she would be taking her sister's place, her life soon to be devoted only to finding a husband who would please her family.

She should be thrilled. Gloriously ecstatic. She'd always wanted to marry a gentleman.

So then why did she only wish to see Mr. Steele?

CHAPTER TWENTY-SEVEN

Marianne did her best not to take that walk to the library. She wandered outside for a moment, ate a morsel of breakfast, even tried stopping by Beatrice's room, but there was no answer to her knock.

Eventually, she gave up on telling her feet what to do, and they led her straight to Mr. Steele, where she hesitated outside of the door.

They had both somehow gotten away with their adventure the day before. Should she really be risking it all by speaking with him?

She peered around the doorway as she had weeks ago upon his first arrival. He carved the edge of the bookshelf, unaware— as far as she could tell—of her presence. His sleeves were rolled up and his waistcoat removed, the braces he wore rising from the center of his back to fork into two, the thick bands accentuating the breadth of his shoulders.

His muscles rolled as he worked, the grooves of his powerful arms pulsing with each tap of the mallet he hit against the chisel. Pulling the tool back, he slid his fingers down the furrows then blew against the wood to remove the excess shavings still clinging to it.

His work was mesmerizing. But was that any surprise when she was captivated by everything he did?

Unable to keep from speaking with him any longer, she fully entered the room.

His face brightened when he found her. "Good morning, Miss Coventry."

His jovial tone and smiling eyes pressed upon her chest.

He must have seen her weak smile, for his disappeared, and he lowered his tools to face her. "Have we been discovered?"

"No, we have not. Somehow we have managed to escape their notice."

Relief rushed across his features, further solidifying Marianne's decision to never reveal the truth about his involvement to her parents.

"Then may I ask what upsets you?" he asked.

She entered the room more fully. "My parents have decided it is time to allow me to enter Society."

His brow raised, his mouth opening, but no words left his lips. Was he too surprised to speak? His expression shifted from shock to...to what? Uncertainty, disappointment? How she wished she could read his mind.

"That is surprising news," he finally replied.

That was all he could say? "Indeed. I am to attend my first dinner party this evening."

He averted his gaze, staring at his carving. "I am pleased for you, Miss Coventry."

His smile seemed forced like hers did. "Thank you."

Their eyes met, then she looked away, ignoring the question looming—why were neither of them happy?

"Have matters changed with your sister? Is that why they've decided to allow it?"

"Quite the opposite. Beatrice is still adamant, but Father appears to have changed his mind about me. I assume Mother was the one to convince him."

He nodded in silence, making no move to say more. Marianne wished he would. She needed to know if his thoughts matched her own.

Or perhaps it was better for them both if they didn't.

She glanced at the carving, noticing for the first time how much he'd completed since she'd been there a little over a week ago.

She wandered closer to the bookshelves, the design resembling the movement of waves rushing inland, ending in swirls of leaves. "You've made quite the progress. Father will be pleased with your work."

"I hope so." He tipped his head back to eye the top of the shelves. The angles in his neck curved. "There is still much to be done. Not only with the carving but the staining as well."

She ran her fingers along the smooth grooves. "It is beautiful, Mr. Steele."

"Thank you," he responded softly. After a moment, his eyes found hers. "I really am happy for you, Miss Coventry. Now you will be able to live the life you so dreamed."

She could feel the truth in his words, but there was a level of somberness she could not deny hearing, for it spoke to her own sorrow.

How she longed for the day before, when his eyes had expressed approval of her ball gown. How she longed for the weeks before when she had been free to speak with him for as long as she wished instead of going to the village with Mama, instead of preparing for dinner parties and dances. Instead of going out into Society.

Now she would marry a gentleman Father could be proud of, and Mr. Steele would leave for Bath with enough money to marry a woman whose family could approve of a match with a woodcarver.

How cruel the world was to change her life just as she realized how happy she had been before.

CHAPTER TWENTY-EIGHT

M iss Coventry's gaze unraveled him like a spool of thread. He had too much work to do to be wasting anymore time staring into her eyes.

Besides, he hadn't any right to be looking at her in such a way. She had always been his employer's daughter, but now she was a fine lady out in Society, ready to marry a just-as-fine gentleman—something Edward could never be.

He drew his chisel toward the carving and tapped the mallet against the back of it. "Are you ready for the dinner party, then?"

"I suppose."

This was her first—rather, second—social outing ever. Why was she not happier? "Are you anxious?"

"No, I believe I am ready."

He hesitated. "Then may I ask why you do not appear thrilled to be attending?"

She crossed her arm over her stomach, holding her elbow with her opposite hand. "Perhaps I am still tired from last evening, Mr. Hickenbottom."

He smiled at her teasing, though the name cast slivers of pain through his chest. Their carefree time together was swiftly drawing to a close, for she would soon take the last name of another.

"I apologize for the delay that yesterday must have caused to your schedule," she said.

"I will be able to make up for it soon enough." Especially now that he'd escaped Mr. Coventry's condemnation for stealing his daughter away.

She watched him in silence for a moment as he pressed the chisel in the curve he'd already created, pushing it deeper with the mallet.

She motioned to his tools. "Is that difficult to do?"

"Not at all." He hesitated saying anything more, allowing her a chance to leave. She had no reason to visit him any longer. No reason to sneak upstairs, to chat with him at sunset, or steal away to a ball together. She'd have a line of gentlemen suitors to do that for her now.

If this was his last chance to be with Miss Coventry, should he not make it count?

He held out the tools toward her. "Would you like to try?"

"Oh, no. I couldn't. I wouldn't wish to ruin your work."

He skimmed the bookshelf, settling on a section he had not yet completed. "If you work the wood there, I will be able to fix it if anything goes astray." He offered her the tools again.

She eyed them warily. "Are you certain about this, Mr. Steele?"

"Absolutely."

She sighed, taking the tools in hand. "I haven't the faintest idea what I am doing."

"Which is why I shall help you." He motioned her closer to the bookshelf. "See these pencil markings?" He ran his fingers along the faint drawings in the bookshelf, still visible from his first few days at Daffley Park. "Take the chisel and press it flat against the thick marking there. Then lightly tap the mallet against the handle of the chisel."

She drew a deep breath, a doubtful look on her brow as she moved forward. With a tight grip, she softly tapped the mallet against the chisel.

When nothing happened, she looked back at Edward. "What did I do wrong?"

He smiled. "Strike it a little harder than that."

With a determined set to her brow, she raised the mallet then hit the chisel with all her might.

The tool dug deep into the wood with a damming thump.

She held up her arm in a gasp, still holding the mallet. But the chisel was lodged so deeply into the wood, it stuck out without movement.

"Oh, heavens."

Edward tried to hold in his laughter, but it escaped as a guttural sound at the back of his throat.

She looked at him then with a barely refrained smile. "I told you I'd destroy your work." She thrust the mallet toward him. "Here, you must take this before I lodge it into the wood next."

He chuckled again, holding up his hands for her to keep the tool. "No, no. You must try again. Simply hit somewhere in the middle of tapping an egg and striking an anvil."

She frowned, though her smile won out again. "Very well, I shall try once more. But if it does not work, I shall retire forever."

"Your father will be so disappointed. I'm certain he'd want his daughter to become a woodcarver." He pulled the chisel from the wood, handing it to her before she stood in position once again. "Loosen your grip," he instructed softly.

She stared at her hands. "If I loosen it, won't the mallet fall?"

"Only if you let go of it completely."

She pulled her lips to the side in frustration. "I do not know about this, Mr. Steele."

He hesitated, knowing just what to do to help the situation. Whether or not it would help his need to stay away from the woman was another matter entirely.

Slowly, he moved behind her and slightly off to the right, placing his hand over hers on the mallet as she held the chisel herself. A warmth blossomed where he touched her, sliding up his arm like a trail of golden light. "Soft, like this," he said in a quiet tone.

Her skin was smooth, and the scent of cherries wafted from her to linger beneath his nose.

She'd been eating tarts again. Would that he could sample them, too.

Marianne's head spun. The callused touch of his hand against hers, his deep voice in her ear—it took everything within her not to fall over with delirium.

"Now hold the chisel securely against the bookshelf," he said softly.

She rested the head of the chisel on one of the markings on the wood. "Right here?"

He nodded, his chin brushing against the back of her hair. Chills erupted near her neck as he rested a hand on her opposite shoulder. One slight step back, and she'd be resting against his chest.

"Relax this arm."

As if she could relax when she could not breathe. As if she could *breathe* when he stood so closely.

"Angle the chisel lower."

She did her best to follow his instructions, but her mind was having great difficulty shifting her focus from his proximity to…what was it they were doing again, carving?

His breath tickled her ear. "Now softly tap the mallet and apply light pressure to the chisel."

His own hand guided hers in lifting the mallet then tapping it against the tool. To her surprise, the chisel slid up a fraction of the bookshelf, shaving off a slight slab of wood.

"It worked," she said with a smile.

She turned to seek Mr. Steele's approval, but as she did so, her brow brushed against his lips, and her breathing stopped altogether.

Their eyes met, and a longing she had never known before rushed through her. Slowly, he released his hold of her hand around the mallet, bringing his fingers to hover beside her cheek before brushing them softly against her skin. Those fingers, they could only belong to a working-class man—callused, worn. Strong.

She longed to turn and face him more fully, but how could she reveal just how greatly she wished to be kissed by him when she did not know if he wished for the same?

As if on cue, his eyes dropped to her mouth. Her lips parted involuntarily, and she raised her chin. As his fingers slid from her cheek to the side of her neck, she was gone.

Unfortunately, so was her grip.

A loud clatter erupted through the room, and she jumped away from Mr. Steele to stare at the ground where she'd dropped the mallet.

Blast. Blast, blast, blast.

She drew in a deep breath and looked to Mr. Steele, who had backed away from her, as well.

What on earth had they been about to do?

She went straight for the door without another look at him. "Excuse me, Mr. Steele," she barely managed to say, then she fled from the room.

Her insides clenched, as if her stomach had been kneaded like bread. She was upset. Deeply.

But as she walked away, she could not decide what she was more upset about—almost kissing the man...or not kissing him at all.

CHAPTER TWENTY-NINE

M arianne enjoyed her time in the village with Mama, purchasing ribbons and choosing fabric for new gowns, but nothing could compare to the laughter and excitement she'd shared with Mr. Steele.

Had she simply enjoyed her time with him more due to the thrill of being caught? Or was it truly Mr. Steele's presence that made everything more enjoyable?

By the time evening arrived, Marianne had managed to convince herself that she had found her answers. Wells had been so enjoyable because it had been her first taste of freedom. Her second taste—tonight at the Clarks'—would be just as wonderful.

"Are you anxious, my dear?" Mother asked as they pulled up to the Clarks' home.

"A little." In truth, she was very anxious. Even more so than at the assembly the night before. No doubt because of the lack of sleep she'd received.

Father smiled over at her. "I understand many of our friends are looking forward to having you join us this evening. Especially Mr. Clark."

Especially Mr. Clark? "What do you mean?"

Her parents exchanged a glance. "Nothing at all," Father said with a knowing smile, turning to stare out the window.

Marianne looked at Mother for an explanation, but she kept silent.

Heavens. They didn't mean to hint that Mr. Clark was interested in Marianne, did they?

She thought back to the occasional moments she'd spent with Miss Clark's brother. She'd only seen him a handful of times in town while out shopping with Beatrice or at church with her family, due to his only recent return from university.

Either way, she should be flattered to have the attention of such an amiable young man, not sick to her stomach. Furthermore, when she entered the Clarks' drawing room with her parents, she dodged past Mr. Clark's swift approach and moved instead to his sister.

"I am so delighted to be joining you tonight, Miss Clark." Marianne paused. "Oh, but it is not Miss Clark any longer, is it, Mrs. Morris?"

Mrs. Morris smiled, admiring her new husband from across the room. "Yes, it is quite the change." She turned to face Marianne with a bright smile. "I am so pleased you are here, my dear. All of us are, in fact. We cannot help but wonder at the sudden change that has occurred."

Marianne had been expecting such questions and had prepared just the response. "I suppose Father simply thought it was time."

Mrs. Morris hardly seemed satisfied with the response. "I trust your sister is well. We were so hoping the both of you would finally be able to join us."

"Yes, I fear she was not feeling up to it this evening." Another rehearsed answer.

Her parents had advised her to keep their family matters to themselves, even though Marianne was just as much in the dark as everyone else in Ashwick. Apparently, only Mother and Father knew the truth behind Beatrice's behavior.

"Now, Miss Coventry," Mrs. Morris said, "you must be eager for your first public outing, but worry not. My brother has graciously offered to be your guide."

She motioned across the room to where Mr. Clark stood speaking with Mr. Morris. Marianne sent him a weakened smile then instantly looked away. That was the last thing she wished for this evening—a guide to remind her just how childish everyone thought her to be.

She looked around for help. If only Beatrice would've accepted Marianne's request to come that evening, but her sister had not answered her knock once again.

Mother was occupied speaking with Mrs. Morris's parents, and Father stood across the room with a tall, handsome gentleman.

For a moment, Marianne forgot all about her plight. "Who is that man?" she asked Mrs. Morris. "I do not believe I've seen him before."

"Oh, that is Mr. Wakefield. He is a friend of your father's. I'm surprised you do not know him."

Marianne tipped her head to the side. Wakefield?

Wakefield. Of course! Mr. Wakefield was the man Father had intended for Beatrice. Of course she would not know him. She was never introduced to father's business associates.

She watched the gentleman closer, wondering what faults of his Beatrice had discovered to set her mind so readily against him—even to push her to say she'd never marry. He seemed kind and well-mannered with a ready smile and engaged expression as he spoke with others. Father had said he was wealthy, too. Indeed, what did Beatrice see that was so offensive?

As the evening progressed, Marianne did her best to discover more about Mr. Wakefield, all while dodging Mr.

Clark's conversation until she was unfortunately seated beside him throughout dinner.

"Miss Coventry, how delighted I am to be so near you."

Why did her name sound so much nicer on Mr. Steele's lips?

"Likewise, Mr. Clark," she forced.

For the first quarter of an hour, the man had needlessly instructed her on which tableware to use and what she ought to expect throughout the duration of the dinner. Then he'd taken to willfully dishing her out food she'd politely declined.

"You will enjoy this, Miss Coventry, I assure you."

She longed to explain to Mr. Clark that though she had not been in Society for twenty years, she did not eat dinner like an uncultured swine. She knew very well the difference between a salad fork and the dessert spoon, as well as what courses were served first. And she *certainly* knew what foods she liked and disliked.

Of course, Mr. Clark was just being attentive, but her patience waned as he rattled off countless stories about university and how he'd played tricks on his friends.

How she longed to speak about anything else. Sunsets. Cherry tarts. Woodcarving...

When dinner ended, Marianne was one of the first of the women to stand, relieved for the excuse to extricate herself from Mr. Clark's conversational grasp.

"Are you enjoying yourself, my dear?" Mother asked as they progressed to the drawing room.

"Yes, of course," Marianne responded.

"You've made quite the impression on Mr. Clark."

Marianne could have groaned. Was this how Beatrice felt? No wonder she was exhausted after ten years in the same regard. No wonder she didn't wish to marry.

"He is kind, is he not?" Mother continued. "And set to inherit this lovely estate."

Marianne nodded. Yes, he was kind. Yes, he would inherit.

But he was not Mr. Steele.

The thought persisted throughout the women's conversation of pianoforte practicing and bonnet trimming. As such, when the gentlemen joined them, she moved to Father's side, if only to provide her with further distraction.

He introduced her to Mr. Wakefield, whom he spoke with once again.

"I was just sharing with Mr. Wakefield about our time in Bath," Father said.

"Oh, yes. It certainly was a delightful time for our family." Especially meeting Mr. Steele for the first time.

"It is a lovely city," Mr. Wakefield said, smiling back at her. He hesitated a moment. "Does-does your sister enjoy Bath?"

Even with Mr. Clark's unending chatter, Marianne had kept one eye on Mr. Wakefield through dinner. He was every bit as amiable as Father had suggested him to be. Why did Beatrice not see this?

"I believe she does," Marianne responded.

The man nodded, his eyes taking on a vulnerable light before he looked away.

Marianne narrowed her eyes. She'd thought Father had pushed for the match out of convenience, but now—

"Ah, here you are, Miss Coventry."

Blast. Mr. Clark had found her again. If only hiding behind a settee was not frowned upon, then she'd not have to speak with him for the rest of the evening.

She listened with boredom as Mr. Clark carried on and on. Mr. Wakefield and Father both wandered away eventually, leaving her to stand alone with the man who seemed to never run out of words.

She ought to give him a chance, really. Perhaps he was simply nervous. She did her best to pretend she cared about his horsemanship and swordsmanship when his conversation abruptly shifted.

"I must say, you are a superb listener, Miss Coventry. It must be all those years confined to Daffley Park that taught you the trait."

Her smile faded. That was rather insensitive of him to say.

"I have been hoping for your presence in Society for so very long," he continued. "But now that it is here, and with your elder sister still unmarried, I'm sure you are aware that questions have arisen as to why you *are* out."

She pressed her teeth together. She would not be speaking of such things with anyone—especially Mr. Clark. She repeated her usual answer. "I suppose my parents simply thought it was time, that is all."

He narrowed his eyes. "Just like that?"

She did not respond.

"I thought…well, there have been rumors about your sister. I'm sure you've heard them."

How on earth was she supposed to have heard them, being tucked away as she was? Why was this gentleman speaking of rumors anyway?

Memories of past conversations with Mr. Steele swirled throughout her mind. Hadn't he said a gentleman had started rumors about his own father that had led to the elder Mr. Steele's death?

Her stomach churned at the thought.

"I'm sure I would not listen to such rumors even if I had heard them," she responded, glancing over her shoulder for an escape.

Mr. Clark grinned. "Oh, come now. Surely you must be curious."

CHAPTER THIRTY

M r. Clark leaned closer, and indignation swirled inside Marianne at his forceful behavior. "It has been said that your sister—"

"Mr. Clark," she interrupted quietly but firmly, "gossip and rumors may not injure the ones who spread them, but surely they are the culprits for wounding countless individuals who are at the brunt of such cruel behavior."

He stared at her wide-eyed, the grin finally gone from his lips.

Thank *heavens.*

It was not as if she wasn't curious about said rumors, but why would she wish to hear the words of another—true or not —about her own sister? If she was to learn about anything in relation to Beatrice, she would hear it from Beatrice's lips, and Beatrice's lips alone.

"Now," she continued in a whisper, "if you were any sort of gentleman, Mr. Clark, you would end the rumors yourself. At the very least, you ought not bring them up to the very sister of the one whom the rumors are about." She raised her chin. "If you'll excuse me. I've had enough of our conversation."

Marianne found Mother and remained by her side the rest of the evening. Doing so kept her safe from Mr. Clark's nagging, but it also opened up her mind to constantly comparing the dinner party to the assembly the night before.

She could no longer deny which one continually triumphed in her estimations.

When the evening finally ended, she rode home in the carriage with Mother and Father, utterly exhausted. Where she'd feared disappointment the night before, she'd certainly received it tonight at the Clarks'.

"You did very well tonight, Marianne," Father said. "We heard nothing but compliments about your behavior and kindness. Of course, we expected nothing less from you."

Marianne looked out of the window with a half-smile. Fortunately, her parents didn't press her to say anything in response.

When they arrived at Daffley, Father moved to the parlor for a cup of tea, but Marianne declined his offer to join them. Before she could retire, however, Mother lingered in the entryway, and the two of them spoke in hushed tones.

"Did you enjoy yourself, Marianne?" she asked, blinking sleepily.

Marianne nodded. How could she respond any differently without appearing ungrateful? "I am tired, though."

"Understandably so. You've done much socializing, and it takes its toll on one who is not used to it."

Marianne couldn't agree less. It was not the socializing that had tired her out but those with whom she had socialized. Was she simply being intolerant? Or...or had her desires changed? Was it not the balls and dinner parties that pulled her any longer but the people—the people she actually wished to converse with, rather than those she was expected to converse with?

Mother kissed her cheek. "Sleep well tonight, my dear."

Marianne nodded, turning, but she paused only a few steps away. "Mother?"

"Yes, my dear?"

"Are dinner parties always like that?"

"Like what?"

She hesitated. Boring. Uneventful. Tiresome. "Never mind. I was simply expecting something different, I suppose."

Mother watched her curiously. "Different in what way?"

She shook her head and smiled. "Never mind. Goodnight, Mother."

She turned away, retrieving an already lit candle from the corridor and heading to her room.

Only, she did not go to her room. Instead, she wandered to the library. She knew Mr. Steele would have left for home already, unable to carve in the dim light produced by the candles, but she was still disappointed when she turned the corner to find the room empty.

She ambled inside, eying the white sheet where Mr. Steele's tools were usually lined perfectly across the small table. Light from her candle illuminated the work he'd accomplished, and she shook her head in awe. He was a talented man. Talented. Kind. Charming. Sweet.

She sighed, shaking her head. Dwelling on Mr. Steele's many first-rate traits would do nothing but keep her up all night long.

Leaving behind the library and the memories of their almost-kiss, Marianne finally reached her room, setting the candle down and plopping onto the bed with an exhausted sigh.

Something crinkled behind her, and she turned to find a rectangular, flat package about the size of her hand situated just below her pillow.

She tipped her head. Was it from Beatrice? A peace-offering for ignoring her for more than a week?

She retrieved the package wrapped in brown paper, tied

together rather scrappily with brown twine. She moved it upside down, but there was no note or writing.

Forgetting all about the dinner party and her terrible evening, she hastily untied the string and unfolded the paper to reveal a handheld, wooden comb sitting atop a folded note. Her lips parted at the detail and beauty of the light-colored wood. She drew it closer to the candle, inspecting it further. As she did so, her heart tripped. Forget-me-nots trailed the top portion of the comb in such minute detail, one might miss them at first glance.

She ran her fingers along the delicate flowers. There was only one person who knew how greatly she loved them.

She retrieved the paper, unfolding it to read the short message.

Mrs. Hickenbottom,

I carved this from a piece of beechwood I found the night we watched the sunset together. May it always remind you of what we spoke of that night, for you deserve every happiness.

E.S.

Tears sprung to her eyes, and her vision blurred as she smiled.

It *was* from him.

She read and reread the small note, stroking the grooves of the comb carved by Mr. Steele himself. Joy filled her soul, and clarity enlightened her mind.

Now she understood why her evening with Mr. Steele had excelled in every possible way. He had listened to her. He had *seen* her, even before she was out in Society. She hadn't loved the dance because it was her first time out in Society. She'd loved it because she loved the woodcarver who'd accompanied her.

Now, even though barriers littered their path toward being together, she could focus on only one question—did he feel the same about her...or did he not?

CHAPTER THIRTY-ONE

E dward never should have given Miss Coventry that comb. He'd finished the forget-me-nots the night of the ball, having been unable to sleep, and brought it with him the next day to Daffley. He'd still been hesitant to bestow the gift, however, deciding to do so only if Jane could deliver it for him.

As luck would have it, he'd happened upon the maid in the corridor the very night Marianne had attended the dinner party, and he'd impulsively thrust the package toward her without a second thought.

Now, the following day, Edward deeply regretted his choice. Suppose Miss Coventry misconstrued the gift as more than what it was—a simple token between friends? For that's surely all it meant to him.

As the day progressed, his mind continually strayed back to Miss Coventry. Had she had an enjoyable time at the dinner party? Would she come to the library and ask Edward what he'd been thinking, giving her such a gift? Would she share with him that she'd already found the love of her life out in Society?

At five o'clock, he dropped his tools haphazardly on the table with a sigh of aggravation, pulling his satchel around his shoulder. He was done for the day. Working was futile if all he did was think about Miss Coventry.

He walked through the large house, keeping his head down to avoid any sight of another person. He'd not heard back from Mr. Chapple yet, but in three days' time, Edward would receive enough money to settle his debts. Any work beyond that would simply further solidify their future at the shop. But should word get out earlier that Edward had given a gift to Miss Coventry, her father would have every right to expel him without a penny.

How Edward could have made such a folly was beyond him —especially after traveling to Wells with her. He had clearly taken leave of his senses.

As he finally left Daffley through the front door, he secured his coat round his shoulders and tucked his hat closer to his head. The rain poured down in droves that evening, rather fitting for Edward's mood. Perhaps it would be just the thing to clear his mind—or make him even more miserable. Either would do.

He crossed the gravel drive, leaving the house behind and blowing out another sigh. How was he to continue carving for the next two months, knowing Miss Coventry was falling in love with another? How was he to bear the grief of knowing she was inside Daffley, preparing for dinner parties and public assemblies and private balls when all he wanted was for her to join him in the library so they might finish that kiss, which had ended before it had even begun?

He was a fool. He'd fallen too hard for a woman he never should have fallen for at all.

"Mr. Steele?"

Edward whirled around as Miss Coventry approached, dressed in her riding habit. Would she mention the comb? His throat constricted.

"What are you doing out in the rain?" he asked.

She raised her voice to be heard above the raindrops plummeting onto the gravel around them. "I rode earlier, before it started up again. I was merely lingering in the stables until I saw you."

So she'd specifically sought him out? She was going to ask him about the comb, he was certain of it. If he wished to avoid the question altogether, he would leave now.

But leaving Miss Coventry after only speaking with her for a moment was like taking a single bite of a fresh pastry—delightful, but never enough to satisfy one's cravings.

"You were riding before dinner?" he asked. "Have you forgone your schedule, then?"

She eyed him curiously, no doubt due to his foolish revelation that he knew her schedule. Blast. He was trying to prove that he did *not* like the woman, not that he was obsessed with her whereabouts like a love-crazed schoolboy.

"I have found that I have a decreased desire to drown my thoughts in routine," she finally replied.

Because she was out in Society, no doubt. He knew he ought to ask after her dinner party last night, but his heart could not bear what she might say—that it had been exactly what she'd been waiting for.

"I am happy you've found the life you've so longed for, Miss Coventry," he said instead, taking a step back. "Now, if you'll excuse me. I shan't keep you in the rain any longer. Good day."

"Oh, but Mr. Steele..." She paused, looking around them before settling her eyes beyond his shoulder. "Might we speak for a moment? If we move beneath the trees, we will be provided with more shelter."

This was not a good idea. In fact, it was a terrible idea. What if her family saw them through Daffley's windows? What would become of them then?

He had a mind to refuse her offer, but when she made for the canopy of trees lining the drive to Daffley, he followed her without question.

A heavy silence hung between them until they reached the shelter the leaves provided. The rain was mostly stopped by the foliage, but the drops that managed to filter through tapped gently against the leaves, like fingertips lightly clicking against a tabletop.

Miss Coventry stared up at him, her gaze stalwart. "I received your gift last night."

He pressed his lips together, nodding in silence. He never should have followed her into the trees.

Her eyes were soft as she peered up at him. "I cannot thank you enough. It is as beautiful as any comb I have ever seen."

He shifted uncomfortably, running his hands across the leather strap of his satchel. "It was nothing, I assure you."

"I find that difficult to believe."

She grew silent, as if willing him to say something more.

But what *could* he say without revealing more than either of them ought to be sharing?

"I simply wished to give you a gift of departure, that is all."

"A gift of departure," she repeated, her words hardly above the sound of the rain. "I see."

He averted his eyes, unable to bear the hurt he'd caused her by his words—his *lies*.

He looked over his shoulder at the lane leading away from Daffley—the lane he ought to be traveling on right now. "I had better take my leave. If your father sees us…"

She was already nodding. "No, we would not wish for him to suspect anything." She backed away. "Good day, Mr. Steele. I shall not bother you again."

She made to leave, but without a second thought, he held out his hand to stop her. "Wait."

She peered up at him, her eyes glossy with tears.

He hesitated, a battle raging inside him, common sense against his heart. He knew which one *ought* to win, and yet, the victor was already clear. For how could he deny his heart what it truly wanted—who *he* truly wanted?

"Please, Miss Coventry, allow me to explain."

CHAPTER THIRTY-TWO

Marianne's cheeks burned with heat despite the cold air nipping at her skin. She never should have mentioned the comb. Deep within her heart, she knew it had meant more than a simple farewell between friends.

And yet, his response had revealed his true desires—that even if he did wish for something more between them, he didn't *want* to want it. That had pained her more than anything.

"All is well, Mr. Steele," she said as he approached. "You were right. We shouldn't be seen out here together."

"No, we shouldn't," he agreed at once. "But I…" He broke off with a sigh, rubbing the back of his neck with his gloved hand. The wariness was etched so clearly across his brow, he could have carved it himself. "I have been an utter cad to allow a friendship to occur between us. You do not even know how you risk your own reputation simply by speaking with me."

Her mind sifted through his words, attempting to make sense of them. "You are speaking in regard to the rumors about your father?"

His silence answered her question.

"But they were false," she said.

He removed his hat, raking his fingers through his hair. "False or not, the reputation remains. I care about you too greatly to allow our association to continue."

Her heart lifted. He *did* care for her. "Surely the rumors will fade as the years pass."

He paced back and forth as if he had not heard her. "If you only knew what has been said, Miss Coventry. You would leave this moment and never converse with me again."

That would not happen, no matter the rumors. But she knew he would not believe her until she had proven her devotion. "Then tell me, Mr. Steele. Tell me what the rumors claim."

He stopped walking and stared at her, clearly debating whether to speak. Finally, with fallen shoulders, the defeat in his stance was apparent. "Father was accused of...being with the wife of one of his employers."

The blood drained from her face, though she forced herself to react unaffected. "But...but *you* were not."

He glanced at her sidelong. "No, my sin is one of mere association. If they believed Father could do such a thing, why would his son not?" He sniffed with derision. "Upper class logic at its finest."

Marianne watched him, the pieces falling into place within her mind. That was why he had been so careful with her, so hesitant in everything he did—because he did not wish to taint her name as his had been tainted.

Was that also why he could not admit his feelings for her? Or was there something more? "Can you tell me more about the rumors?" she asked with care. "How they came about?"

He stared off toward the gravel lane nearby, rain bouncing up from the small rocks in minuscule splashes. "Mr. French commissioned work from Father for many years. Mrs. French would often speak with Father when he'd install various furnishings around their house, but she began to linger too greatly in his presence. Father always brought me along or sent me alone to try to ward the woman off, but one day, when I was occupied elsewhere, Mrs. French attempted to...to encourage Father to behave improperly. Father instantly refused, declaring his devoted love for his own wife and his respect for Mr. French."

His lip twitched down in disgust. "Mrs. French, obviously humiliated, told her husband that Father had been the culprit. Mr. French was furious, and rightly so—had she been speaking the truth. Unfortunately, the gentleman created story after story, discouraging anyone from accepting work from *Steele and Son* again."

He shook his head, still clearly affected by the horrifying details. "Mrs. French's conscience eventually got the better of her, and she apologized to Father in a correspondence, declaring his innocence in the whole situation. But it was too late. We lost every last one of our well-paying, long-standing customers." His eyes took on a faraway look. "The physician said Father died from a fever, but Mother and I know what really killed him was his grief. He simply could not understand how his friends and associates, people he had known for years, could truly believe he would do something so heinous."

Marianne's chest ached as she imagined the anguish his family must have endured. She longed to reach out, to caress Mr. Steele's furrowed brow and ease his wounds. "I'm so sorry. I cannot imagine having to go through such a terrible experience. But...not everyone believes such things."

His eyes found hers.

"As you can see, I am still here," she continued, "despite the rumors, despite what it might do to my name and reputation. Surely that tells you something."

He sobered, a gaunt look in his eye. "Yes, it tells me that I was selfish to seek a connection with you from the start, knowing your name would be sullied if connected with mine."

He shook his head. "I should have been honest with you. And I certainly never should have given you that blasted comb."

The words fractured her heart, and she scrambled to put the pieces back together. She could see Mr. Steele's reasoning. If he pursued any sort of relationship with Marianne, he would lose any chance of maintaining his work at Daffley, thereby forfeiting his and his mother's home and his own future at his shop.

She could not ask him to do that.

She took a step away from him, embarrassment rushing through her limbs as swiftly as the drops fell from the sky. How could she have been so selfish to have even considered them being together?

"Forgive me, Mr. Steele. I could never ask you to choose between me and your livelihood. I never should have put you through this."

She shook her head, backing away then turning on her heel and fleeing from beneath the cover of the trees.

This time, Mr. Steele didn't attempt to stop her.

Rain poured down over the brim of her hat and fell against her shoulders, the cold seeping through her riding habit. In contrast, warm tears blurred her vision, and she squeezed her eyes to be rid of them.

How could she have been so foolish? So heartless to have put him through such torment? So *stupid* to have believed there was some chance of them being happy together, of both receiving what they wanted and needed?

"Miss Coventry?"

She gritted her teeth, trying to run faster than his words, but he called out to her again.

"Miss Coventry, please!"

She spoke over her shoulder, though she plowed ahead through the rain. "No, Mr. Steele. You needn't explain your reasoning. I understand it all too well."

"No, you do not. Please, do not leave like this."

The pleading in his voice tugged at her conscience. She did not wish to leave like this either, but then, what were they to do?

Slowly, she turned to face him. He stood more than ten feet away, his boots planted in the sopping grass, his hat and satchel nowhere to be seen. Had he left them beneath the tree? Rain slipped from his hair to his brow, trailing down the angles of his nose, lips, and jawline, and his dark jacket shone all the darker due to the rain.

"The comb." He paused, swallowing as the lines in his neck angled. "It was not a mere token of friendship or farewell. It was the only way I could express my feelings for you. The only way I could share how deeply I love you."

The words took root in her heart, swirling slow warmth throughout each of her limbs before she had the chance to stop it.

"But you would have no future with me as your husband," Mr. Steele continued, his eyes red-rimmed and shining with moisture.

She struggled to accept his words, her common sense failing her as she stared at his pained expression. "I know I would have more of a future with you than I would with anyone else."

"You do not know what you say. We would be poor. Destitute."

And she would make them all the poorer. She didn't wish to put such a strain on him and his mother. But how could she bid farewell to the one man who knew her, the one man who *loved* her?

Her heart thumped painfully against her chest, each tap like a mallet to the chisel, carving his name into her soul forever. "I don't want to lose you," she said, her voice breaking.

His chest rose and fell beneath his waistcoat, his breath puffing out in white clouds as the cold air encircled them both.

"Nor I, you, my love," he said. His lips parted again as if he wished to say something more, but they closed a moment later as he winced.

Shaking his head, his jaw twitched, and he advanced upon her, closing the distance in a few strides. Swiftly, he pulled off his gloves and dropped them to the ground, reaching out and holding her face gently in his hands.

Silence pulsed between them, the rain softly tapping against the grass, their eyes unmoving from one another's until his gaze dropped to her mouth. He moved his thumb along her bottom lip before he leaned forward.

No more words were spoken—no more words were *needed*. They were of the same mind, same heart, same desires. She closed her eyes, tipping her head to the side at his soft urging and waited with anticipation until his lips finally pressed against hers.

Rain pattered against her cheek, sliding down her skin and leaving a cold trail behind the drops. How the sensation contrasted sharply to the warmth infusing her entire being as Mr. Steele kissed her. With his heated breath against her cheek, his hands cradling her face, Marianne had never felt more loved.

She slid her arms around his shoulders, tipping her head further to the side as their kiss continued. She felt at home in his arms, as if this was what she'd been missing her entire life. How had she ever lived without this man? How was she to live without him now?

Reality settled its way into Marianne's thoughts once more, though she did her best to set it aside. Mr. Steele must have noticed the change in her focus, for his kisses slowed, and he pulled back, resting his brow against hers.

They remained still for a moment, his hands resting at her hips, hers on his shoulders, neither of them wishing to dispel the peace around them.

But the spell had already been broken merely by a simple thought.

"What are we to do?" she whispered.

"I do not know. We could speak with your father..."

The very idea made her throat constrict.

He pulled his brow back from hers. "He will not listen to us, though," he finished.

She nodded. Father was far too aggravated with Beatrice's choice to never marry. Marianne saying that she had decided to marry a woodcarver would be even worse.

"We cannot keep it a secret," she said, though she longed for that to be a viable option.

He nodded at once in agreement. "Speaking the truth will only infuriate your father to the point that I will no longer be employed here."

That could not occur. Too much was at stake for him and his mother to risk losing any amount of pay from Father.

"What options are we left with, then?" she asked, despair swiftly swallowing her hope in one large gulp.

He must have sensed her worry, for he reached forward, gently wiping away the moisture sliding down her cheek. "We keep up our hope and pray for a sunset."

Warmth settled again into her heart, and she raised on the tips of her toes to press a lingering kiss to his lips.

But a voice disrupted their moment of solitude, deep and loud...and coming directly from the house. "Marianne!"

CHAPTER THIRTY-THREE

F ear clenched Edward's chest, refusing to release its hold. This was not how Mr. Coventry was supposed to find out. This was not how at all.

The man stormed toward them, the door to Daffley Park swinging wide open behind him. He wore neither jacket nor hat, his waistcoat unbuttoned and cravat clinging to his shoulder from the rain.

"Mr. Steele," Miss Coventry breathed.

"It will be all right," he said, though he did not believe the words himself. He reached down, taking Miss Coventry's hand in his, willing his fingers not to tremble.

How could he have allowed this to happen? How could he have been so stupid, so careless? Mr. Coventry would, in no way, allow Edward to keep his job. His future as a woodcarver was lost. How would he care for Mother? How could he be with Miss Coventry?

His hope spiraled down like a bird diving toward land, only he could not spread his feathers and swoop back into the sky. He was grounded, stranded upon the earth for he, like a fool, thought he could sail without wings.

Mr. Coventry shouted from across the grounds once again. "Remove yourself from my daughter at once, Steele!"

But Edward held fast, and so did Miss Coventry, her grip on his hand even tighter.

This was the last way Edward had wished to go about matters, but time could not be turned. He and Miss Coventry had chosen their path, and he would not regret it—even if the fury in Mr. Coventry's stride made the hair on Edward's neck stand on end.

"What in the devil do you think you are doing, Steele?" Mr. Coventry shouted, fire in his eyes as he approached.

Edward held up a hand. "Sir, allow us to explain—"

"Oh, you are past explaining," he growled.

The closer Mr. Coventry raged, the more Edward realized the man was not stopping. Would he take a swing at Edward? Pull Miss Coventry back into the house? He moved his shoulder in front of her to protect her no matter what her father did.

"How dare you!" Mr. Coventry shouted, stopping inches from Edward's face. "How dare you come under my roof and steal away my daughter."

Edward drew a steadying breath. He longed to shove Mr. Coventry back to a respectable level, but the father had every right to be angry. Edward had acted abominably.

"Father," Miss Coventry began, "he did not steal me away. We are—"

"I will speak with you later!" he shouted, pointing his finger at her.

Miss Coventry shrunk back, her hand gripping Edward's.

"Do not shout at her, Mr. Coventry," Edward advised, his voice deep and slow. "Direct your anger at me, not your daughter."

Mr. Coventry's eyes widened. "You have no right to tell me what to do."

Edward paused, finding the humility he knew was needed in

this situation. He was in the wrong, and they all knew it. "You are right, sir. But I will beg of you to listen to your daughter."

Mr. Coventry carried on as if he did not hear a word Edward said. "I should have known better than to keep you on. I should have dismissed you the moment Lord Ryecombe wrote to me nearly a week ago, informing me of the rumors."

Lord Ryecombe? Edward fisted his free hand. He should have known. That earl would be the death of him yet.

"But no," Mr. Coventry spat out, rainwater flying from his lips as he shouted the words. "I foolishly believed in your merits. I chose to trust that after a month of work, you had proven your worth. Of course that was not the case. Now you have injured my family with your filthy name, behaving the same as your worthless father."

Anger surged through Edward's veins, as it always did at any poor mention of Father. Edward had wanted to copy Mrs. French's letter and distribute it to all of Somerset in order to clear their name, but they knew it would do very little. People believed what they wished to believe, and lies bellowed louder than the soft-spoken whispers of truth.

"I would advise against speaking of what you do not know, sir," Edward said.

A sneer stretched across Mr. Coventry's lips. "Just as I thought. You haven't shared that with my daughter, have you? Is that how you deceived her, with your lies?" He faced Miss Coventry. "This man has been dishonest with you from the beginning. When I returned from Bath, I was finally informed of the horrific scandal involving his family."

Edward had never been more grateful that he'd spoken the truth.

Miss Coventry shook her head, coming to stand side-by-side with Edward. "He *has* told me, Father. They were falsehoods spread about by a disenchanted gentleman."

Edward's love for the woman grew tenfold. She had not

once questioned his words, believing him from the start. How had he ever earned the love of such a woman? How would he ever live without her?

She took a step forward. "You cannot—"

"Silence, Marianne! I will not hear another word from you."

Edward squeezed Miss Coventry's hand in support. "You must stop shouting at her, sir."

"Or what?" Mr. Coventry growled. "You have nothing, Steele. You've a sullied reputation, a ruined business, and not a penny to your name. You'll not receive a penny from me, either."

Edward had been expecting the threat. When would he learn to never trust the word of a gentleman? He forced his mind to the present, though the burden of providing for his mother, for keeping *Steele and Son* afloat, pressed upon his chest like a pile of uncarvable stones. He had been so close to receiving that payment. So close.

"Father, that isn't fair," she cried out. "Mr. Steele has done the job admirably, exactly as you asked—"

"I did not ask for him to steal away my daughter in the middle of the night!"

Miss Coventry pulled back with a startled expression. "You knew?"

"Of course I knew. Did you truly think you could get away with such misconduct?"

She winced. "I was going to tell you, Father."

"Yes, but you didn't, did you? Instead, I had to hear it from the gossip of my own servants." He narrowed his eyes. "Imagine my disgust when I learned of my most obedient daughter's subterfuge, convincing a maid and a woodcarver to go along with it." He turned on Edward then. "I thought Mr. Morley had been mistaken in what he brought to me from below stairs. I was even inclined to speak with you to set the record straight. Then I see the both of you out here, cavorting disgustingly together. How could you risk her reputation in such a way, coming to Daffley, being in full possession of the knowledge of what those rumors could do to us? You had better pray the news has not yet spread about Ashwick."

Regret rushed over Edward in droves stronger than the waves of the sea. "I have prayed for such, sir. I cannot tell you how I regret risking her name at all. I am deeply sorry." He peered down at Miss Coventry. "To both of you."

Her eyebrows pulled close together, and she shook her head, as if to say he did not need to apologize, but Mr. Coventry's barked laughter cut through her words before they could begin.

"An apology means nothing when said out of duty."

Miss Coventry removed her hand from Edward's, wrapping her fingers around his forearm instead. "Mr. Steele has done nothing wrong, Father. I am the one at fault. It was I who convinced him to go to Wells, and it was I who spoke with him from the beginning."

Mr. Coventry frowned, his eyes flicking between them as he clearly struggled to decide who to direct his anger at now. With a growl of frustration, he shook his head. "Return inside, Marianne."

"Father, please, listen—"

"I will not ask you again." Mr. Coventry took a step forward, reaching for her arm. "Return indoors and wait until I am finished with this worthless woodcarver."

She tried to pull her arm away, but her father held tight, pulling her forward. Edward's desire to protect her surged through his body, a raging fire consuming his every thought.

"Release her," he spoke as calmly as possible.

Mr. Coventry turned livid eyes on Edward. As if Heaven helped him, he could almost see the man's fist flying toward him just before it occurred. In swift movements, Edward pushed Miss Coventry out of the way as gently as possible, ducking in time for Mr. Coventry's blow to sail through the rain.

"Father!" Miss Coventry cried out in despair. "Stop!"

Mr. Coventry did not listen, attempting to hit Edward again, but Edward jumped away with arms raised in defense. He refused to engage in a physical fight with Miss Coventry's father. He loved her too much to hit him back.

Shouts came from across the wet grass as Mrs. Coventry, the elder Miss Coventry, and the butler rushed forward.

Mr. Morley was a large man, and Edward's heart thumped in his ears. Edward would not stand a chance between both him and Mr. Coventry.

"Jacob!" Mrs. Coventry shouted out toward her husband. "What is going on?"

Mr. Coventry stopped advancing on Edward, though his fists clenched tightly in front of him. "I am defending the honor of our daughter!"

The others came to stand just behind him, eyes wide as they glanced from Edward to Miss Coventry.

"This does not need to escalate further, sir," Edward said, raising an open hand toward Mr. Coventry as if to tame a wild animal. "If you will but listen to what your daughter has to say."

Moments ticked by, the tension as dense as the rain clouds above until Mr. Coventry's fists lowered. He glanced at Marianne, and Edward held his breath before the man spoke again.

"Get on with it then."

CHAPTER THIRTY-FOUR

Marianne's control of the situation had unraveled before her very eyes. How had things escalated so swiftly? How had everything fallen apart so tragically? Her stomach contorted alongside her heart.

Mother watched her with confusion, Beatrice's eyes rounded with concern, and Father looked at her with such disgust, she feared she'd never earn his favor again.

"I'm so sorry." She brushed the rain from her cheeks with the back of her gloved hand. "I'm sorry for all of this. I never intended..." She shook her head. The time for regret had ended. She needed to be open and honest for the first time in her life.

Slowly, she moved to Mr. Steele's side, taking his hand once more in hers. "I love him."

Mr. Morley turned away with wide eyes, no doubt wondering if he ought to be there for such a conversation. Beatrice's mouth gaped open, her eyes flying to Mr. Steele as Mother let out a gasp. Father merely blinked mutely in a clear attempt to hide his own shock.

"But-but how?" Mother stammered. She blinked away the moisture in her eyes. "Marianne, I do not understand."

Marianne paused with a glance at Mr. Morley. Clearly, the servants had been speaking with Jane and Jane's sister. She did not blame the girls for sharing what had occurred, but she did not wish to give them more to gossip over.

Mr. Morley seemed to catch on to her concern, and he turned to Father. "Are you well, sir?"

Father nodded and waved him away. "Yes, please ensure Mr. Steele has left nothing behind in the library. He will no longer be employed here."

Mr. Morley hesitated a moment longer, a wary eye on Mr. Steele, then he returned indoors.

"Father, you cannot expel Mr. Steele," Marianne said at once. Her explanation could wait, Mr. Steele's future could not.

"I can, and I will."

"But he has done nothing wrong—"

"He has broken my trust in you, Marianne!" The pain cracked his voice and cut through her core.

She drew in a steadying breath. "No, he did not, Father. I did that on my own. *I* sought his friendship first. *I* asked him to accompany me to Wells for the assembly. *I* fell in love with him."

"Wells?" Mother's eyes widened. "You traveled to Wells?"

Mr. Steele tightened his hold around her fingers, infusing courage within her when she needed it most. "I did. I would do so again, if I knew I was not risking Mr. Steele's livelihood."

"Whyever would you do such a thing?" Mother asked, coming to stand beside Father. Beatrice remained silent, her mouth clamped shut as she wrapped her shawl tighter around her shoulders. Her blonde hair stuck to her temples from the rain.

"I know my behavior was reckless," Marianne responded truthfully. "But you must understand, I was under the assumption that I would never be allowed into Society. I was desperate."

Disappointment filled Mother's eyes but also the purest

form of understanding. Marianne knew she would receive such empathy from her. Would that all her family could react the very same.

Beatrice remained silent, her eyes red with tears. Was she more disappointed that Marianne had not spoken with her earlier—or that Marianne had fallen in love with a woodcarver?

Father spoke first, anger returning to his tone. "How you could have risked our family's standing with Society, your very future, is beyond me."

"My future is standing beside me, Father."

He scoffed. "You believe that I will allow a marriage to occur between you and Mr. Steele? I have told you before, you will marry a gentleman, Marianne, or no one at all."

"Father, that is not—"

"Mr. Steele," Father interrupted, looking him up and down. "I've heard your piece and Marianne's, too. Now you will leave Daffley Park immediately, as you are no longer welcome here."

"Father, you cannot—"

He turned on Marianne with sharp eyes. "No. I will hear no more of this nonsense."

Marianne looked up at Mr. Steele, but he stared at her father.

"Are you so focused on what Society thinks of you that you are willing to set aside the desires of your daughters?" Mr. Steele asked.

Marianne held her breath. Father's nostrils flared, his eyes narrowing as Mr. Steele continued. "You ought to be proud of being a working-class man raised up to be a gentleman, not ashamed of where you began. Now you turn your back on others in the same position as you once were—the very way many gentlemen treat you simply because of where you started."

Father's eyes flicked away, his feet shifting as his frown deepened. "You do not know of what you speak."

Mr. Steele nodded. "Perhaps I do not. And yet, I know that

you had the great opportunity to choose the direction your life would take. So why do you not allow your daughter the same liberty?"

Father blew out a disbelieving breath. "I did not sacrifice everything to have both of my daughters revert back to their lives in a lower class."

"But, Father, surely..." Marianne paused. *Both* his daughters? What did he mean?

She glanced at Beatrice. Surely it was a slip of the tongue. Surely Beatrice did not...

Their eyes met, and the pain in Beatrice's eyes reflected Marianne's so clearly, the breath rushed from her lungs.

"You?" Marianne breathed.

Mother and Father exchanged glances. "Perhaps we ought to continue this indoors," Mother suggested.

"I'll not have that man step foot once more in my house," Father said.

Beatrice's gaze did not waver from Marianne's.

"I don't understand." Marianne said. Had Beatrice fallen in love with Mr. Steele? Or was she referring to someone else?

Silence continued, and her frustration mounted. How could they survive as a family with such secrecy? Without communication and sharing the truth?

"Please," she said, looking at each of them, her voice breaking, "please, someone tell me what is going on."

CHAPTER THIRTY-FIVE

Marianne's family remained silent.

"She has a right to know," Mother said.

Father shook his head. "No, she does not."

Beatrice's gaze did not falter from Marianne's. Rain filtered down from the ends of her blonde locks. "I am in love."

Marianne's breathing stopped. "With whom?"

Beatrice winced.

"Charlie Macrae," Father responded with disgust.

Marianne searched her mind for the name but could not place it.

"The Clark's stable hand," Mother said softly.

Heavens. Marianne could hardly believe her ears, darting her eyes toward Beatrice. Her sister looked away in shame. She'd always been as adamant as Father about marrying a gentleman. Surely she was in jest.

But as her red eyes met Marianne's once more, the truth was confirmed. "I met him months before we left for Bath," Beatrice explained. "I told him we could never marry, but he pursued me anyway."

Thoughts streamed forth as Marianne attempted to make sense of the revelation. This was why Beatrice had not wished to participate in Marianne's game to find eligible gentlemen at the cricket match. This was why she'd spent so long at the Clarks' without anyone's knowledge. This was why she'd cried before dinner that one evening in the drawing room—no doubt from heartbreak. Had Marianne truly been so blind, so preoccupied with her own life that she'd missed Beatrice's grief altogether?

She grimaced, turning to Father. "How can you do this to us —to both of us? Can you not see we wish to be with the men we love?"

Father raised his chin. "Beatrice has chosen for herself not to marry Charlie Macrae."

Marianne looked to Beatrice. "Surely that cannot be true."

Beatrice sniffed away the moisture trailing down her nose. "I do not wish to be the wife of a stable hand." She shivered, hugging herself closer. "And you would not wish to be the wife of a woodcarver."

Marianne pulled back. How could Beatrice claim such a thing if she did not know how deeply Marianne's love for Mr. Steele ran through her very soul?

Before she could protest, Beatrice turned on her heel and made for the house in silence.

"I think we had better follow her and return indoors," Mother said softly, compassion filling her eyes. "Come, Marianne."

Marianne frowned. This was not how it was supposed to end. Her parents were supposed to have listened to her, to understand her love for Mr. Steele was true. They were supposed to accept him and their future together, not ignore the very desires of her heart.

She looked to Mr. Steele in a panic. His jaw was set, though his eyes reflected the dismay they both shared.

"Marianne," Father prompted next in a firm but softened tone.

How could she have allowed this to occur? Mr. Steele would lose his property, his only way to work. How would he and his mother survive? With fleeting hope, she turned toward Father. "Please. Do not punish Mr. Steele for my own actions. He is not at fault."

Father looked away, his jaw twitching. "That may be so. But I will not allow that man to work under my roof any longer." With his gaze still averted, he spoke to Mr. Steele. "I will pay you for the work you've completed. Not a penny more. Now leave, and do not return."

Marianne's relief was short-lived as she faced Mr. Steele again. How could this be happening? Surely he wouldn't leave. Surely they would work this out.

The sorrow in his eyes spoke measures. Nothing could be done. Marianne could not leave her family with nowhere to go, burdening Mr. Steele and his mother with another mouth to feed, and Mr. Steele could not stay in Ashwick without work.

"Mr. Steele," she whispered, unable to finish another word.

"Marianne," Father pressed again.

Mr. Steele stared down at her, taking a step away so her hand around his arm dropped to her side. The cold air swirling around her paled in comparison to the ice forming at the center of her heart.

Was this truly goodbye? Would she never see him again?

"I love you," he whispered for only her ears to hear, then with a reassuring nod, he retrieved the tools from Mr. Morley and walked away from Daffley Park.

Marianne watched him depart, his head hanging as low as her heart.

"Marianne…" Father began.

She whirled around to him, frustration encompassing her.

"How could you?" she cried out, then she fled past his flinching eyes and made for the house.

She would never be whole again.

CHAPTER THIRTY-SIX

Edward returned to Bath late that night, soaked and weary to the bone. Mother was, of course, stunned as he entered through the door of their small home.

"Edward?" she exclaimed, rushing to his side at once, her tattered dressing robe wrapped securely around her shoulders. "What on earth are you doing back?" She kissed his cheek, taking his portmanteau and satchel at once. "Heavens, you are sopping wet, son."

Edward had hoped to arrive after she'd fallen asleep, if only to avoid the rush of questions awaiting him, but of course that would not be in his fortune.

He allowed her to usher him straight to the fire, pulling forward the chair he and Father had first made together, oak with rigid angles showcasing Edward's young, unskilled carvings. How he wished Father was there now.

"Remove your boots and stockings," Mother instructed. "I will heat up the broth I made earlier."

"Thank you, but there is no need, Mother." He had no appetite, which was just as well. Before long, they would have no money for food. Once word got out about what had happened between him and Miss Coventry, no one would ever hire him again.

Mother paused, returning to his side at once. She did not speak for a moment, her eyes searching his, but he averted his gaze. Mother had always excelled at reading his mood, even sometimes his thoughts.

But his thoughts needed to be his own tonight. If they escaped, he did not know how he would ever get them under control again.

"What happened, son? You were not to arrive for another two months."

He drew a deep breath but said nothing. She watched him then moved to place two small logs onto the fire in the hearth.

"Did you return to ensure Mr. Chapple did not evict us?" she guessed. "I told you I could manage the man. He has not contacted me in weeks."

"That is because I wrote him a letter, promising to pay our rent in full by the end of next week."

Mother stared. "And…and can you make good on that promise?"

He stuck his tongue in his cheek, feeling the bite marks he'd created on the stagecoach, attempting to prevent his mind from dwelling on the woman he'd left behind—the woman who had pushed for his and Mother's livelihood.

"I will be able to satisfy the rent for the last few months. But if I do so, nothing will remain of what Mr. Coventry paid me." He would now spend the rest of his days searching for one commission after another.

Mother hesitated, stoking the fire as Edward stared into the growing flames. "Did you finish your work at the Coventrys' early?"

There would be no end to the questions that evening. In truth, Mother deserved to know what he'd done, how he'd destroyed their lives and their future.

"No, Mother. I was asked to leave."

She was not surprised, the fire lighting the weary lines in her brow and beneath her tired eyes. "They heard word of the rumors then?"

Edward laughed mirthlessly. "That was only part of the reason." His stomach churned, the emptiness inside as barren as his heart. How could he admit to Mother that he had irreversibly damaged their one chance to rise above their struggles? There was no possible way Mr. Coventry would keep silent on the entire matter. Once word spread, Edward would surely never receive a commission again.

"Edward, tell me," she urged softly.

He leaned forward, scrubbing his hands up and down his face. "They asked me to leave because...because I fell in love with Mr. Coventry's daughter."

Mother didn't respond, sitting back against her chair in shock, no doubt wondering what she'd done to have ever been cursed with such a selfish son.

For he *was* selfish. What other man would risk his mother's livelihood in such a way?

He hung his head in shame as her silence continued. "Forgive me, Mother. I did everything within my power to stop my feelings from growing. I knew the costs and the risks. But Miss Coventry..." His mind flooded with memories of her—her striking green eyes, her ability to find joy in the mundane, her selflessness and goodness. "She is everything to me."

The fire snapped, embers shooting into the air as Mother sniffed.

He glanced up with a wince. Sure enough, tears filled her eyes. "I'm sorry to have caused you such grief," he said, knowing her tears were born from their lost future. "I only pray you may one day forgive me."

"Oh, Ed..." Mother leaned forward in her chair, close enough to place her hands over his. "That is not what upsets me." She sniffed again. "We will get by, as we always have. What upsets me is the lack of hope I see within your eyes."

He stared, his brow pursed as she continued.

"I can hardly comprehend everything you've shared," she said with a small laugh. "So many things to understand. But none so shocking as the fact that my son has finally fallen in love." She smiled, a tear trailing from her squinted eyes. "She must be quite a woman to have earned your admiration."

His heart pinched. "She is the best of women," he whispered. "She has conquered much hardship in her life, and still her smile remains. She is enthusiastic about everything. She believed me without hesitation when I told her about Father."

Mother shook her head in awe. "No wonder you love her."

Edward looked down at her aged hands still resting atop his. "Yes, but to no avail. Her father will not allow it, and I cannot afford it."

"Would she be happy marrying into this life, do you think?"

"If we were not absolutely destitute, yes, I believe she would. She is not materialistic, nor is she frivolous in her behavior. But I could not bring her down so low."

Mother winced, sorrow tugging her lips into a frown. "I'm sorry this burden has been placed upon you, to run *Steele and Son*. To care for me. A man your age ought not be worrying about such matters. You ought to be free to fall in love, to live carefree and happily. To marry the woman you want. Not weighed down by false rumors and a widowed mother."

Edward took her hand at once. "You mustn't ever think that I resent you, Mother, or that I have ever resented the opportunity I have to care for you. You are not to be blamed for any of this, so do not take it to heart."

She nodded, though her weary brow remained. "So what is to be done of the matter?"

Edward sighed. "I will pay Mr. Chapple the rent in full

tomorrow. Then I will begin work on the commissions you've made in my behalf and pray the money will last. Then I—"

"No, Ed," Mother interrupted with a smile. "What is to be done about Miss Coventry?"

He stared. "Nothing is to be done."

"I cannot believe such a thing."

"It is true. I've been through every possible situation. Even if my workload increases and our situation improves, Miss Coventry will no doubt be coerced into marrying a gentleman —one of whom her father would approve."

He wanted Miss Coventry's happiness more than anything, but the thought of her marrying another made his chest shrivel like a dying flower. Still, what could be done if all he had to offer her was a penniless marriage?

"There is no chance Mr. Coventry will see to your plight?" Mother asked next.

He laughed mirthlessly. "No. No, he is adamant his daughters will marry gentlemen."

Mother grimaced, then after a moment, she planted her hands on her knees and straightened her back. "Well, I am going to warm up that broth for myself. You may as well enjoy a bowl, too."

His stomach rumbled as if on cue.

She stood, speaking as she moved to the adjoining kitchen. "While I do so, perhaps you may take my mind off my work by telling me more about this Miss Coventry."

Edward hesitated. Speaking of the woman would surely do him more harm than good. But then...didn't a mother have the right to know more about the woman her son had fallen for, even if there was no chance of marriage?

With a heavy heart, he joined her in the kitchen before his depressed thoughts could swallow him whole.

CHAPTER THIRTY-SEVEN

M arianne had refused to join her family in the dining room for days. Father had requested her presence especially, but she'd sent a message straight back that she would not join them. She could not face them after all that had occurred.

She still had not received any word from Mr. Steele, and though three days was not an eternity, it felt like one without him at Daffley Park.

She needed to take care, to resign herself that this was her future now. That Mr. Steele was not to be a part of it because he had other responsibilities.

But had he given up on her?

As another day passed by with her lodged securely in her room, she stared at the dark clouds preventing any sight of the sun. In one hand, she held the comb Mr. Steele had carved for her, her free fingers tracing the small flowers across the top of it.

She needed to look for the sunsets in her life, but what if the clouds were simply too thick to penetrate? What if there was no hope to be found?

A knock sounded at her door. That would be Jane with her food.

Marianne slipped down from her seat by the window and opened the door, frowning as Beatrice stood before her instead of Jane, a tray of food in her hands.

"What are you doing up here?" Marianne asked.

They had not spoken since that rainy day outside of Daffley.

"Mother sent me with the tray to see if you would speak to me, as you won't speak to anyone else."

Marianne hesitated. She was not in the mood to speak, especially with Beatrice, who apparently seemed to think she knew Marianne's mind better than Marianne herself.

Still, she could not shut her out forever. With a sigh, she opened her door farther and allowed her in.

Beatrice entered, closing the door behind her with a soft tap of her heel. Silently, she set the tray on the table near Marianne's bed.

"How have you been?" she asked softly.

Marianne shrugged. Surely Beatrice should know. Had she not just experienced a heartbreak of her own?

Beatrice sighed. "I know the pain you must be feeling now is rather poignant, but trust me when I say that it eases with time."

Marianne turned away, sitting down on the window ledge. "Or you simply learn to live with the grief Father has caused."

Beatrice hesitated, then she came to sit beside Marianne. "He only wants what is best for us, Marianne."

"I know. But he does not always know what *is* best for us."

"You truly believe marrying the woodcarver would benefit you?"

Her question was unassuming, but it nibbled at Marianne's patience. "How can you think it would not?"

"Marianne, listen to yourself. He is poor. He will no doubt struggle with money for the rest of his life. And..." Her brow furrowed. "Father told us about the rumors surrounding his name."

Marianne stood from the ledge at once, walking away with a growl of frustration. "The rumors were false! Why is that so difficult for this family to understand?"

Beatrice continued in a soft voice. "It matters not if they were false. His reputation—"

Marianne raised a hand, refusing to listen any longer. "Mr. Steele's character speaks far more than what the world views as his reputation. I know my name would be brought lower by association. I know I would be poor. I know we would no doubt struggle. But..." She broke off with a sigh, her shoulders falling forward as a feeling of hopelessness overcame her. Why could her family not understand? "But what marriage comes without a struggle? And what love is not worth the fight?"

A small, faint line formed in Beatrice's brow as she frowned. "I don't understand. You would not mind, then, returning to the life we lived before Father made his fortune?"

Marianne knew her answer at once. "No. Not if that meant I could be with the man I love."

Beatrice stared out of the window, her lips pulled down.

"Would you not do the same to be with Charlie Macrae?" Marianne asked.

She still had yet to process the fact that Beatrice had fallen in love with a stable hand. But surely that ought to connect the sisters more than anything.

"In truth?" Beatrice asked. "I don't believe I would."

Marianne pulled back, the answer foreign to her own desires. "Do you not love him?"

Beatrice raised her lips into half a smile. "I believe I do. Or rather, I did. At least to a degree. I found freedom with him. Something I had never experienced before. But that faded as I realized that I could not give my heart fully to a man with whom I could not truly be happy."

Marianne's heart reached out to her. Beatrice had been looking for freedom, just as Marianne had. They'd suffered such a similar grief, yet they'd each had to mourn alone. How could they have both been struggling without the other knowing?

Beatrice's eyes took on a distant look. "But even though I prevented myself from fully falling, that does not mean it did not hurt to say goodbye. That night we spoke in the drawing room?" Marianne nodded before Beatrice continued. "Charlie had proposed. I declined, telling him what I had told him from the beginning—that we could not marry."

Marianne's heart bowed at the pain still reflecting in Beatrice's eyes. No wonder their argument had been so bitter, so raw. "Is that why you told Father you would never marry?"

"Yes." Beatrice winced. "I am not proud of this, but I was saying so to injure Father. When he discovered that I'd fallen for a stable hand, he'd reacted the very same as he had with you, shouting and threatening. He did not give me the opportunity to tell him that I had already decided against marrying Charlie. In impulsive retaliation, I proclaimed that I would never marry. In truth, I still have hope to do so one day."

Marianne thought for a moment, an errant smile spreading across her lips. "That must have been satisfying to let Father stew in such a way."

Beatrice gave a half-smile. "As I said, I am not proud of my behavior...but it was rather satisfying to have his face turn so unflattering a shade of red."

She shared a small laugh before Beatrice sobered. "I truly am sorry for your loss, sister. If I had known you were falling for Mr. Steele, I could have warned you to prevent any injury."

Marianne hesitated, her defenses falling in time with her shoulders as she sat beside Beatrice at the window seat. "Your warning would not have helped. You may have prevented yourself from fully falling for Charlie. But I gave my whole heart to Mr. Steele, and I will never get it back." Tears filled her eyes as the pain returned. "I love him. I will hold out hope and pray harder than I ever have for matters to be resolved so we can have the life we wish to share together."

Saying the words aloud infused her with renewed hope. But was what she wanted even possible with the world against them both?

"You really love him."

Marianne nodded. "I will always love him."

Beatrice studied her for a few moments in silence, as if to determine the truth, then her brow softened. "I'm sorry I did not know your true feelings before all of this. But now that I do, well, I did not marry my stable hand, but we can certainly get you your woodcarver."

CHAPTER THIRTY-EIGHT

Edward never thought he'd be back. It was a strange sensation, walking through Daffley Park again after being expelled from its premises only a week before.

Mr. Morley allowed him inside when he returned, no one else from the family or household in sight, though Edward kept his eyes peeled for any glimpse of Miss Coventry.

Of course, she was nowhere to be found. Mr. Coventry would have made sure of that.

Edward still couldn't comprehend why he'd been brought back. Mr. Coventry's correspondence had not explained much at all.

Mr. Steele,

I am certain this letter will come as a surprise to you. After all, I had determined to never make contact with you again. But as matters have slowly been brought to my attention, I have need to speak with you, one man to another. Therefore, I request your presence at Daffley Park at your earliest convenience.

There is no need to send your agreement via correspondence, as I am certain you will readily concur with meeting me.

Lastly, I ask that you do not misconstrue this invitation to return to Daffley as forgiveness for your treatment of my family. I assure you, that matter has not been laid to rest in the slightest.

Signed,
Mr. Jacob Coventry

Edward's head had spun faster than the ratchet wheel of a sawmill when he'd first read the man's words. Obviously, Mr. Coventry hadn't changed his mind in regard to Edward being worthy enough to wed Miss Coventry. But then, to what end had he requested his presence?

He'd expressed his worries to Mother, for he did not wish to see Miss Coventry if he could not *be* with Miss Coventry. But Mother, of course, had encouraged him to drop everything and leave the moment he'd received word. "The commissions will wait, son," she'd said. "Love will not."

Edward had boarded the coach the very next day, unwilling to lose his chance at possibly fighting for the love of his life.

Still, as he followed Mr. Morley through the corridors, Edward's stomach roiled left to right. What could Mr. Coventry want of him? And why was Mr. Morley leading him to the library?

The butler motioned for him to enter, and Edward did so cautiously, though his feet froze a few steps into the room. Mr. Coventry stood directly before him, his hands clasped behind his back, a steady expression on his face.

Memories of their last conversation floated before Edward, and heat slipped up his neck. "Sir," he greeted with a stilted bow.

Mr. Coventry barely gave the slightest of nods in response.

The door clicked behind him, and Edward glanced back to find that Mr. Morley had left. Unease crept upon Edward like a silent shadow. Did anyone else know he was in the room with Mr. Coventry?

"I will bring him back if you prefer," Mr. Coventry said. "Though I will treat you with civility if you pledge to do the same."

Edward hardly believed the man. After all, how could he? "I can promise that, Mr. Coventry."

The man drew a deep breath, looking none too pleased. "Much has happened between us, Mr. Steele. I would like to say that I have overcome the mistrust you've caused between me and my family, but as you know, that is not the case."

So Edward had been brought here to simply be berated further? His heart deflated, what little hope he'd allowed himself slipping from his grasp. Why had he even bothered to come? The man would not yield. Edward would never be with Miss Coventry.

He glanced to the bookshelf, his fingers twitching as he took in the sight of the unfinished carving. He did not enjoy leaving things incomplete, and yet, Mr. Coventry had spoken.

"Is that all you wish to say to me, sir?" he asked, his tone clipped. "If so, I will be on my way, as I've a stagecoach to catch."

He'd come so far, was so close to Miss Coventry. He could almost smell the cherries on her breath, see the joy in her smile, feel the warmth of her love.

"If only I *could* allow you to depart," Mr. Coventry murmured with a look of regret. "As it is, I have brought you here for another reason."

Edward's jaw tightened as he waited impatiently for the man to continue. Would Mr. Coventry ask him to finish the carving without pay? To return the money he'd given him? To swear on his life to never see Miss Coventry again?

"What reason is that, sir?"

"To answer two very pressing questions."

Edward's brow drew low. Questions? He'd traveled twenty miles, hadn't slept a wink, and abandoned Mother again for two questions? Could this man be any more inconsiderate? "Very well. I will do my best to answer them."

Mr. Coventry's stare intensified. "Has anything improper occurred between you and my daughter?"

Edward drew in a steady breath, his whole face aflame in seconds. What a thing to be asked by the man whose daughter he longed to marry. "Apart from speaking alone and"—he cleared his throat—"the kiss we shared last week, nothing else happened between us, sir."

Mr. Coventry seemed to contemplate the answer. "That is just what Marianne has told me."

How Edward yearned to see the woman. "It is the truth, sir."

"Hm." Mr. Coventry's gaze did not falter. "You are fortunate I believe her. For if I did not, you would not be standing alive before me today, I assure you."

Edward's cravat seemed to tighten on its own at Mr. Coventry's mirthless smile. "I am well aware of that fact, sir."

The man remained silent.

"Have you another question for me, sir?"

"I do. I must know if your feelings for my daughter are true. Do you love Marianne?"

Edward had never been asked a more important question in his life—nor had he been asked an easier one. With all the love in his heart, he replied. "Yes. Yes, I do."

Mr. Coventry was silent for what seemed an eternity, his eyes—green, like Miss Coventry's—delving into Edward's before he finally nodded. "I believe you." A beat passed. "But that does not mean you are right for my daughter."

The words did not come as a surprise—indeed, Edward had expected them. And yet, the wind had been sapped from his sails once again. How much more torture would this man put him through?

"Fortunately, for your sake," Mr. Coventry continued, "my opinion holds very little weight, as Marianne is adamant in her love for you, as well. She believes that she will be far happier *with* you than without."

Edward refused to make room for hope in his heart. He could not believe the man had changed so drastically, so swiftly, to allow Edward any chance at being with Miss Coventry.

Mr. Coventry stepped across the room toward the bookshelf, running his fingers along the smooth section Edward had not yet carved. "When you left Daffley Park, I was determined to announce your despicable behavior to all of Somerset. I did not believe you deserved the chance to work again, given your actions. Fortunately, for your sake, my daughters spoke to my conscience." He glanced at Edward sidelong. "It would seem that you have finally found advocates in this world."

Edward blinked in silence. *Both* daughters had spoken in his defense? What he would not give to know what had been said.

Mr. Coventry continued. "I was made aware of the fact that if I brought your name down further than it already is, the Coventry name would follow suit. As it is, I would prefer not to add more rumors about my family, as my eldest has given me more than enough to deal with." He grimaced. "At any rate, for those reasons and others, I will keep silent about your behavior —so long as I have your word that you will behave in a manner more akin to a gentleman than a cad."

Edward swallowed his pride as best he could. Speaking with this man was like speaking with Lord Ryecombe. How they managed such a level of condescension was beyond him.

Still, he could not provoke him further by denying his offer. Mr. Coventry would keep quiet about the rumors. That meant Edward might have some chance at keeping *Steele and Son* afloat.

And Edward *had* behaved like a cad.

"You have my word, sir. And thank you. I am indebted to you."

Mr. Coventry studied him for a moment. "Contrary to your belief, I do not wish to bring others down. And as you have also accused me of being ashamed of my past, I will readily deny that as well. My actions, like yours, are dictated by Society's standards. And I must rise to meet them—or fall." He focused his gaze. "I would advise you to do the same, Mr. Steele."

Edward's chest emptied of all anger, humility rushing to fill the void left behind. He could not agree with the way the man controlled his daughters, but Mr. Coventry—like Edward—was doing the best he could with what life had dealt him. Though, their struggles were miles apart.

"I admire your ability to rise above your circumstances, sir," he spoke gingerly. "But striving to overcome the whispers of unworthiness is different than rising above false, damning rumors."

Mr. Coventry watched him, and Edward could have sworn a flicker of compassion flashed through his eyes. "I am inclined to agree with you, Mr. Steele. Which is why I am willing to help you."

Help him? The man was offering to help him?

Mr. Coventry eyed the ceiling and shelves. "I will hire you back to finish the carving here—under strict supervision by a member of my household, of course—and if you perform your work admirably, I will offer you my insight and advice on how to raise *Steele and Son* from the ashes you are working with now."

Edward stared, dumbfounded. He could not deny the appeal of having the clearly business-minded Mr. Coventry help him rise above his destitution. But had the man not just criticized him and demeaned his worth, said he was unworthy of marrying his daughter? No father would bring an offending man back into his home, and there was no possible way Edward *wouldn't* see Miss Coventry at one point or another.

His hands fisted together at the thought of her. He wished to see her so badly his heart ached. But he would not allow himself to believe the man was in earnest. Mr. Coventry must have some ulterior motive. The only problem was, Edward could think of nothing that made sense. Was he simply playing a trick on Edward? Or was this an act of pity?

"I appreciate the gesture, sir, but I cannot accept charity."

Mr. Coventry scoffed, dropping his hand from the mahogany. "Charity? That is the last thing I would offer you, Mr. Steele. You will work to earn my help."

That was fair enough, he supposed. Still, something niggled at his conscience. "If it is not charity, then what other reason have you for offering your help?"

With a pointed look, Mr. Coventry responded. "I will not have my name associated with a failing woodworker. Just because my daughter made a poor choice in deciding to marry you, that does not mean I wish her to suffer for it."

The words struck Edward dumb. Had Mr. Coventry just said...? No, surely, he could not have. "Sir?"

Mr. Coventry continued with an annoyed expression. "Against my better judgment, I will agree to your union with my daughter."

Edward's mouth dropped open. This could not be true. It was too wonderful to be true, too perfect. Too...unbelievable.

"I-I do not understand, Mr. Coventry," he stammered.

"What is there to not understand? You wish for my daughter's hand in marriage, do you not?"

"More than anything."

"Then you may have it."

Edward stared, still reeling. Before he could stop it, light poured into the darkness that had encompassed Edward's heart for days, filling his soul with an airiness he had not known possible. "But…why?"

"Are you questioning your own worth, Mr. Steele?"

"No, of course not. I will treat your daughter better than anyone on this earth. But I do not understand what has occurred to make you change your mind. I know you cannot approve of the union."

"No, indeed I do not. But I wish for my daughter's happiness. And she believes you can give that to her."

Something about the way he spoke made Edward hesitate—his shifting gaze, how anxious he was to move past the conversation. Had his daughters truly just appealed to their father's conscience—or had something more been offered? Edward was sure there was more to it than Mr. Coventry let on, but then, what did it matter if he could be with Miss Coventry?

"So what say you, Mr. Steele? Will you accept these terms to obtain my daughter's hand?"

Edward could have laughed. What an arrangement he was agreeing to—marrying the woman he loved and receiving help from her business-minded father. "Yes, sir. I will absolutely accept the terms you've set."

Mr. Coventry's lips thinned with clear displeasure. "Then might I suggest you remain here for a moment? I will return shortly."

Edward watched him walk from the room, staring at the open doorway in utter shock. What on earth had just happened? And how?

He chuckled, rubbing the back of his neck. That was certainly a turn of events he had *not* been expecting.

Now the question burgeoned in his mind—when would he get to speak with Miss Coventry?

He glanced at the oversized chair in the corner of the room, no books nor crumbs in sight. She hadn't returned when he'd left?

"I read in the library at nine o'clock."

Edward swung around at the sound of her voice. His breath caught in his throat. He'd thought of her every day, every moment, since they'd parted. Yet, somehow, he was overcome with even more love by the mere sight of her.

She smiled, her hands clasped together, dimples deepening at the edges of her mouth. Her father stood behind her with eyes narrowed at Edward.

"You have less than a quarter of an hour," he said with a stern brow, then he gave a brief nod, and his footsteps retreated down the corridor.

Finally, Edward was left alone with Miss Coventry.

CHAPTER THIRTY-NINE

Edward had longed for this moment, to see Miss Coventry again, to be graced by her presence. But now that it was here, he hesitated. Would moving toward her break the spell between them? Scare her away as it once had when he'd imagined her to be the ghost of Daffley Park?

As she stood before him with an unwavering smile, tears glistening in her green eyes, he knew at once she would not leave—just as he would never leave *her* again.

He bowed in greeting. "Miss Coventry."

She did not return with a curtsy. Instead, she rushed toward him without hesitation, her grin matching his own. He met her with open arms, encircling them round her to welcome her back where she belonged.

"Oh, how I have missed you!" she breathed against his ear, her fingers sliding through his hair at the nape of his neck, her soft cheek against his.

He closed his eyes, pressing his nose into her neck and breathing in the scent of her. "And I, you," he murmured against her skin.

He could never have imagined loving this woman more than

he had when he left Daffley, but now as he held her in his arms, his love delved deeper into his heart, never to be removed, never to be forgotten.

A moment passed, neither of them speaking as they drew in each other's presence. How he longed for this to last, to never release her from his arms again.

But Mr. Coventry had been firm. They did not have long—and Edward had one very important matter to accomplish.

Slowly, he straightened, leaning back to take in the sight of her. "I never thought I would see you again," he said, brushing back a stray curl from her brow. "But however did you make this come about? I assume your father did not change his mind of his own accord."

Slowly, her smile faded away, her arms sliding down to rest on his. Edward's stomach churned. "What has happened?"

She shook her head. "It was not I who changed Father's mind but Beatrice."

Edward narrowed his eyes. Had the elder Miss Coventry some great influence over her father? "I do not understand. Your father was adamant. As set as any man I had ever seen. He wanted you to marry a gentleman."

"He did. But Beatrice offered him something he wanted even more—a connection to an earl."

"But how could he obtain such a thing? Your sister is in love with the stable hand, is she not?" he asked, recalling the shock he'd experienced when she'd admitted such a thing to Marianne.

"She is. Or at least, she was. But that marriage will not occur. You see, she has agreed to marry Mr. Wakefield, who is a cousin of Lord Ryecombe's."

Edward cringed. He would never escape that man. "Why would she promise such a thing if she does not love Mr. Wakefield?"

Miss Coventry drew a saddened smile on her lips. "She made

an arrangement with Father. If she marries Mr. Wakefield, Father will allow our own marriage to occur."

Heavens. Edward's jaw went slack. Slowly, the pieces fell into place before his eyes. That was why Mr. Coventry had allowed him to return and for their marriage to happen, because he was getting something far greater in return—proof that he belonged in the upper class by obtaining a relation to an earl.

"Did the arrangement also include bringing me back to work on the library?" he asked, already knowing the answer.

"It had taken a great deal of coercion to convince Father to allow our marriage, but he was resolute in not hiring you on again. That is, until Beatrice told him that he could control the narrative of his family at a greater level if he raised you up in Society's eyes, as he did for himself."

Edward should have known. Mr. Coventry had said as much, but knowing he'd sacrificed the happiness of his eldest daughter to get what he wanted…Edward shook his head. Should he be blessed to have any daughters, he would never put them in such a position as to bargain their future to make himself appear better than he was.

"I am sorry," Miss Coventry said hesitantly, eying Edward's scowl. "As you know, I do not care about your status, but Beatrice knew that logic would speak to Father more than anything." She winced. "Are you angry?"

Edward shook his head, softening his frown. "No. I know your intent was pure, as well as your sister's." He paused. "I will admit, though, that I have a mind to run *Steele and Son* into the ground on purpose, if only to teach your father that class means nothing to me…" Thankfully, Miss Coventry caught his teasing eye and smiled.

He blew out a breath, running his fingers through his hair. What a morning. What a drastic change to how he'd expected the day to turn out. Who would have thought they would owe everything to Miss Beatrice Coventry. A wave of gratitude rushed over him. "You are certain your sister is decided on the matter?" he asked. "She really does not wish to be with the stable hand?"

Miss Coventry shook her head, her eyes taking on a distant look. "No. Her desire to have ease of life was always stronger than her desire to be with him."

———⟨∽⟩———

Marianne thought back to her conversation with Beatrice, her heart still aching at the memory. She had tried so hard to convince her sister to not give up her future, but Beatrice had been adamant.

"I always had a mind to marry Mr. Wakefield anyway," she had said as the two had conversed days before. "I was simply denying the opportunity as a means of ruffling Father's feathers. Now that Charlie is no longer in my life, it will be easier to move on. And Mr. Wakefield is kind. He will treat me right."

Marianne had reluctantly agreed as the plan had progressed, though she had since prayed with all her might that Mr. Wakefield would make her sister happy.

After their strategy had been laid out, they'd taken the proposal to Mother, who had reluctantly agreed, for she knew, as well as Marianne, that Beatrice would move forward with or without her consent.

As a united front, the three Coventry women had set upon Father, invoking his compassion as well as his business-oriented mind. Marianne could not have been more grateful that everything had worked out for the best. She never could have agreed to marry Mr. Steele had she not done something to ease the financial burden she was sure to place upon him as his new wife.

Still, Beatrice's sacrifice could not be erased from Marianne's mind.

"You've given up your life for me," she'd said only the night before.

"And you gave up five years for *me*," Beatrice had returned.

"That hardly equates to the same. I will be indebted to you forever."

Beatrice had been silent for a moment, moisture brimming in her eyes. "Then do one thing for me, Marianne."

"Anything."

She reached out, holding Marianne's hands in her own. "Promise me to live. Be happy and *live*."

Thinking of the memory now still brought tears to Marianne's eyes, and as Mr. Steele reached up, brushing the moisture fallen to her cheeks, she was pulled back to the present—her glorious, blessed present.

"What is it?" he asked in a whisper, wiping away another of her tears.

She shook her head with a solemn smile. "I am merely thinking of our future together—and how happy I will be with you."

A wave of uncertainty flickered over his features. "*Will* you be happy?" She tipped her head in question, and he averted his gaze. "You said your sister wished for ease of life. I cannot help but fear that you will wish for the very same. I can promise you a life full of love and hard work, but even with your father's help, we may be destitute forever. And even if I had wealth, I would always be but a humble woodcarver."

How she longed to erase his vulnerability forever, to ensure he knew that her love was steadfast and true, no matter their wealth or lack thereof. She reached forward, lacing her fingers together at the back of his neck.

"I never did get to tell you about the dinner I attended, did I?"

He shook his head, resting his hands on her hips.

"I do not exaggerate when I say that it was utterly and absolutely miserable."

He sniffed out a laugh at her dramatic response. "And why was that?"

"Because every single moment I was there, every single person with whom I spoke, I compared to my time with you in Wells. Your company, your kindness, and your attentiveness are unmatched." She trailed her finger down the side of his jawline, and his eyes closed for a moment, as if to enjoy her touch more fully. "Over the last five years, I have painted, I have read books, and I have sketched and sewn and everything else on that blessed schedule. But do you know of what I was thinking during every moment of my daily routine before you came to Daffley?" He shook his head. "I was hoping—praying—that the time would come that I would finally be seen. *Truly* seen. Then one day at a cricket match, I was."

Tears pricked her eyes. Mr. Steele's expression softened to where she could truly see his love for her—for it matched her own for him. "You have continued to see me, Mr. Steele. The real Marianne Coventry. That is why you are worth more than a thousand gentlemen to me. That is why I wish for you to always be a humble woodcarver. *My* humble woodcarver."

As she finished, he pulled her closer, his hands at the small of her back. "If your sister's negotiation skills are anything like yours, Miss Coventry, I can see now why your father relented."

She laughed. "I am merely speaking the truth, sir."

He sobered, his brow raised. "Then I shall speak the truth to you next. I did not live—truly live—until I met you. You have made me happier than I have ever been before. So..." He paused, drawing in a deep breath, and with all the sincerity in the world, he asked, "Will you marry me, Mrs. Hickenbottom?"

Laughter erupted from her lips at his unexpected words. She stood on the tips of her toes and pressed her nose to his. "Of course, I will, Mr. *Higgenbottom*."

He pulled back. "You've forgotten my name already?"

They shared a smile, and Mr. Steele leaned toward her, pressing a sound kiss to her lips.

After a moment, he pulled away. "How I wish I could kiss you forever. But I would hate for your father to return, only to find us in each other's arms again."

Marianne smiled, stepping back, though it took everything within her to do so. "You're right," she said, pulling on a look of feigned austerity. "Now get to work on finishing this library, woodcarver."

He instantly straightened with a stiff nod. "Yes, ma'am." Then he sent her a wink. "Though, I must admit, I far prefer carving for Miss Coventry than for this stern, future Mrs. Steele." He glanced at her sidelong, and a smile inched across his lips.

Unable to help herself any longer, she reached forward, bringing his face down to hers to share in his affection again. It was worth the risk, for Mr. Steele kissed as well as he carved, and that was saying something, indeed.

EPILOGUE

Marianne tucked her arm through Edward's and followed him toward their awaiting carriage, their smiles unceasing.

The wedding that morning had been perfection, and the gathering afterward at Daffley Park had been even better. The guests—upper and working classes alike—had mingled as they'd sampled various pastries, a wedding cake, and, of course, cherry tarts.

"Why not have the typical breakfast affair?" Father had protested when plans were being made.

Beatrice had piped up in an instant. "Because Marianne and Mr. Steele love pastries, Father." She gave him a pointed look. "Worry not, when Mr. Wakefield and I wed, we shall have the dreary meal *you* prefer."

That had seemed enough to satisfy Father, and Marianne had sent her sister a grateful smile.

Over the last few weeks, Marianne's life had changed dramatically. Her relationship with Beatrice had returned to what it had been before, Mother was in her element planning *two* weddings, and Father, well, he was as happy as the circumstances allowed.

Their footsteps crunched against the gravel drive as she and Edward turned, facing their families who had trailed after them. Beatrice and Mr. Wakefield stepped forward first.

"I wish you both a very pleasant trip," Mr. Wakefield said with his usual kind smile, which Marianne had grown used to seeing. He'd proposed to Beatrice only a week after Edward and Marianne had become engaged. "Though do not delay your return. I'm certain your sister will be eager to see you again."

"Indeed, I will." Beatrice removed her arm from her betrothed's and reached to hold Marianne's hands in her own. "Enjoy the sea air for me, sister."

"I will."

Marianne and Edward would travel to Cornwall to spend a week there in just each other's company. She was more than looking forward to their time away—no carving, no responsibilities, no Father ensuring they'd never spend a second alone together.

Mr. Wakefield and Edward engaged in conversation about where their first stop in Cornwall would be—Tregalwen Beach, then off to St. Just. Beatrice's tightening fingers drew Marianne's attention toward her.

"You will be back for the wedding," Beatrice stated in a whisper, though uncertainty flickered in her light blue eyes.

"Of course," Marianne assured her. "You know we will return from Cornwall here, rather than Bath. I would not miss your wedding for anything."

Beatrice smiled, blowing out a soft sigh of relief. The Steeles would have made straight for Bath and Edward's wood shop, but Edward still had a month and a half of carving before he completed the library. Though looking forward to beginning their new life, Marianne was pleased she could remain at

Daffley Park a little while longer—if only to spend further time drawing closer to her family.

Chuckling from Edward and Mr. Wakefield drew their attention toward the men, then Beatrice and Marianne shared a smile.

"I hope you will be happy with him," Beatrice whispered, "even though he is a working man."

She winked, and Marianne shook her head in amusement. "I hope you will be happy with *him*," she returned in a low voice, tipping her head toward Mr. Wakefield, "even though he is the cousin of a lord."

They shared a smile, then Beatrice sobered. "Do not worry about me, Marianne. He is a good man. I will be happy with him. I'm certain of it."

Marianne could only pray that was true.

The sisters shared a departing embrace, then Beatrice moved toward Mr. Wakefield, bidding her farewell to Edward next.

Marianne made to stand beside her husband, the distance between them—merely a few feet—too far for her comfort, though they would be confined in their borrowed carriage from Father over the next few days. But when Edward's mother came up to speak with her next, she remained where she stood, her smile brightening.

"What a lovely day it has been," Mrs. Steele said, "and what a beautiful bride you make."

Mrs. Steele had only arrived in Ashwick a few days before the wedding, but in what little time Marianne had spent with her, she knew she was going to bond with the woman splendidly. Mrs. Steele's confidence, kindness, and strength exuded from her character like the sunshine had broken through the clouds that morning.

"Thank you, Mrs. Steele. I am so pleased you could come. I very much look forward to getting to know you better."

"After everything my son has shared with me about you, I

already know we shall be the best of friends." She leaned closer. "You see, I, too, have a penchant for pastries."

She winked, and Marianne's heart warmed. Yes, the two Steele women were going to get on splendidly.

Mrs. Steele moved away then, Mother and Father stepping up next. "Take care, Marianne," Father said with a rigid nod, his eyes moving about as if afraid to meet her gaze. "Of the carriage, the team, and yourself."

"I will, Father."

They stood in silence for a moment. Matters had been strained between them since before the proposal had taken place, but Marianne had expected as much. That was another reason she was grateful she and Edward would remain at Daffley for a while longer, if only to force Father to see that she was still his daughter, and that Edward was a respectable man.

"Mr. Steele will ensure everything is taken care of as well," she said, almost pointedly.

Father nodded, though he looked pained to agree with her on such a matter. Then he reached for her hand and placed a kiss to the back of it. "I…I love you, my dear. And I wish you every happiness."

He dropped her hand as if it was scalding, then he moved to address Edward.

She stared after him. Would he ever forgive her for betraying his trust? For marrying a woodcarver?

"His pride will be alleviated at some point," Mother said with a shake of her head, as if she heard Marianne's plight. "Until then, you and I shall veritably beat him over the head with your new husband's various accomplishments and good qualities."

"I do love that plan."

They shared a small laugh, and Mother embraced her. "I'm so pleased you will be with us when you return and that you shall not be living so very far away. I've already spoken with Father about spending a few months in Bath next year. Queen's

Square is not too far away from Mr. Steele's shop, I understand. We shall have a grand time exploring more of Bath together. Perhaps we may convince the Wakefields to join us, too."

The very notion sounded too good to be true. But then, her life seemed too good to be true. Thankfully, it was. "That would be delightful, Mother."

The rigid stances of Edward and Father caught her eyes again, the two men speaking with stinted words and impassive expressions—characteristic of each of their conversations over the last few weeks.

"Well," Mother whispered, "at least the two of them could rival one another's pride."

"Indeed, at least they are both on their best behavior, though."

"Mm." Mother shook her head. "They are ridiculous, are they not? And yet, are we not the more ridiculous ones to have fallen for them?" She glanced sidelong at Marianne, a twinkle in her eyes. "I suppose for the Coventry women, there is something irresistible about a working-class man, is there not?"

Marianne smiled. She could not have agreed more.

⁓

"I will ensure she returns in one piece, sir, yes."

Edward stood across from Mr. Coventry, each of them holding their hands behind their backs—no doubt each of them wishing for their painful conversation to finally come to a close.

And yet, they both knew they had to make some effort with one another—if only for Marianne's sake.

"Very good." Mr. Coventry took a step back. "Then I wish you a safe journey. Goodbye, Mr. Steele."

He walked away, and Edward blew out a silent breath. The two had managed to speak on a few business matters regarding the carving of the library and the future of *Steele and Son*, but that had been the extent of their conversations. They certainly would not be friends in the nearby future, but that was more than fine with Edward.

He was only grateful the man had finally allowed Edward to marry Marianne.

He glanced toward his new wife, Marianne laughing with her mother—about what, he could hardly even speculate. His heart was full, words unable to express the joy Marianne had brought into his life in so short a time. How he had ever lived without her was beyond him.

"You have married a remarkable woman, Ed," Mother said, coming up to stand beside him. "Your father would have loved her."

Edward nodded, swallowing the moisture rising in his throat. He'd thought the very same the past few weeks, but especially today.

"He always enjoyed a fine celebration," Edward said. "He would have had a marvelous time today, had he been here."

Mother squeezed Edward's hand in hers. "He was here, Ed. I have to believe that he was."

Their eyes met, tears brimming in her own. Edward reached down, embracing his mother with a quick kiss to her cheek.

"Now enough of that," she said, pulling away to fix his cravat. "Be sure to watch over yourselves while on your journey, son. And eat often to—"

"To maintain our high spirits?" he finished for her.

She smiled up at him. "Just so."

"We will, Mother. Worry not. You have taught me well."

As the last of the farewells were said, Marianne and Edward entered the carriage and gave one final departing wave through the glass before the horses pulled them away from Daffley and toward their future.

Marianne instantly shuffled closer to him, wrapping her arms around his.

"Are you looking forward to the journey, my dear?" he asked, resting a hand on her knee.

"Mm. Very much so. If only to escape Father for a moment." She ended in a small laugh. He couldn't have agreed with her more. "I saw you speaking to him. I trust he was able to keep the conversation amiable."

"He did. He assured me that we would discuss business matters upon our return."

"Oh, wonderful."

Edward nodded, peering out of the window at the green countryside passing them by. He did not relish the prospect of Mr. Coventry helping him with his woodworking, if only because he expected condescension at every turn.

But Edward would be daft, indeed, if he refused his help. He had Mother *and* Marianne to think of now, not just himself.

"I hope he will have a few ideas on how to improve matters," he said.

"I'm certain he will. At any rate, anything will be better than the help I allotted you in carving the shelves in the library."

He chuckled. "I can still see that chisel sticking out from the side of it."

She sat upright, swatting his leg with a laugh of her own. "I tried, did I not?"

"Indeed. I'm still not convinced you could not do better. Though I think I shall not be changing it to Steele and Wife anytime soon."

"Mm. I suspect not." She looked up at him. "Will you still change the name, do you think?"

He shrugged. "I've considered it, but I think I may as well keep it now. After all, we may have a son yet."

She beamed up at him. "Or *sons*," she said, accentuating the end of the word.

"Indeed." He tipped her chin up with his finger, pressing a kiss to her lips.

As the moments passed by with Marianne in his arms and his lips on hers, love overflowed from his heart, spilling into every inch of his soul. Sons, daughters, a wife. How Edward could ever be so fortunate, he did not know. But he would spend the rest of his days ensuring that he deserved them all. For he loved Marianne, her vivacity for life, and the delightful way her kisses always tasted of cherry tarts.

THE END

Order the next book in the Sons of Somerset series
The Stable Master's Son by Mindy Burbidge Strunk

AUTHOR'S NOTE

I brainstormed for months about which job Edward should have, finding that I had already used—or will use—many of them already. (Apparently, like the Coventry women, working-class men are my weakness.)

No job was fitting for Edward until I came across carpentry. I knew at once that I didn't wish to write about woodworking in the traditional furniture-making sense. Why? Well, frankly, I didn't have time for the research to do the job justice. Luckily, being a woodcarver fit Edward even better.

Even with his job, though, my research took weeks. I was able to find a few books that went into detail about the tools and techniques used for woodcarving in the 18th and 19th centuries. I didn't even scratch the surface of what woodworkers can really do, though—their gorgeous work is simply inspiring!

As many of you know, I like to put little Easter eggs into my stories, and this one was no different. Edward mentioned the Golden Mermaid Inn in Devonshire that he stayed at with his father. This is a nod to an upcoming story of mine that will be released at the end of 2021. You'll have to keep your eye out for the mention of the same inn!

I'm sure you all noticed the most obvious Easter egg—my inevitable mention of Cornwall. I had to add that in, of course. This story ended up getting *two* mentions. Did you find them both?

The name Daffley Park isn't so much an Easter egg as it is my liking to create names and give them more meaning. I imagined Daffley from daffodils, the flowers symbolizing new beginnings. Daffley Park is certainly where the Coventrys have their new beginning—and Mr. Steele, too.

Lastly, Ashwick *is* a real town in Somerset, as well as Inglesbatch and, of course, Bath. I didn't wish to change the history of those places, so fictional houses were created to that purpose.

Well, that's it from me! I do hope you enjoyed the book! If so, you are always welcome to leave a review on Amazon. If you haven't signed up for my newsletter yet, you can sign up to receive the latest news about my upcoming novels.

My favorite places to be are Instagram and Facebook, so if you aren't following me yet, please do! I always love connecting with readers and sharing more about my writing.

I hope to connect with you soon!

Deborah

ACKNOWLEDGMENTS

I feel like each new book gets harder and harder to write. Shouldn't that be the opposite?? Oh well. I'm just extremely grateful for all those who have helped me—and continue to help me even when I'm crazy.

First, my author friends. Ladies, what would I do without you?

Martha Keyes, I gotta give you props, you Whitney-Award-Winner, you. Months ago, you gave me permission for my story to have a morning and a night coachman's route so I wouldn't have any plot holes. You also gave me permission for something else…but now I can't remember what it was. Oh, well. Thanks a bunch. You're the best.

Kasey Stockton, you read the worst draft of this story known to man. I'm seriously so sorry. I can't even imagine the patience you had to have to read through it. Thanks for not telling me it totally sucked, even though it totally did. You're also the best.

Joanna Barker, I've said it before, and I'll say it again—I love that we have the same sense of humor. Your edits are my favorite because you laugh at all my dumb jokes. I mean, my hilariously hilarious jokes. And you're the best, too.

Arlem Hawks, you have taught me from the beginning that details matter to a story—and I'll be forever grateful for it! I'm so blessed to have you in my life, my friend. You're the best, as well.

Jess Heileman. When I was freaking out about this story, thinking it was the worst thing I had ever written and that it had zero romance in it, you volunteered to read the story ON YOUR FLIPPING VACATION. Who does that? The most selfless person on earth, that's who. Thank you so much. You're the best also.

Jenny Proctor. It gives me so much comfort to know that I have you backing me up and supporting my story, helping it to shine so I don't have to whine. That didn't even make sense. Maybe I should have you edit my acknowledgements, too.

A quick shout out needs to go to every single one of my ARC readers and to my Bookstagram friends. Tasha (@the_-clean_read_book_club), Mandy (@probablybookinit), Ashlee (@bookswithnopictures), Madi & Meg (@apageofpeace), Marilee (@marilee.loves.to.read), and so many more of you. Thank you for the laughs, the shares, and the support. You make my life unbelievably easier. Thank you for loving my books!

Next, I need to thank my family.

Mom and Dad, your trust and confidence in me, your support of me, and your love for me mean everything to me! I don't know what I would do without you both.

My sister, Joanna. I am so grateful for your friendship. I always looked up to you when I was a little girl—and I do so even more now. Thank you for your continued support in everything I do. I'm so glad we live close to each other. You have always been such a blessing in my life. Love you!

Finally, Christian. Thank you for your unending patience with me as I finished this book. I'm sure you *never* get tired of me saying how each book I write is the worst book I've ever written. Or how I'm never going to write again. (Sorry about that.) You may not carve wood, but you are still *my* working class man. *kissy face emoji*

BOOKS BY DEBORAH M. HATHAWAY

A Cornish Romance Series
On the Shores of Tregalwen, a Prequel Novella
Behind the Light of Golowduyn, Book One
For the Lady of Lowena, Book Two
Near the Ruins of Penharrow, Book Three
In the Waves of Tristwick, Book Four (Pre-Order)
Book Five, Coming Soon

Belles of Christmas Multi-Author Series
Nine Ladies Dancing, Book Four
On the Second Day of Christmas, Book Four

Seasons of Change Multi-Author Series
The Cottage by Coniston, Book Five

Sons of Somerset Multi-Author Series
Carving for Miss Coventry, Book One

ABOUT THE AUTHOR

 Deborah M. Hathaway graduated from Utah State University with a BA in English, Creative Writing. As a young girl, she devoured Jane Austen's novels while watching and re-watching every adaptation of Pride & Prejudice she could, entirely captured by all things Regency and romance.

Throughout her early life, she wrote many short stories, poems, and essays, but it was not until after her marriage that she was finally able to complete her first romance novel, attributing the completion to her courtship with, and love of, her charming, English husband. Deborah finds her inspiration for her novels in her everyday experiences with her husband and children and during her travels to the United Kingdom, where she draws on the beauty of the country in such places as Scotland, Somerset, and her beloved Cornwall.

Made in the USA
Middletown, DE
08 September 2021